They Don't Love You Like I Love You

CARLIE JONES

Edited by Lena Jones

Hope & Jones, LLC

THEY DON'T LOVE YOU LIKE I LOVE YOU

CONTENTS

3

GOOD TIMES (WE WILL NEVER FORGET)

4

GOOD GRIEF

5

WOODY AND BUZZ (BF4L)

6
VIOLENT CRIMES (KARMA)

7
YEE

8

THE LINE OF FIRE

9

PROJECT MAYHEM

10

THE ORIGINAL MS. JACKSON

11
IT'S ONLY LOVE THAT GETS YOU THROUGH

12
THUGLIFE

*DEDICATED TO **US***

"If there's a book that you want to read but it hasn't been written yet, then you must write it."
- Toni Morrison

Acknowledgements

The completion of this undertaking could not have been possible without the participation and assistance of many family members, friends, mentors, and supporters. Your contributions are deeply appreciated and gratefully acknowledged– I am privileged to have you all in my circle. **A special thank you and particular indebtedness is owed to the following:**

To the editor, *Lena Jones*, you are the man. The time, care, and intentionality you poured into the Love family was unmatched. Thank you for helping me use my voice– even when it shakes– on this project and in every lifetime.

To the front cover artist, *Temilola Sobomehin*, your vision is one of a kind. Seeing the Love sisters through your eyes was transformative. Thank you for collaborating with me to translate this story into incredible digital art.

To the back cover photographer, *Deija Walker*, you have a special way of seeing the world. Thank you for capturing my bliss during this time. I will forever love this headshot.

To the mentors, *Harry Kalvin* (Artist, 10+ yrs) and *Nan Thibodeaux* (LMFT, 30+ years), nobody sees me like you both do. Your professional insight and feedback critically elevated this story. The continued authenticity, love, and grace you share with others makes the world a better place. Thank you.

To the beta readers, *Aaliyah Sanders, Ani Janssen, Esther Smith, Tati-ola Sobomehin*, and *Tayo Sobomehin*, your insightful, brutal, and hilarious feedback made this project. Thank you for gifting me your wisdom. Y'all were the cherry on top of this beautifully messy sundae.

To all family, friends, and teachers who in one way or another shared themselves with me, either literally or figuratively, to make this project happen, thank you!

Trigger Warning

This book contains descriptions of scenes that some may find disturbing, if not triggering. In mental health terms, being "triggered" refers to a broad collection of mental, physical, emotional, and/or behavioral reactions that someone may experience when presented with a reminder of past trauma.

The graphic scenes include, but are not limited to, substance abuse, disordered eating habits, self harm, abandonment, sexual assault, abortion, domestic abuse, and gun violence.

If you crave support processing any of these topics, please complete the Reflection Questions in the back of this book. For additional support, review the list of Resources, also at the back of this book.

This book is intended for mature audiences.

1

IF YOU SCURRED GO TO CHURCH

| 1 |

Chapter One

August 5th, 2007

This eternal sunshine and blue skies bullshit is obnoxious. I feel like everyone around me is smiling. Or, worse, in love. What for? Did I miss something? Did *SNL* post another viral skit and the algorithm thought I didn't deserve to see it?

I keep walking around with my eyes squinched up and my lips pouting out to the world's general direction. I don't even think anyone has noticed -- let alone cared. I don't know. I must be the only person who thinks this world is burning down in flames as we speak. But, I'm just a fifteen year old tragic mulatto, so the world doesn't really care about whatever I'm thinking -- right? "Well, that's just too damn bad," as Mr. Sir would say.

When you have an addict as a parent you don't get to be a five year old kid, let alone a normal teenager, and you learn everything about life at warp speed. Everyone always tells me I'm "so mature for my age," and I know they aren't just gassing me up either, you know? I really *am* hella mature. And, I understand how lame that sounds, but, at least I'm mature enough to recognize that. Plus, I know the *whole* world isn't completely hopeless. It's only *my* microscopic world that is disintegrating into a total shitcident.

Ninety-nine percent of the time I feel like I'm about to have a total breakdown, but, for the other three percent of the time I'm just fine. It never quite adds up, but I guess that's alright, right? That's just life. Besides, watching a person crack up into million little puzzle pieces while eating popcorn from the comfort of your home is Our modern form of entertainment, amiright?

Or am I right?

See, the problem with having a parent who eats narcotics through his nose for breakfast, lunch, and dinner before washing it down with tequila, is that you never quite know what to expect.

Take, for example, my Dad -- which I'm sure you already knew about. Lawrence was generally the type of wholesome, Black, church-going family guy you expect to spend his days at home, you know what I mean? Like Denzel in *The Preacher's Wife*.

But, just like Denzel, Lawrence could suddenly switch roles on you. Remember, like in *Training Day* or *John Q*? Lawrence liked to call all the shots. He liked to pick out my hair before bed, and ensure everybody knelt at the waterbed to pray before baby Jesus every night. But, at some point, I think it was right before "Semi-Charmed Life" and *Fools Rush In* were released, Lawrence started fading out. All of a sudden he didn't give two shits about coming home late. Sometimes, he wouldn't even come home at all.

In that time, during the foggy midst of Lawrence's benders, I basically operated like a zombie. The only thing I remember was waiting for him to come back home. I don't remember the days when he resurfaced, and, to be honest, I don't remember a lot of things. It's like one day I woke up and knew a big ass chunk of time was missing from my memory. I've never been able to understand why. Last year they told me most people don't usually end up remembering the chunks that went missing until much later in life. They said your brain won't let your body remember things sometimes, but I always ignore *those* people.

Last year, the not knowing almost drove me unmistakably bat shit crazy, but it didn't. After a while I realized I don't actually want to know what happened during those days. Then, I realized I don't care if the strung out shadow of Lawrence ever came around again or not. If you really want to know the truth, I realized I didn't want the ghost around at all.

All those nights you spend praying for a safe return flip flop on you and you become obsessed with praying for the opposite. You pray for things you'd never dare mention out loud, so, you end up bottling it all in. Then, you focus all of your energy on thinking about the things you'll do differently when you grow up, about the ways you'll stand up for yourself and your family when you're old enough, and most importantly, about all the ways you won't end up like them.

Does that sound about right? I guess a large part of the problem is that whenever someone asks me about my past I don't know where to begin. Beyond the fact that I don't remember, the story is so age old, so stereotypical, it feels irrelevant. Plus, I don't even know how to properly articulate the enormity of such an invisible weight. It's just not that easy.

My little sister, Elle, is probably my biggest help. She's only five, so she's like my ten years younger identical twin who I didn't actually start paying attention to until recently. Elle makes everything better. Her life is easier, less stressful, and way more fun than mine. She can handle anything and anyone. Take last night, for example. All night Elle kept asking Vivian where Lawrence was.

"Where's Daddy?" Elle asked.

Vivian, who always has tabs on everybody, responded that she "didn't know," which immediately made me suspicious. But, I didn't say anything.

I was too hung up on Elle still referring to Lawrence as, "Daddy." I *still* can't remember the last time I referred to Lawrence as anything beyond "Dad," or, "Sir." I use his first name -- only in secret. But, Elle is a daddy's girl. She likes to pretend she doesn't know what's really going on. Despite that one annoying character flaw, I know Elle better than she knows herself. I basically am Elle. I know she still thinks animals and humans can be best friends. I know she prefers rainbows and butterflies over superheroes and princesses. And, worst of all, I know she'll adopt the most obviously toxic people because she'll want to save them with her love and positivity -- even though she can't.

Initially, I couldn't tell if Vivian was lying or not, since she's such an experienced storyteller. But, when Vivian was swooping up our plates from the yellow kids table and Lawrence still wasn't home, I knew she had been telling us the truth. She really didn't know where he was.

I continued digging for answers regardless, "Mom, when is Dad coming home?"

I only started calling Vivian by her first name this summer, but that's still in secret too.

"I told you earlier that I don't know where your Dad is. Just don't worry about him right now and focus on yourself. What else do you need to do before you can get to bed?" Vivian was trying to keep Elle busy to stop her innocent mind from wandering. You know, she was doing that good old distract-the-child-with-a-different-question technique that never actually works. All it does is subliminally teach children to stop communicating with their parents about their feelings. I hate that. I'll never do that when I'm a mom.

Either way, I was committed to maintaining the peace. In an effort to keep up the act like everything was normal, I left Vivian in the kitchen to be alone with the dishes and I ventured into our moldy ass bathroom to start a tub for Elle. Vivian loves to clean the kitchen and scrub things when she gets anxious, especially in our low-budget apartment that gives her too many things to fixate on. She'll slap on some rubber yellow gloves and go to town -- speaking to herself in tongues and wiping everything down until it's guaranteed to pass her white glove test.

Elle, on the other hand, uses playtime to dissociate from reality. Elle reminds me of a yellow ducky type of bright yellow. She's an annoying yellow that is squeaky clean and pure and always happy, you know what I mean? Elle's got soft brown skin, the shade of brown sugar, hazel eyes like me, and short nappy hair that she likes styled into an Afro so as to symbolize her elite status.

Elle is still so young she brings plastic dolls and animals into the bathtub to play. Plus, nine out of ten times she stays in way longer than Vivian allotted. Elle's imagination is as big, beautiful, and boundless as her kinks that won't lay down flat no matter how much coconut oil is applied. So, she naturally loves playing in the alternate realities she creates for herself. Elle uses baths as an opportunity to expand her imagination. On an average night, Elle stays in the bathtub playing with her newest, latest, greatest fashion dolls until the water turns ice cold and her fingers look like an 86 year old man's.

Once Elle finally got out of the bathtub I had to convince her to get dressed. While the act of picking out pajamas may be a simple and short-lived task for some, for Elle, it can be a deep and life-altering decision. When Elle realized Lisa Lopez was her doppelganger she committed herself to becoming a 24/7 fashionista "for the rest of [her] whole life." Now, each outfit has to "make a statement." On the plus side, Elle's hair is still in cornrows from last week, so I only had to find her a night cap. Eventually, Elle decided to wear her silk bright pink Barbie nighty with lace frills lining the skirt and sleeves.

Elle skipped through the apartment singing "Say You'll Be There" by the Spice Girls. She was so stoked to be wearing her most elegant pjs that she only stopped running around long enough to twirl for us in the living room. But, I won't front, it was hella sweet. Vivian even pulled out her Safeway-bought throw away camera and took a couple pictures. Elle readily struck a some poses, then persuaded us to let her perform before going to bed.

We set the stage for Elle. Vivian dimmed the lights down low in the living room. I grabbed a hairbrush for Elle to sing into. And, then Vivian tossed on a "Now This is What I Call Music" mixtape. Vivian grabbed the microphone hairbrush from Elle and introduced her to "the crowd," with arms spread wide open -- even though it was just us and our dog, a black and white-spotted Pitbull named Jasper.

"And now performing for you folks live *is* Ellesha Love Grove!" Vivian turned back towards Elle, who had been hiding, and said, "Elle, you only get three songs and I mean it! OK? It's a weekday and we all have to get up in the morning."

Elle nodded her head in agreement, and Vivian sat down next to me. We sat on our orange and navy decorated futon that was folded up into the couch position. I think the navy pattern was supposed to be a flower, or a fruit of some sort, but I honestly can't even remember. We got that couch at one of my Grandma Soul's estate sales a long time ago, so who even knows.

Vivian interrupted Elle with one last parenting tip from the couch, "we have neighbors we don't want to wake up."

"O-kay, okay! May I begin now?" Elle chimed in over Vivian.

It was actually already past our bedtime at this point. I think Vivian was just so distracted with Elle's show she forgot it was already sort of late -- like 9 PM or so. Vivian had delayed serving dinner because she was waiting for Lawrence to show up and eat with us. As a result, our dinner was cold when we ate *and* our whole nightly routine had been thrown off. Plus, Elle performed ten songs instead of just three. But, that's a minor little detail. By the time Elle was actually calmed down enough to brush her teeth without laughing and drooling all the toothpaste out of her mouth, to listen to a goodnight story, and to lay down to go to bed, it had to be near 10:45 PM. On a Monday.

Just when Vivian started tucking Elle in for bed, Lawrence strutted through the front door. During this era when Lawrence was rarely around, he'd seldom come home in a casual or normal manner. Instead, he'd dominate the whole space. He'd make a scene of his being on the scene, as if some imaginary director had just yelled "ACTION" from afar.

Lawrence was sure to approach with a friend. "Uncle" Brad trailed along as a surprise special guest to the evening. Within an instant, the Monday Night Football recap started to broadcast throughout our apartment; Jasper started barking and running around in circles;

and, mid-conversation laughing broke through the wall into our back bedroom.

Elle sprinted out of bed like it was a race. Vivian quickly made the effort to restrain her, but it was futile. Elle escaped. Vivian pressed her hands on the waterbed, too tired to lift herself from the floor without assistance, and pushed up to chase after Elle. Vivian grunted out a half-hearted muffled command as she exited the bedroom, "Elle, come on back here, Honey. It's bedtime."

A few moments later, I silently inched up the hallway to meet everyone in the living room. Brad was sitting in our orange director's chair that matched the orange fold up couch. It used to be my favorite chair, for obvious reasons, but, now it's Elles favorite. So, whatever. Elle was trying to convince Jasper to dance with her in the middle of the living room floor. Lawrence was sitting on our futon rolling a blunt, and Vivian was standing in the corner with her arms folded tightly in front of her chest.

Brad cheerfully said hello before feigning a wave my way. I ignored Brad by not responding and acting like I didn't hear him. Mom gave Brad a cold upward head nod and basically didn't respond to him either, so I didn't get in trouble.

"How was everybody, Elle? Did you make sure everybody behaved while I was gone?" Lawrence liked to leave Elle "in charge" when he goes out. So, last night he had her wrapped up in his arms, and they were having a private conversation, per usual. Then he turned his attention outward to interrupt Brad's small talk with Vivian.

"Brad just got this new bike a few weeks ago, Vivian. Did I ever tell you that?" Lawrence demanded her attention.

"It was about a week ago," Brad corrected.

"No, you didn't tell me." Vivian seemed uninterested and stared past Lawrence.

"Yeah." Lawrence turned his chin up at Vivian, then pivoted his attention back towards Brad and the football on screen. Smiling mischievously, Lawrence continued, "it's real nice, Viv, you should see it. I think you'd like it."

"Oh yeah?"

"Yeah."

"Why's that?"

"Well, why *is* that, Brad? Why do *you* think she'll like it?"

"Well, Lawrence, since you ask, the bike is basically brand new."

"It's basically brand new, Viv."

"Yup, and it's got a bunch of space so a couple folks can sit on there comfortably, if you know what I mean," Brad and Lawrence riled each other up like teenage boys. His caramel complexion was further amplified by his orange, freshly jerry curled hair, and freckled face. Brad has some missing teeth, and the others are a gnarly yellowish brown, so he usually wears a metal grill. Last night was no different.

"See, Viv, it's got a ton of space! You should really go outside and see it."

Vivian scoffed, audibly, Elle kept dancing with our dog like she didn't feel the tension in the room rising, and I was basically not there. Lawrence pouted, upset that Vivian had the audacity to shrug him off. Mom continued, "are you serious right now, Lawrence? It's past 11 o'clock! I'm not going outside to see a bike this late at night."

All five feet and two inches of Vivian is filled with free-will. When Lawrence first found out Vivian was pregnant he bought her a ruby ring and asked her to be his wife. She still sometimes wears it on her wedding finger, but she would never *actually* get married. Especially to Lawrence. She's a living, breathing, Woodstock-attending hippie with long ash brown hair that she swears is curly -- even though it's really straight. Vivian has green eyes and a warm smile that makes everybody entrust her with their innermost thoughts. If I could give Vivian a color it would be a cool black -- like a black leather blazer or 90's-style trench coat. Vivian is smooth. Everyone I know wants to be like her, even my best friends! She's a trend setter who walks to the sound of her own beat -- "Walk Don't Walk" by Prince, if you were to ask her. Vivian spouts messages of female empowerment all day long, even though she's miserably in love with my Dad. Plus, last but not least, she's also my best friend.

"Why not?" Lawrence sharply snapped his head to lock eyes with Vivian, who had been repeatedly stabbing daggers into the side of his head with her eyes.

"Because, Lawrence, it's too late to even see anything. Plus, I'm tired. We're all tired! We were just trying to go to sleep before you two came in here and riled everybody up. It's *past* bedtime." The tone in Vivian's voice didn't let up, but her body language told me she was sinking in her standing ground like it was quicksand. Mom's toes shifted in the carpet hairs and her arms controllably unfolded to a resting position on either side of her hips. She knew Lawrence would keep pushing.

"It's not too late for anything, Viv. We're adults. *We* make up the rules around here, right? Nobody tells me when *I* need to go to bed -- ain't that right?"

He was speaking to the crowd but nobody directly responded. Elle swung her arms up in the air and called for her partner in crime to play, "come on, Jasper! Come on!" Elle whistled.

Everyone in the room could see that Jasper wanted to dance. But, instead he stayed stationary, looked backwards to Lawrence on the couch, and continued laying on the ground with his tail tightly tucked. Lawrence stared down at Jasper, as if daring him to play with Elle. Jasper quickly forfeited and rested his square head back down between his paws on the floor. The sound of football highlight reels carried on in the background while Vivian and Lawrence's bickering continued to take center stage.

"So, who wants to go for a ride on the bike?"

Vivian immediately exclaimed, "What?!"

"What do you mean, 'what'?" Lawrence mocked. "The girls want to go out for a ride, Vivian!" He looked Vivian up and down as if he were disgusted with her.

"What are you talking about, Lawrence?! It's late, the girls have school in the morning, and they're in their pjs!" Vivian's entire body had tensed up while the thunder of her voice had started washing away.

She sounded soft, "come on, Lawrence."

He just stared at Vivian without saying a word. Instead, he communicated with her telepathically for a few moments while we all stood still in time -- waiting.

"I said 'the girls want to go on a ride,' Vivian. Not tomorrow, or after school sometime, or whenever you get home from work. It's not when *you* decide you have the time to pay attention, it's when *I* decide. You got it?"

"You're too messed up right now, Lawrence. It's not safe. You can't be driving around with the kids on a motorcycle that's not even yours!" By this point Vivian was pleading with him.

"Ahht-! Ahht-! I don't wanna hear it, Vivian." Lawrence turned to Elle and exploited the fact that she's a daddy's girl. "E wants to go on a midnight motorcycle night ride with her Papa, doesn't she?"

Elle cheered him on screaming, "yeah, Daddy! Yeah! I wanna go!"

To be honest, the thing that fucked me up most that night was the way they were fighting this time. I had seen Vivian and Lawrence argue over plenty of serious things before -- like, Lawrence's other girlfriends and him not making money. But, I'd never seen Vivian, or Lawrence for that matter, act so stone cold towards each other. Usually Vivian can get through to Lawrence and calm him back down to a rational state of mind. But, instead of Vivian advocating for her perspective until she had won Lawrence over, she was retreating and reluctant. And, instead of storming out of the house to cool off, Lawrence unabashedly locked in. It's like he was constantly experimenting with how much space he could take up in our already tiny apartment. As if he *wanted* to shut everyone out.

Anyways, Vivian basically just started pacing back and forth in the living room. Occasionally she'd make a few comments under her breath like, "this isn't right", "what is he *doing*", and, "he doesn't have a license to drive this thing." But, before I knew it we were all outside huddled around Brad's new motorcycle.

The bike was shiny, bright red, and huge. It was potentially even heavier than me, Vivian, and Elle all put together -- no bs. There aren't any street lights on our back street I think because it's just a small narrow alley. Or, maybe because people don't want to see what happens in neighborhoods like mine. But, the cherry redness of the bike shone like Dorothy's red slippers even in the darkness of the night. The seats were black and lined with a deep matching red leather, and the bike was leaning towards the kick stand.

"So, whatcha think, girls?" Lawrence's white teeth glowed in the dark in contrast to his dark Brown skin. It was beautifully sinister and uncomfortably appropriate. Brad stood on the furthest side of the bike facing all of us while smiling proudly as Elle ran her fingers over the bike, sliding her stubs from the back to the front. I stood still with my arms crossed and feet hips width apart in my warrior stance. I was imitating Vivian who stood in position, oozing with unfulfilled expectations. Nobody directly responded to Lawrence, again, so he continued seeking validation.

"Viv, it's nice isn't it?" Lawrence sounded as excited as Elle does when she hears the ice cream truck outside. Vivian remained quiet, and soon, Lawrence's eyes opened so widely they almost jumped out of their sockets and punched her in the mouth for him.

"Vivian, I said what do you think of Brad's bike? Fucking answer me, woman."

Vivian cleared her throat before speaking, "yup, Lawrence, I can see it," she motioned to the bike in front of her like it was obvious, "it's nice."

Lawrence snarled back in a way that demonstrated he was fed up, "yuh huh."

My parents were still acting cooler toward each other than the midnight not-quite-summer-anymore breeze slapping across my face. Lawrence swung over Brad's motorcycle and straddled it between his legs, kicking the stand up from the ground.

"Just give her to me, Brad," Lawrence instructed, pointing to Elle. Brad picked Elle up and passed her over to Lawrence like a football. Once he got Elle settled on his lap Lawrence called out for me, and I nervously obliged.

"Aww, now look at ch'all sandwiched together there on my motorcycle looking like the Black royalty that ch'all are. MMM MM MMM." Brad started clapping at us like Mama Klump, "God't damn."

I sat up front with my hands on both the handlebars while Elle sat in the middle squeezing my abs into absolute nothingness. She kicked her legs back and forth excitedly on either side of the bike -- completely fearless. Elle seemed like she was having a great time. Lawrence sat all the way in the back and strained to reach his arms up to the front handlebars. To accommodate, he tightened one arm around me and Elle, and stretched the other arm out further to hold the right handlebar of the lion-powered bike.

"Ok, girls, you gotta hold on now. E, you go ahead and grab on. Olivia, you're going to steer us and make sure we don't crash into anything, alright?"

I told him "ok," but I was really just scared shitless and didn't know what else to say, you know? It's not really like I had any other option.

Right before we took off Vivian spoke up, "just one time around the block, alright Lawrence?"

"Sure, Viv." Dad turned his attention to Brad and started laughing at the expense of my Mom, "don't go holding your breath on that." Uncle Brad started snickering with Lawrence like they were childish ass children, and Lawrence continued berating Vivian. "You can just go on back inside and go to bed, Vivian. You said 'it's bedtime,' right? We'll be back when we're back."

Then, boom. The engine started to gargle, Lawrence hit the throttle, and we vroomed down the dark gravel alley. I was so furious, disgusted, and enraged with Lawrence and the way he had disparaged Vivian that I could barely see in front of me. My eyesight blurred up with water, but I couldn't manage to wipe away the tears streaming down both cheeks because of my death grip on the bike. The whole time I could hear Lawrence screaming out with enthusiasm from the back, sounding like he was having the best time of his entire life. "Wooo hooo!! That's it girls!! Let's go faster!"

"No, Daddy! I don't want to," Elle shouted over the already accelerating engine.

Lawrence was having a blast. One of the things I love most about Lawrence is his deep barrel belly laugh that he never ever holds back -- no matter how inappropriate his Black joy is at any given moment. Lawrence looks as if he could be a real bouncer, like his little brother, my Uncle Marlon. Lawrence hovers over almost everyone because he stretches up six-feet six inches tall, and it has instilled a false sense of security that Black men his age typically no longer have. Lawrence keeps his hair short, and one of my favorite characteristics about him is that he likes to experiment with different styles when shaping up his hair and his beard.

Still, hearing Lawrence's laugh from the back of the motorcycle last night made me feel ill. All in a moment I realized Lawrence knew how to use his laugh against people. He knew how to hurt and to tear people down with his laugh just as much as he knew how to build them up. Last night I finally realized Lawrence was using his laugh against me... and Elle.

Why else was he obnoxiously laughing so hard when Elle and I were shaking so visibly? I think Lawrence was trying to trick us into not being scared. Trying to make us forget what was happening. Trying to manipulate us into not feeling anything besides whatever he wanted us to feel. But, it wasn't *really* working. I felt terrified, and angry, and confused -- and I didn't forget it.

Lawrence continued screaming, "put your arms out, Olivia! Go on!"

I was so mad I couldn't even speak. I could barely even breathe. I just kept crying, silently, allowing my tears to freeze like icicles to my cheeks. My teeth clicked together in a shiver, but I felt like I was flying.

I was flying from one blacked out alley to the next, not minding any big rocks, any branches, or any intersections in my way. The cold wind on my face actively alerted me to the fact that I was still alive, and

I felt every inhale infiltrate the holes burned through my throat. Elle's tiny fingers clenched on to the sides of my Barbie nightgown at my torso and she buried her face into my back so she didn't have to look. Lawrence continued howling at the stars. Hungry like the wolf.

"Wooo hooo!!!"

I wasn't sure if I was having fun, if I was having a panic attack, or if I was even actually there at all -- just like most memories. When we got home, Lawrence dropped Elle and me off in the back alley, but didn't come inside with us. I heard the bike gurgling behind me until I reached the sliding glass door, and then, without looking, I heard it speed off.

The color from Vivian's face had faded. I watched her sit on the orange futon, petting Jasper and staring at the lifeless black television screen for a few moments before getting back into character. Once she realized Elle and I were home, she hurried up off the folded futon and greeted us with cheer.

"How did it go?! Are you alright?" Vivian smushed Elle into her silky light blue nightgown and back out again, as if to verify the results.

I walked to the back bedroom without answering. Elle had it all under control. As I closed in on the bed I heard Elle telling Vivian, "it was so much fun, Mommy! You really missed out!"

| 2 |

Chapter Two

How do you spend your Sundays? In my family Sundays are unique. They reserve a special little spot in my heart. Elle always wakes up before I do, and springs out of bed unintentionally disrespecting the sanctimonious tradition of sleeping in. Still in her Barbie pajamas, she almost immediately runs out to the kitchen to start up the fairy fountain.

Our fairy fountain is magical. On each level sits a ballerina, or a fairy, or something I can't quite remember, spinning at different speeds. The top layer is the fastest, oh, and, each layer lights up too! There are green lights on the bottom, pink in the middle, and yellowy-whites on top. Elle's ideal way of setting the mood is to turn off all the lights in the apartment, close the blinds, add a little water to the top layer, and watch the sparkling water show unfold.

The fairy fountain sits on our yellow kids table with royal blue legs. There isn't space for it anywhere else, and Elle would become unhinged if we ever threw it away. But, it kept making us late in the mornings when we were eating, so Vivian put a sheet over the thing and said, "Sunday mornings only, Elle."

Now, Elle rallies the troops early every Sunday. I usually won't wake up until I hear the singing. If we're skipping church, I can immediately feel the chill vibes. I'll be able to smell the bacon, eggs, and sweet-style grits cooking. I'll be able to hear Lawrence and Vivian having a karaoke-style sing off to James Brown or James Taylor from the kitchen. And, when I come out to meet the crew still in a sleepy haze, I double take and see them all dancing. Vivian will be swaying her hips and shaking her shoulders to the beat. Lawrence will be leaning down so his face can be near Vivian's as he takes on the role of a pop-singer. Even Elle, who is still very distracted by the fairy fountain, will be bouncing up and down in her seat or singing into the fountain. Sometimes she'll even break away from the fountain to dance with Jasper. To an outsider, that might be a real head scratcher, but in our blended family it all makes sense. Things are alright, good even. Nobody will be uptight or in a rush.

But, if we're going to church things are different. There's nothing but coffee in the air. You immediately feel the tension caused by exhaustion and resentment. My parents have polar opposite religious beliefs. Where Vivian is free, and believes in all versions of any higher power, Lawrence is constantly trying to save Elle's *and* my impure souls. So, on church mornings I only hear Lawrence sing, he's intentionally loud, and it's only gospel. When I join the group in the kitchen, I see everybody else sunken and sullen, even Jasper just lays tiredly on the floor. Vivian will be drinking coffee and tapping her foot as she waits for Elle's frozen burrito to heat up in the microwave. Elle will be staring blankly at the fairy fountain while Lawrence tugs her hair into some braids. Things are unsociable and my parents are on edge.

In the car, we'll listen to various sermons on church radio stations. Lawrence usually works up a pre-church sweat-cry combination while banging on the roof of the car to symbolize his praise. He's abnormally amped. In the meantime, Vivian and I silently fight the feeling of sleep creeping up from Elle snoring in her car seat. We're typically late, so finding parking becomes near impossible. This presents an opportunity for Lawrence to drop us at the front of the church while he "finds a spot to park the car." I think he usually just splits and then comes back in a few hours when service is about to end, but I immediately go to Sunday school so I don't really know what he does. All I know is that one time Vivian and I had to wait with the pastor and Grandma Soul for a long time after church was over until Lawrence came back.

Our church is small but multilayered. The women occupy the basement-level kitchen that shares a wall with the youngest group of Sunday school students. Elle is in that baby group. I think they mostly learn stories about God in pamphlet-styled coloring handouts. But, Elle pretty much just spaces out. The basement is sorta scary because we're so far from our parents. You're sitting in a room filled with the kids of parents who also inconsistently attend while trying to dig into some really deep, personal beliefs. If you ask me, I'd much rather be upstairs sitting with the adult congregation in the mahogany stained aisles. I'd rather spend the extra time with my parents.

Usually when I'm with the adults I silence out the pastor any-way. I'll dissociate by staring at the art. Especially because a more-than-life size porcelain statue of That Man on a Cross is hung on the wall directly behind the pastor's podium. It straight up scares the shit outta me. So, I like to look at the stained glass windows instead. I like to focus on how the light alters all the different colors depending on how awake the sun is at any given moment. I've never seen the sun look as gentle as it does shining through those colored church windows. I swear -- it just sits there and glistens making the blues bluer and the greens greener. Now *that's* what I call a holy experience.

My color study is typically interrupted by the congregation. I'll look up and see an elder Madea-looking lady in a floral purple dress and matching hat at the front of the stage. She's either already fainted or is going to faint, and the teenage usher boys will lunge to grab her from up under the armpits before she hits the ground. Folks will be up dancing around her. Sometimes the elder lady will be switched out with a man, typically crying, in an off-color suit. Either way, folks dance around, with one hand in the air and the other waving their fans in their faces. People start howling out saying, "yes Lawd," and "Amen." Sometimes shouting in tongues.

I've learned that if I don't look at the ground in these moments, I'll look at Vivian. All it takes is one second of locking eye contact before we're both in a fit of giggles, which, rightfully so, enrages Lawrence; and, usually the people directly in front of us too. To avoid this, Vivian and I typically sit opposite one another with Lawrence sitting smack down in the middle, so we don't "encourage each other." Us laughing wouldn't be such a big deal if Vivian weren't White *and* if we weren't always that one *mixed* family.

"She can't just be out here acting like every other kid in that church, Vivian," Lawrence will yell on the way home.

"As a Black woman, and especially being mixed race, honey, you have to be careful. People are always going to be waiting for you to be vulnerable so they can pick you apart, and that's a promise. Never let your guard down, Olivia," Lawrence coaches me from the rearview mirror, "you hear me?"

I'll nod because he always says that.

After service, everybody meets outside, which is my favorite part. You spend hours and hours in silence, with your eyes closed and head bowed, on a Sunday morning, and they really expect you *not* to fall asleep?! I can't. Even when I was Elle's age I had a difficult time with the whole setup. But, I've always loved the part after service when my family congregates on the lawn and finalizes our plans for dinner. It's usually still so cold that the grass is frozen over and we can see our breaths lingering in the air out in front of us. So, my cousins and I will play around spelling out words for each other and guessing what it is for a minute. We giggle and chase each other around, weaving in and out of my Grandma Soul's legs until she finally barks at us to "knock it off."

Even though the kids are all playing around, I still keep an ear open to the adult conversation. I think we all do. There's nothing too spicy ever being exchanged on such holy grounds, but if something is going down in the family one of the adults will say, "let's get together for Sunday dinner tonight, who's down?" and then they'll all start collaborating on which dishes to bring. Someone will casually say "I'll bring some beans," before another pops in with, "alright, and I've got the slaw," and then another with, "and I'll do the fried chicken." Grandma Soul drops the hammer every time with, "yeah, and I'll bet y'all want me to make the mac and cheese, the cheesecake, the BBQ ribs, the mashed potatoes, the greens, and pretty much everything else, right?"

She's right. We're all waiting to go to "Big Mama's House."

Even though I drag my feet getting up and out of the house, I live for the colorful family moments that make my mouth water. There's nothing like Black church on Sunday.

| 3 |

Chapter Three

August 19th, 2007

I miss the summer, and the feeling of being woken up by warm wind during an afternoon nap. I miss the sound of kids playing and adults messing up the lyrics to great music. I miss feeling the excitement that's felt when standing behind a BBQer. I miss being outside all day, and breaking into random pools at random apartment complexes. I don't miss Nikky comparing her skin tone to mine, but I miss everything else.

Yesterday, I went to my friend Nikky's house with my best friends Charlotte and Laurie. We've been trying our best to put the summer behind us and get into the swing of a new school year. It's the start of our sophomore year of high school and every moment feels like a big deal. We're all so excited that we've already collectively decided to make this year be our best one yet.

Especially because all summer we fucked around. I live in this super small town that's like four square miles and is infiltrated with 32 parks. Just enough to make a person go insane, yaddamean? It's cool though because all the annoying parents can't be at the same parks at the same time. So when my friends and I sense a bad parent we'll usually just migrate to a different park.

Either way, I don't know when I'll have another summer like this last one. Every day was gorgeous, and colossal. It was pretty much Miles, Charlotte, Nikky, Steve, Mark, and me. We were inseparable. Laurie and Justin came around every so often. But, Laurie was busy most of the summer skiing in France like it was nothing; and, Justin was either begrudgingly attending the Jewish summer camp his parents made him go to, or hanging out with his other friends doing more wholesome shit.

Justin and I used to date, but Steve and I are the ones currently giving our generation hope that love exists. We've liked each other since we were ten years old. Steve was one of the first people I met when we moved to California. We were neighbors, and his brother is the same age as one of my sisters. So, we bonded pretty quickly over alla that. I made sure not to mention Elle, but we sorta lost touch any-way. Then, once I got socially settled at school, I randomly saw Steve again when I was out with my girls. It was crazy, almost like the world stopped. I still remember that day like it was yesterday, but I doubt Steve does. Turns out, my friends were already friends with Steve's friends. So, we all started kicking it.

This past summer was probably our last one all together. Steve and I flirted every day. Nothing ever manifested though, so don't worry. We mostly just hung out as friends skating around and laying out in the sun with the group. We'd walk in circles around town from one park to the next, ding-dong-ditching a few rotten eggs along the way. Sometimes we'd retreat to our own homes for dinner, and some-times we'd double up at someone else's house, but most of the time we just pulled together whatever cash we could pull and ate out. KFC was our *favorite* spot. We were notorious there. We used to order out their supply of ready-made snackers, speak too loud, and toss biscuits at each other from our individual booths. We left the place a total mess but only because it felt like home. Until the manager stopped letting us dine in after ordering, that is.

Mark was usually the one to stir things up first. He's the baby of our group. So, he's naturally the type of teenager who thinks it's cool to throw rocks at cars. Steve is the type of teenager who joins without hesitation, cracking undeniably hilarious jokes along the way to cover up his insecurities. They're each other's hypemen. When they're together they can become explosive. But, Miles is different. He's the type of teenager who doesn't mind moving to the beat of his own drum. He's unavoidably soulful. You can just tell everybody respects him, especially because he makes it seem so effortless. Justin, the wholesome Jew, is upper class. Something about him oozes pretentious college frat boy, and something about me is attracted to it.

Nikky and I are two peas in a pod, Raven and Chelsea, Left Eye and T-Boz. We're super close, but we also have our issues. I'm most honest and down to earth with my friends Laurie and Charlotte. Laurie, the one who lives a second life abroad during most breaks, is the crépe to my Nutella. I can always rely on her. Charlotte is my *Legally Blonde* sister. We're going to be justice fighting *Charlie's Angels* together one day. The four of us girls are the types of teenagers who can relate to the urge to throw rocks at unnecessarily expensive cars, but who will keep each other in check. Instead, we befriend and nurture the actual rock throwers to assist us in the moments our mouths get us into some things our asses can't handle.

It's great to see us all interact together! It's crazy how people can be so different and yet still be the best of friends. Lawrence always tells me "you lose friends as you get older and make different decisions in life," but I know everything he says is a lie. He likes to go on and on about how my friends are going to betray me, teach me to hate myself, and steer me down some horrible path -- it's all bs. He's barely even met all my friends! I think he's just jealous because I spend more time with them than I do with him. I don't even consider myself a "me" without my friends. We're a forever thing and that's on true commitment, something Lawrence doesn't know jack about.

Whatever. There I go talking about last summer again.

Anyway, yesterday we were at Nikky's listening to music and talking about the new school year. All of a sudden it turned into us talking about exactly how we were going to level up this year. We were goalstorming real big, and out of nowhere I turned all Vivian on them. "Charlotte, can you grab us some paper and pens? I want us to write all of this out so we really commit to it," I repeated without being able to stop myself.

"OK," Charlotte readily responded before returning to the carpet with three different shades of pink ballpoint washables and an open blank-paged binder. She looked up at me for further instruction.

"Alright," I assigned each of us a shade of pink and started taking notes from a half-extended child's pose over my knees.

We were covering topics like cars, boys, school, travel, and mental growth. Then, before I knew it, we were using the pens as microphones and dancing on Nikky's taupe colored L-shaped couch cushions. Honestly, I think "Beautiful Soul" got the train going, as it does. Then, "Get It Shawty" had us practicing our body rolls. Before I knew it we were making up choreography to "Shortie Like Mine." After we hit the "Girlfriend (Remix)" we were finally able to get back into our goalstorming session.

"Olivia, this year, you need to hook up with Steve! Give the people what they really want!" Nikky jeered while jumping off the couch and heading back to the open binder on the floor. She continued writing on our list while I coyishly laughed, "oh, really? Is that what 'the people' really want?"

"YES," they *all* annoyingly said in unison.

"And I'm going to finally hook up with Mark," Nikky declared.

"Gross, dude," Charlotte said while faking a gag. Mark and Charlotte are brother and sister, "the twins."

"Yeah? Well I want to hook up with a random hot guy," Laurie said rebelliously, true to her character.

Nikky squished her eyebrows as close together as she possibly could and stared the threat of a thousand social death towards Laurie, "you're such a whole whore, Laurie! Oh my gosh!"

"Nikky, what the fuck!" I barked. See, this is why we have issues. Nikky can be a real, mistaken, outta pocket, lowercase-"f" type of "friend" sometimes. I can't stand it! I have no space for friends who think it's funny to be mean to one another, and Nikky does that all day errday.

"Sorry, whatever," Nikky responded under her breath and rolled her eyes to herself, which Charlotte called out and said, "ew" to. I was much gentler in my approach than Nikky. I mean-mugged Nikky, rolled my eyes to Charlotte for support, and then looked at Laurie with a normal smiling face, chuckled, and said, "are you being serious, Foreigner? A complete *stranger?*"

"Yeah! You guys, I'm being serious! I don't want to hook up with anyone from our group. Everything's perfect just as it is right now. I don't want to mess anything up with *that.* It's not worth the three minutes."

"True," Nikky said quietly to herself.

"Plus, I want to meet someone completely new. I want to hook up with someone taller, funnier, and way better looking than anyone in our group." Laurie flipped her hair and said, "come on, we're sophomores now! We gotta step it up!"

"Oh, okay, Laur! We hear you, gurl!" I joked. Laurie's always raising the bar and opening our perspectives.

"I agree with Laurie," Charlotte cheered!

Do you want to know our final list of goals for the year? I'll tell you --

1. Go to a club and a house party
2. Get "my" version of a perfect body
3. Ride the Zipper at the next arts festival
4. Get good grades -- As and Bs only -- and stop partying so much
5. Get tan (that's only Nikky's goal. Laurie and Charlotte are happy being pale, and I was obviously already born tan)
6. Hook up with Mark
7. Hook up with Steve
8. Hook up with a random hot guy (Laurie and Charlotte's goal)
9. Get over the guys we're currently stuck on
10. Stop being mean to one another

11. Buy a 2008 Nissan Altima for 16th bday (my goal)
12. Date a fantastic boyfriend
13. Actually go out on a date (preferably with a guy who has a car)
14. Go to Cabo together for Spring Break
15. Fuck! (Nikky's goal, she's still a virgin)
16. Get into a Fight
17. Pay Charlotte 1 million dollars (Charlotte's goal for us)

Wish me luck.

2

NIKKI REED

| 4 |

Chapter Four

August 23rd, 2007

You want to know about the "boyfriends in the wall" argument? It was just another shitty thing that happened at home on a Monday. I'm pretty sure Mondays are internationally known as the worst day of the week, but that doesn't really change what happened. So, I guess I'll stop stalling and just tell you.

I have one more question before I begin though.

Why do the worst days always start off so normal? It's like you start sinking into your routine, and then, all the sudden -- WHAM!

That's how this one shitty Monday felt -- like just another normal night. Even when I got home things felt normal. Vivian was waiting for me in the living room, cautiously spread out on the orange futon folded out into a bed. She was alone watching *Ally McBeal* reruns. I joined Vivian on the futon for a bit, but, as soon as perpetually heartbroken Ally was crushed by a giant wrecking ball in the unisex bathroom, we left to go pick up Elle from school.

"Let's just go," Vivian said, sounding as disappointed as a properly seasoned viewer might. She knew what was coming next: Billy being married.

We usually walk to and from Elle's daycare together, since it's only a couple blocks from our apartment. But, yesterday Vivian wanted to take a taxi instead. She said her feet hurt from wearing her new heels to work. Honestly, Vivian said she wanted to drive, but Lawrence had taken the family car and Vivian didn't know where he was, so…

Vivian is one of those super professional women who wears a different snazzy suit to work every day. She has the best accessories and typically wears little makeup because she doesn't really need it. Vivian is always more than enough all on her own. "Makeup would ruin it," as Lawrence says.

I think the whole ride to pick up Elle only took like fifteen minutes total? But, it still didn't matter. The taxi driver tried to hit on Vivian within the first five seconds.

When we asked the driver to take us to Elle's daycare the greasy-haired douchebag turned back towards us and smiled. He didn't smile at me, the fifteen year old girl actually within the guy's range. Oh no. He very distinctly only smiled at Vivian. The prepubescent-looking driver pretty much ignored my existence altogether, winked at Vivian, and then asked, "so, how much do you charge for babysitting? I have a little sister too."

Vivian barely even laughed. She answered flatly, clearly not flattered. "Oh please, I'm picking up my second daughter. Just drive, kid." Vivian motioned ahead to encourage the guy to start driving. He sobered up and quickly followed Vivian's command.

When we picked Elle up from daycare she was living her best five-year-old life to the absolute fullest. Hovering over ten perfectly-seated toddlers, Elle instructed, "remember you have to do what I say, remember?"

It became increasingly evident that Elle was leading a pretend play session. So, I clung to the walls and decided to watch from behind the glass. If you haven't already gathered, Elle is a complete force of nature and is not to be crossed -- I don't care who you are. Elle is consistently sweet, sassy, and goofy, *and* she has a heart full of pure gold. I mean, who else can get a group of toddler-tweeners to sit still?

Even the staff can't get them to listen like Elle can -- they love it when she plays principal! Vivian gets embarrassed at how headstrong Elle is sometimes, probably because Vivian tries to remain opposite that trait to make others comfortable, but *I* love it. Elle is a force.

Vivian approaches Elle differently than I do -- as "the Mom" and all. Like, when Vivian saw Elle bossing all the kids around and the two teachers sitting together in a corner talking. Instead of standing to the side like me, Vivian bravely entered the room.

"Can't you see we're busy here, Lady?!" Elle said as she shoved her hands to her hips and sent her head forward like a clucking chicken.

Vivian laughed but ignored Elle's inaccurately presumed authority, she gathered up Elle's jacket and lunch box. Mom waved goodbye to the teachers and signed Elle out while efficiently escorting her 60lbs adult-like spirited daughter out of the daycare. Just like that, and all at once, Elle was no longer the boss.

During the car ride home I asked Elle what game she was playing with the other kids, even though I already knew. "I was being the principal," she said, "and they were *all* in trouble." Elle shook her head relaying to us all that she was actually disappointed in her peers for not buying into her dream world. Everyone except Elle started laughing -- even our taxi driver looked up at us in the rearview mirror and started in. Our driver was too busy searching for Vivian's eyes in the rearview mirror to focus on the road, but she didn't see him. Vivian was just looking out the window counting the trees. Elle pouted, and my hand flew up and down outside the window. I remember envying Elle's naivety and confidence, but otherwise, it was a pretty boring ride on another normal night.

It was so normal I felt comfortable to make a completely lame joke over dinner about our taxi driver having the hots for Vivian. We were all joking and arguing one of our normal family play arguments about who is the best looking in the family. Elle was sassing from the kids table, per usual, when Lawrence chimed in that he was the best looking. Elle snapped back at him without hesitation, "uhh uhnnn, Dad! Mom is the prettiest in the whole world!"

His deep belly Dad laugh rumbled through our entire apartment building, "psht, girl you don't know what you're talkin' about!"

I just tried to keep the laughs flowing, "our taxi driver sure thought so!" Totally forgettable and harmless, right? Well, only Elle and I continued laughing. Quickly it was just Elle, and then nobody except the crickets singing outside. Vivian looked indirectly towards Lawrence, who looked like Ali after being challenged to a weight-lifting contest. He didn't fully lose his temper until later that night -- right after Mom put us down to sleep. Still, I should have known Lawrence would get angry at a joke about some guy thinking Mom was cute. I just let my guard down and wanted to make sure everyone kept on laughing.

I swear, trying to prepare for an addict parent's upcoming emotional state is like playing Marco Polo. You think you're a great swimmer, or that you know all the parent's triggers, so you'll never be tagged. But then, all of a sudden, you get tapped out. And it's not ever really just a "tap," it's a punch in the gut that completely takes you out of the game for the next few days. You can try to duck the swings and swim away quickly, but you can't actually plan ahead enough to not get tagged out in the first place. It's one big cyclical "game" of causing anxiety to whoever you're in the pool with -- typically family and friends. I like playing the game Marco Polo in the pool, but never with Lawrence, and never in real life.

I made sure Elle stayed asleep next to me in the back bedroom. Elle can sleep through almost anything, even the waterbed swishing back and forth, but Lawrence's accusations were excruciating. I cuffed my hands around Elle's ears, pressed as hard as I could, and prayed to Whoever. I didn't want Elle to wake up to the sound of Lawrence's emotions erupting all over our apartment like I did. Even though there was obviously *no way* Vivian was throwing her cooch anywhere near the taxi driver, Lawrence wouldn't let it go.

I heard him scream, "how are you gonna be bringin' guys back here, Vivian?!"

Any accusation that Vivian was cheating was totally ludicrous. Lawrence was beyond uncontrollable and I could hear Vivian crying. Well, honestly, she was more whimpering. Sort of like how Jasper does when he has the runs. It was a cry that, at least from the back bedroom, sounded as if she were in a deep uncomfortable pain. So, I left Elle sleeping peacefully under the covers with Jasper and climbed out of bed to sneak a check on Vivian. The lights in the hallway were off and it was dark enough to cling to the wall and watch without either of my parents noticing.

"I know you've been hiding men in here!" Lawrence roared.

"No, I haven't! Please listen to me, Love!"

Vivian calls Lawrence "Love" for short most of the time. Apparently the "L" stands for Lawrence and the "ove" comes from our last name, Grove, so when put together it spells "love." Vivian and Dad used to be really into making up pet names for each other by combining their names. Take my name, for example, "Olivia" is the combination of Larenzo (a variation of Lawrence) and Vivian. When Vivian got pregnant with Elle my parents made sure to choose a name that started with an "E" so all of our names put together spell out "LOVE." They really took it too deep if you ask me, but, anyways, I've digressed.

"Don't you fucking lie to me, Vivian!" Lawrence was screaming. As I discreetly approached them from the hallway, I could see Lawrence had his hands shaped like a gun and he was pointing it in Vivian's face. He was screaming, "I know you've been fuckin' other people! I know it! You're fucking them in my bed and then hiding them somewhere." He was relentless and persistent.

"Love, listen to yourself."

"You're hiding them! Where are they, Vivian?"

"Listen. I'm not hiding anyone." Mom was blubbering and her snot was spreading everywhere. "When do you think I have the time for someone else, Love? Keeping this family together takes up all my time."

"*Vivian!*" He screamed as if the act of shouting her name alone would prove his point. I'm sure he felt she was egging him on, like he always does. But, a high pitched tone from Lawrence indicates he is beginning to consciously squirm in his baseless accusations, so I went back to the room, recruited Jasper, and made sure Elle was still sleeping. She was tucked under the blankets, seemingly asleep, with her eyes and lips pressed closed tight.

After I made sure Elle was settled, I found a spot on the hallway wall to plaster myself along with Jasper. We snuggled into the floor like bugs in a rug under my blanket and watched over Vivian from around the corner together. I still didn't want to be alone, even though I was older this time around.

"Where do you think I'm hiding someone, Lawrence? Look around! There's nobody here except us and the girls! There *is* nowhere to hide! There's nowhere for me to hide myself, let alone anybody else!"

"In the fucking corner, Vivian!"

"What?"

Lawrence stormed over to the blood orange futon, now folded up into the couch position and leaning against the wall near our front door.

"There's space right here!"

"Where?" Mom was perplexed rather than simply scared, sad, and confused like in past arguments.

"In the fucking corner, Vivian, you probably got a little ass nigga scrunched up right there."

"Lawrence," Mom paused and then trailed off, "what the..."

I could tell Lawrence was about to go out partying, to some woman's house, or to wherever he goes when he's gone. Lawrence wore a fresh black flannel shirt, he calls it his "cowboy shirt," his Timberland boots, and a dark wash pair of jeans. His cologne was strong but his insecurities were stronger -- tonight he reeked.

"Oh, so you want me to go check in that back room then, huh? He's probably pressed up in there!" Lawrence started towards the hallway, but Vivian stopped him. I think she saw me because her eyes got pretty big and she begged him to calm down, "so the neighbors don't call the cops on us *again*," she pleaded.

Vivian always looked more petite next to Lawrence than normal when they fought. Vivian was wearing her soft light pink shirt that ruffled at the end of the sleeves, and the type of high-waisted mom jeans that Maya Rudolph, Tina Fey, Amy Pohler, and Rachel Dratch rocked so well on *SNL*. I only saw the back of her head shaking but I could tell Vivian's eyes were darting back and forth on Lawrence -- scanning for a physical indication of how much longer the drugs would make him crazy.

"Back off, Vivian!" Lawrence broke eye contact with her, grabbed the set of porcelain stacking dolls in front of the TV from the dresser top, and casually shattered them on the ground. Those porcelain stacking dolls were a gift from Vivian's older sister, Aunt Deb. Vivian says her and Aunt Deb used to play with the dolls as young girls, like Elle and I do now. But, Lawrence didn't care; he just spun around, snickering, and wrecking everything. He was so busy tearing our home apart he didn't notice me, like Vivian clearly had, crying scared in the shadows.

Lawrence stopped spinning around, looked down at the mess he had made, and then blew through the front door. A normal night turned nightmare-ish.

I didn't really care though, I'm used to it. I was just upset because Elle loved playing with those dolls, ya know? She cried in the morning when she realized they were really still gone and she cried intermittently throughout the day; but, whatever. I'm not really trippin'. I just hate that we didn't tell her what really happened. Instead, in the morning, Mom just said, "there was an accident, Honey, I knocked them over last night," and left it at that.

| 5 |

Chapter Five

August 30th, 2007

After processing all of the bullshit that happened the other night -- I'm pretty fucking lit. I just don't understand how parents think their own kids don't know anything. I swear! They really think they can lie, steal, cheat, and do whatever in the world they want to, but we just won't notice? Yaddamean? Like, some parents really truly believe they know more than you just because they're older. They think *you,* specifically, don't know anything because you're "too young" to know about shitty universal truths.

Why is that?

Personally, I have instincts and full thoughts, but what I lack is the desire, and, no doubt, sometimes the ability, to express them. Parents fake themselves into believing their kids are angels. We're not. As if I've never gotten too drunk and puked up my lunch in front of my family and friends -- like Lawrence did last weekend.

My first time puking was two years ago. I upchucked a wad of spaghetti. The most graceful worm-like thing a person could ever yack in front of her friends, huh? Of course, I couldn't have just had some light soup ahead of time? Nope, not I. Also, Elle was there. I mean, she was 3 years-old at the time, so, obviously she probably doesn't even fully remember what happened -- if at all. But, I won't lie to you, she did see me drunkenly get sick a couple times. The look of disappointment in her eyes still stays with me today. In my defense, I was only like 13 years-old, so I really didn't know any better. Plus, I learned my lesson and made sure she wasn't around the first time I smoked weed a couple months later.

Anyway, some parents just really don't think you see all the stuff happening right in front of your face! Some parents are oblivious to you and they assume it's mutual -- which, like, come on. That couldn't be further from the truth. Some adults just straight up think they're more valuable than you, as if there's really some holy hierarchy placing adults far above kids and teenagers. It's crazy! Some parents think they're smarter than you, some parents walk around with their heads in the clouds, and some parents are so wrapped up in doing their own lives they forget you have one too. It's like we're fundamentally at a sometimes-civil war and built to remain in conflict. To tell you the truth, I honestly just think they're all scared.

My parents, they're the best examples of alla this. I think Lawrence is totally checked out by this point in life, and Vivian is refusing to accept the severity of his addiction. She keeps lying to me saying "everything is fine," when in truth, Lawrence has been spiraling for years now. Our home has turned into the type of place you'd never want to invite people over to. It's boiling red like hot lava. I can't focus on trivial things like my school work when the house is burning down.

It's hard to believe my grades really matter when I'm learning how to dodge the atomic bombs raining down all around me. All these interruptions throughout my days are just that. They're throwing me off my path. My plan. The whole thing makes me so full of rage I could scream at the sun until my lungs catch fire and I blow the whole sky out -- forever.

But, sure, "everything is fine."

| 6 |

Chapter Six

September 6th, 2007

Truth is, I actually started having sex last year when I was fourteen years old. Justin, the same guy I mentioned to you a while ago, has been my friend since I was eleven years old. I don't remember the first time I met Justin, it just feels like we were always in the same group of friends who hung out after school. But, I guess we started getting closer as we got older. All of a sudden, I looked around and he had become my best friend who I told everything to and loved being with. So, I leaned into that feeling. Besides, teenagers don't do what our parents *tell* us, we do what our parents actually *do*.

Or, at least we try.

Justin is a tan, dirty-blonde haired, Jewish guy who carries a strange amount of confidence despite his underdog status. I see forest green when I think of Justin and his hazel eyes that change color depending on whatever shirt he's wearing for the day. Justin has always been incredibly unexpectedly hilarious. So, it's no surprise he was also the first boyfriend that I actually started doing stuff with.

Anyway, one time at a school dance Justin asked me to slow dance. Back then, we really didn't slow dance like in the movies because we were too young and too shy. Instead, we'd just hold our arms

43

out straight, barely tap each other's shoulders, and not quite make eye contact. But, Justin and I knew each other. So, when we danced it felt comfortable, his hands tapped my hips, *and* we made eye contact.

The. Whole. Time.

Whew! Sorry, sometimes it still makes me fan myself when I think of that first slow dance of ours. During the dance, Justin asked me to be his girlfriend. I didn't answer, but I held his hand in front of all our friends the whole walk up to McDonalds after the dance. When Mom picked me up I texted him "yes" as soon as I got in the car. Then, Justin called me when he got home and told me he loved me. I just said "ditto" and hung up.

The more I started getting used to the idea he was my boyfriend, the closer we got. We started passing notes in between classes, being inseparable at lunch, hanging out together after school, and staying up all night talking to each other on the phone. Justin went from being my best friend to becoming my *best*, best friend. Even though Nikky, Charlotte, and Laurie got jealous.

Eventually, Elle caught me whispering on the phone all night and started interrupting. She kept me up all night sharing about her memories, and I couldn't concentrate on Justin anymore. So, Justin and I took some space, and soon after we were fighting like cats and dogs. We fought about random things, like who hung up first and who loved the other more. But then, all of a sudden, we started fighting about real things like flirting with other people, not being supportive of each other, and, even if one person wanted to hangout with the other or not.

Our first real fight broke out because of Mark. We were all at KFC eating our Snackers, when Mark and Justin started going in on each other, "for fun." Mark took it too far, per usual, and he told Justin to "go get back in the oven, Kike."

Justin was pissed; he turned up and started chasing Mark around the entire KFC until the manager finally came over and kicked them out. Justin felt slighted and protested the perceived injustice while Mark just laughed. Once Justin left KFC he started chasing Mark around the parking lot, and then up on the sidewalk of the actual road until they disappeared around the block.

Mark came back first, sweating and wearing a snarl across his face. Justin arrived shortly after. His shirt was stretched and looked rugged. He walked in, grabbed his backpack off the ground, snatched his jacket off the back of his chair, and then left without saying a word. Zero eye contact with any of us.

I went to the bathroom to text and call Justin, but he wasn't answering me. So, I was super surprised when he later showed up at the skate park where all our friends were foreseeably already gathered. Justin was stepping back into our world, but he still didn't talk to any one of our friends. After pushing down a few ramps Justin texted me. With his skateboard in one hand, and hat to the back. He asked, "wanna talk?"

"Yeah..." I texted back.

We walked out of the skate park, in concert, and sat together on the concrete against the handball wall. Justin wore the hood of his black hoodie on top of his hat, he continued avoiding eye contact, and was tugging at the grass growing from the cracks in the concrete as he spoke.

"Why didn't you stand up for me?" he said.

"What do you mean?"

"What Mark said about me going in the oven was fucked up. You know he only said that because I'm Jewish. You didn't say anything."

I didn't have an answer for him, so I just got mad at him for blaming me about the fight with Mark, and then stormed off. I regretted it almost immediately. I still do. Justin just followed me into the skate park and hugged me in front of everybody; I knew we were fine. I only said sorry to him inside my head but I know he heard me.

Anyways, I was the first one to ask about having sex. Lawrence had been stressing me out about sex and loosing my virginity since I was a kid, so I just wanted to get it over with. Plus, Justin was the kindest, sweetest, and smoothest guy on the planet. I knew the time was right *for me.*

The day I lost my virginity was a cloudy and grey Wednesday. Justin and I had cut school together after lunch on a whim one day. I guess it was pretty risky, but I had to take my shot. Justin and I had talked about having sex before, but we never knew when the right time would be. I texted Justin about the idea to skip school the night before.

"It's our only open window!" I persuaded.

I wore my white t-shirt that spelled "Don't Trip" in orange cursive and showed off a bit of midriff. My light wash jeans were distressed and I had slipped on my olive green checkered Vans. If I hadn't been so frantic thinking about the fact that I was going to lose my virginity when getting ready that morning, I would have stolen a pair of lace panties from Vivian! I would have at least worn a bra that matched whatever clean unders I could find. But, Justin didn't seem to mind my chocolate brown bra and pink teddy bear panties. Justin just wore a white t-shirt and his favorite medium wash jeans that he wore pretty much every day. I guess we sorta matched. He wore blue and white plaid boxers underneath it all. Justin looked great no matter what he wore -- even in just socks.

You know, nobody ever wants to talk about the fact that having sex isn't actually all that easy. The movies don't show all the awkward moments and they always make it seem like a trouble-free grand ol' Axe commercial, but *I* didn't have that experience during my first time. Also, the whole thing only lasted about thirteen minutes, and in the movies they make it seem like the sex just goes on and on and on forever and ever. Geez. Take this truer-than-true public service an-nouncement from me: sex is *not* like how they show it in the movies.

First of all, we were both *so, so* nervous. Second, I sweat out my straightened hair and my hair became all curly and poofy, which nobody ever warns about. Justin had never seen me all raw like that, but he said I looked great -- even though I knew he was lying. Then, third, we turned the TV in the living room down too low so it was awkwardly quiet; and, fourth, the condom was too big. Justin swore he didn't get an extra big size or anything, but it was still way too big, and he stumbled putting it on.

"What the fuck," he said, which broke the tension and we both started laughing. He's the greatest.

The sound of the light rain pattering on the window reminded me of Seattle. I felt my mind drift back in time while Justin finished wrapping it up. But, then another hurdle arose. Neither of us could figure out how to actually "connect," if you know what I mean. Eventually I did the flicking the switch move, and we found some sort of groove.

Even though we both kept periodically nervously giggling throughout the whole thing, it felt special to me. Justin kept asking, "am I doing this right?" and "are you OK?" Hearing him express how much he cared about my experience was so sweet, and sexy, and it made me want him even more. I felt as full as a cream filled doughnut.

The second time we had sex felt pretty nice, and the third time was actually great! I still think my homework of us both watching some *Sex and the City* and listening to Sade's "Flow" so many times beforehand definitely helped us improve. Over time, Justin even agreed with me and said the extracurricular exercises "helped teach us the proper form."

Anyway, after we were really and fully done that first time I walked Justin home. Justin only lives on the other side of the bridge, but it's such a nicer neighborhood. On the walk to his place we held hands and we decided "Your Song" by Elton John would be our song.

"I had a great time," he said.

I looked up towards *The Simpsons*-like grey blue sky and laughed out loud. I said "duh," and then kissed him softly on the neck a few times on the way up to his lips. "Me too."

Lawrence always tells me that I'll forget the memories I make from the time before I'm twenty years old. "Just wait," he says, "you're still just a kid, Olivia, you still don't really know anything yet."

On the off chance that Lawrence is actually right, I hope I never forget the smile on Justin's face as we said goodbye that day. And I may not know anything, but I don't think you have to be an adult to know about love. I still really, *really* believe that Justin and I were in real-life love, and he wasn't just using me to cum. But, who really knows?

| 7 |

Chapter Seven

Last Friday Vivian and I picked Elle up from daycare. It was a grey day, but it hadn't rained, and the fall Washington winds were warm -- practically pleasant. The three of us were walking on the sidewalk heading home, when Mom busted out singing our famous family Friday night song.

"It's Friday night and I've got my girls," she sang, hunching down towards me and Elle slanging her arms over our shoulders.

Vivian continued singing, "I said it's Friday night, and I've got my girls! And we are gonna all head home, and sing, and take a bath, and have fun all night long."

Vivian sang this song to us on most Fridays upon picking Elle up from preschool. It's a corny ass little jingle, but I love it, OK? After the "and we are gonna all head home" part, we fill it in with whatever the plans are for the evening. We usually do the same thing every Friday night though, so when I hear the song it signals we're about to go home, pop some corn, snuggle in bed together, and watch some Ally McBeal -- *our* favorite show.

Vivian is practically a single mother. She works in finance, or technology, or training. Something like that. I think she trains people on how to invest their finances? I'm not one hundred percent sure. But, I know she works in the second tallest building downtown Seattle. The one with the American flag on top. Either way, Vivian is one of the few people in her office who knows how to fix the computers so she's always staying late and always on the phone. Sometimes she even goes in on the weekends, and lets Elle and me play in the conference room.

But, last week when we got home from picking up Elle, our Friday night routine was thrown off. Vivian's older sister, Aunt Deb, called and needed help. Our Aunt Deb is in remission from the breast cancer she beat last year, so sometimes she needs help at home. Especially since her husband, my Uncle Mike, is also an addict and can't really be relied on. Vivian called Lawrence and, after explaining the situation, insisted he come home.

"I don't care where you are, Lawrence, just hurry up and come home so I can take the car to go help my sister," she said before hanging up. We used to have two family cars to avoid situations like these. But, earlier this year Lawrence wrapped one of them around a telephone pole. It was after a few nights of not coming home, so I don't really know what happened beyond Vivan's insurance not paying anything. I'm assuming the accident was Lawrence-binge-induced, but who knows? Ever since that accident Vivian takes the light rails into the transit tunnel because Lawrence needs a car to drive from one window washing gig to the next.

Usually he just sits at home and watches Elle and me.

Like last week. When Lawrence finally got home it was completely dark outside and Vivian was in a rush to Aunt Deb's. I was hopeful Vivian would take us with her, but she didn't, so we were stuck with Lawrence. He tugged the futon down into bed position with just one hand, then grabbed some pillows and our big bright pink blanket out from the hallway cupboard. The four of us -- Lawrence, Elle, Jasper, and myself -- all squished in together on the futon. Jasper sprawled out spanning our jagged line of feet, and Dad powered up the television.

Lawrence leaned his head on Elle's shoulder, itched at his nose, put on MTV, and closed his eyes. Eventually some weird ass music video started bumping throughout the apartment. It was Michael Jackson's "Thriller." I could tell Elle was freaking out because she didn't understand we were watching a music video, but Lawrence was snoozing. Even though she was playing it cool, I could tell Elle thought we were watching a real story about a man turning into a zombie wolf and trying to attack his girlfriend. To her defense, the video damn near runs a whole fifteen minutes -- so it's not your average music video.

After "Thriller" ended things got worse. Lawrence woke up and said he wanted to watch movies for the rest of the night. We started with a horror movie called *Bride of Chucky*, which starred this wild, orange headed, psychopathic babydoll in overalls. Have you ever seen any of the Chucky movies? Have you ever watched them as a five year old child? It was yet another scary movie about a guy, a freaking male babydoll no less, killing his girlfriend. I guess technically Chucky killed his *ex-girlfriend*, Tiffany, but hopefully you're seeing the important pattern of what Lawrence finds entertaining -- right?

In case you missed it, his taste is any sort of entertainment where chauvinistic male dominance is normalized. Elle was curled up in Lawrence's arms, hiding under the blanket, and singing softly to herself. At the most intense moments of the movie Lawrence would flex the muscles throughout his body, squeezing Elle close, and scream out as if a monster was coming to attack us. Each time Elle and I screamed at the top of our lungs for someone to come save us. But, somehow Lawrence's big barrel laugh drowned us out. He was always so much louder.

The last movie we had time to watch together before Vivian came home was "Jaws." Before the movie started, Lawrence started in on lecturing us. His face was as serious as when he's leading us through a prayer, so both Elle and I made sure to not break eye contact and to listen to him carefully.

"I want to show you girls this important movie about sharks." Lawrence explained. "I need you girls to know what a shark is capable of doing and to take it seriously. You know we have a water bed."

I was so perplexed I let out a semi-sassy, "so?"

"So, young lady, sharks live in the water. We have a water bed. That obviously means we have sharks living in our water bed. They sleep during the day and then they come out and go hunting for food at night. *We're* their food."

Elle gasped and covered her mouth in utter shock.

"Oh no, Daddy!"

"Yes, E. It's true. Now watch this. Learn what a shark can do to you if you're not careful." Lawrence started *Jaws*. He continued his supposed-to-be comedic bit as Chrissie is attacked by Jaws while swimming in the ocean. Lawrence's voice trailed on in the background while Chrissie was being raggedly tugged back and forth across the screen.

"That's why we have to always cover up the holes Jasper pokes in our bed as soon as possible, Elle. We don't want the sharks to come get us through the holes!"

After that first scene, Lawrence disappeared into the bathroom. He kept the movie running for us in the living room in his absence. Elle and I talked about turning the TV off, but we were scared we would get yelled at when Lawrence came back out to join us. He didn't end up joining us until the end of the movie when the guys were trying to kill Jaws on the unrealistically small fishing boat.

Anyway, when Lawrence came out of the bathroom he made Elle and me promise not to tell Vivian about what he "let us" watch. He had given us some bullshit spiel about how he trusted that we were mature enough to watch movies like *Bride of Chucky* and *Jaws*. When really he was just trying to manipulate us into not telling Vivian what we had seen. Especially Elle, since she was obviously bound to be scared out of her rational mind for weeks to come.

Elle kept the secret, but it all came out to Vivian that same Friday night anyways. The way Elle acted made it obvious something had gone down. She started clinging to Vivian as soon as Vivian got home, and she was hesitant to go into the dark back bedroom by herself. Then, after she fell asleep, Elle woke the entire complex up by screaming at the Chucky in her sleep.

"Chucky, don't hurt me! I love all my dolls equally!"

Vivian rolled over in bed and faced towards me. Mom's face was simultaneously annoyed and angry.

"What the hell was that?" Mom whispered to me while rubbing Elle's belly as she laid between Vivian and I.

I whispered back, "we watched *Bride of Chucky* tonight with Dad."

Vivian rolled her eyes, signaling her disappointment, so I continued.

"And 'Thriller,' and '*Jaws.*'"

"Oh my gosh, your Dad is so -"

We were interrupted by water quickly spreading underneath us. I looked at Mom and cocked my head sideways while rolling my eyes back to her. Jasper was laying out in the living room, waiting for Lawrence at the door. So, we both knew it wasn't Jasper who was making the bed leak this time -- it was Elle. Then, Vivian let out a grunt and said in her normally volumed voice, "of fucking course."

Elle jolted up from sleeping position into seated position within an instant. Elle looked panicked and was flushed from sweating in her sleep. As Elle transitioned to full consciousness she started frantically turning her head back and forth between Vivian and me on either side to be sure we were still really there.

"The sharks are coming! I feel the sharks coming, Ollie! We *have* to get out of here!"

"Don't worry, Ellie Bear, we're safe. We're at home and you were just having a really bad dream. Try to focus on your breathing and forget about the sharks and Chucky and anything else bad."

Our waterbed was leaking. But, for the first time in a long time Jasper's long nails hadn't punctured the bed and caused it to start leaking. This time the water was coming from Elle. My sweet girl had had such a scary nightmare that she peed the bed in her sleep. Elle was the first preschooler in her entire cohort to master potty training, so the occurrence of her wetting the bed had been unheard of for at least the past two years.

I felt bad because Elle was super embarrassed about it.

"I'm sorry, Mommy. I didn't mean to."

"That's OK, Ellie" Vivian hit the lights on in the bedroom and started gathering up the sheets spread across the bed. Jasper heard us moving around, so he ran to the back room to check on the commotion. "Here, get up, baby." Vivian helped Elle up and off the wobbling bed.

Elle and I stood a bit behind Vivian perpendicular to the bed. I hugged Elle as we stood watching Vivian wrestle the waves and blankets.

"Olivia, would you mind helping your little sister get clean?"

"Naw, I gotchu."

I softly took Elle's hand in mine and led her to the bathroom where I plugged the tub and started a bath. I tried to stay calm and keep my breathing steady because I realized I was starting to feel over-whelmingly resentful. I couldn't speak, and I was beyond being able to small talk like Elle needed me to. All I wanted to do was smash things into tiny, microscopic pieces of dust. I didn't even care what I smashed -- the hand mirror seemed enticing, the porcelain bowl that holds our soap felt appropriate, the bottle of Dad's cologne sitting on the side of the sink looked like a perfectly sized object. The feeling of fury was so overwhelming it scared me. It scared me so much I didn't even tell Vivian how horrible I felt.

Instead, I took a deep breath and let it pass.

After Elle was cleaned off, and Vivian had laid down new sheets, Vivian made us hot chocolates. "I think we all need some chocolate before going back to bed, don't you?"

Jasper followed us out to the kitchen and flopped down on the linoleum floor. Elle scurried to the back bedroom and then returned to the kitchen with a soft pink baby blanket. It was the same blanket my parents carried her home from the hospital in. The blanket hadn't been peed on -- so it was folded up on Elle's pillow waiting for her in bed. Elle shook her baby blanket out and covered Jasper with it. She kissed Jasper's cheek a couple times, pet him on his square head, and then laid down behind him becoming the big spoon. Elle fell asleep right there on the floor before our hot chocolates were even ready.

| 8 |

Chapter Eight

September 20th, 2007

I swear some of the most messed up stuff in the world happens at my house. This time I caught Lawrence doing something really shady and, in response, he went on a smear campaign, then made sure to erupt the whole apartment. Elle was scared shitless, but I'm not even sure if that's the right way to fully capture the intensity.

I guess it all started when Elle and I were playing with her dolls on the bed in our back bedroom. Lawrence, just an arm's reach away from us, was ironing out his silky red button up shirt. Prince's "Gett Off" was playing, even though I think "Wake Me Up When September Ends" would have been way more appropriate! Lawrence was swaying from side to side with a spliff hanging from his bottom lip. He was smiling, while intermittently guzzling down his 40oz.

On too frequent an occasion, Lawrence pounded his fist down on the ironing board in unison with the bass. I'm not sure if you've ever heard "Gett Off" or not, but at the top of every four counts there's a hard bass sound that goes, "BOOM." So, every other eight counts or so Lawrence would hit the ironing board all dramatically like it was a tambourine, then stop and continue on ironing like nothing had ever happened.

Elle and I tried to ignore him; but, Lawrence is impossible to ignore when he wants attention. He really loves making a scene and repeating his processes, you know what I mean?

I know Lawrence is prepping for a night out drinking whenever the music vibrates through the apartment, Vivian glues herself to the couch watching Ally McBeal, and the apartment fills with his sexy man cologne. If getting ready for a night out was a person, it would definitely be number one in Lawrence's top eight. To be honest, I think it's the process of shedding fatherhood, monogamy, and the tedious responsibilities of adulthood that he's actually addicted to. It's not even about the actual narcotics.

Anyways, last night Lawrence was dancing to his favorite, nastiest Prince songs. As I said, he was clapping, banging on the ironing board, swaying his hips, drinking *and* smoking a joint. Basically, he was taking up all the space he possibly could just to see how far he could go. At certain points Lawrence would sorta bend over, and scream out, "Uhhhn! You hear that girls, did you hear what he just said?! Woo!" Then, he'd just crack up laughing -- mostly to himself. Of course Elle smiled without making eye contact. But, it was only out of pity. I remember when I used to act the same way.

Duh! We could obviously hear the music, you know? It was like 9 PM on a Tuesday night and the music was so loud I couldn't even hear John Cage channeling Barry White in the living room. Lawrence was being ridiculously unnecessary and fucking childish, blatantly inconsiderate and rude, but I just kept playing with Elle.

"Sorry, Elle, I gotta go pee," I whispered into her ear. "Just pretend my Brat is sleeping right now. Be right back"

"But, Ollie, it's day time! She can't go to sleep right now!" Elle looked up at me with her insatiable puppy eyes, and, under her breath so Lawrence couldn't hear, she whispered, "don't leave me."

"You're right," I told her. "So, let's say my dolls are at school right now, Ellie. My bad, I forgot. Mine is sick. She's going to visit the school nurse really quick."

Elle looked down at her Brat dolls. "I'll be right back, Elle, OK?" I kissed her on top of the head after whispering, "I'm not leaving you. I just have to pee."

Elle is so scared of Lawrence she's afraid to even admit it out loud. It's sick, but I guess I get it. As a kid, I wasn't always able to talk about what was happening around me when I was alone with Lawrence. I think Elle is like that too.

"Be right back," I reassured loudly enough for both Elle and Lawrence to hear.

Elle was ignoring me but I wasn't worried. I knew she'd be alright alone with Lawrence for at least a little bit. Within a 500 square foot apartment there really *is* no leaving her alone with any one of us, let alone our loud ass Dad, yaddamean? Elle only felt alone because she's so young that our crappy little basement apartment tucked into the middle of Nowhere Important still feels like a castle to her. Even though the carpets are stained, the hallways are too narrow for two people to comfortably pass each other, the bathtub is lined with an inch and a half of mold that resists all of Vivian's scrubbing, and our waterbed pops and leaks all over our "clean" piles of clothes about every other week. Four people, a dog, and an aquarium just don't all fit in together like that and still live with any sort of privacy.

One time, I even caught Vivian say, "this place is fucking disgusting." She was talking to herself while we were doing our "Clean-Up Clean-Up" Barney-inspired routine on a random Saturday morning and she just let it slip. I think because Lawrence wasn't home she didn't really think there was anybody left to listen to her in a serious way, but I heard her.

Anyways, anyways, sorry.

After peeing I returned to the bedroom pretty quickly. Everything was different -- it stopped me in the doorway. In an instant it had all changed. Lawrence wasn't ironing his red button up shirt anymore and the music was still playing, but the room was totally still. *I* was the one thrown off balance. I felt sick in a way similar to when I black out. Elle wasn't playing with her dolls any more. I stood there in the doorway, silently, just taking it all in. It took me a minute to fully process what I was seeing. I blinked hard hoping my vision had blurred.

Lawrence was sitting on the corner of the bed bouncing Elle on his knee while talking softly in her ear. Both Elle and Lawrence gazed downward. It felt suspiciously sweet. Elle wasn't smiling, but she didn't look upset either. To be honest, I don't remember her face really at all.

All I remember is that Lawrence was smiling, like a slithering snake, and he had his snake arms wrapped around my little Elle. His arms glided down past Elle's baby face and crossed against her tiny chest locking her in like a rollercoaster ride. My eyes followed the snake arms downward and I realized Lawrence didn't have hands, but rather, he had the heads of snakes -- life-threateningly poisonous Inland Taipans, no less -- where either hand would be. One Inland was holding Vivian's purse open for Elle, and the other was helping her sift through it. He was on a mission with a clear objective: he wanted sssome money.

Soon, I was able to sort out his actual words.

He was saying, "ok good, that's her lipstick! Now, let's find her wallet!"

I just watched them. Lawrence and Elle scavenging through Vivian's *Mary Poppins* miracle purse, racing to find Vivian's money. It was a *Rat Race* that Elle "won" by finding Vivian's wallet first, even though it was clear the snake hand let her win. Lawrence had a much better vantage point and I felt his eye widen when he first spotted the goldmine.

He didn't even feign defeat. He just said, "good job baby! That's it! Now, go ahead and open it up. Let's see what she's got in there!"

Elle pulled out pictures, cards, and random little papers. Vivian had secretly kept her ticket from last year when we all went to the movies for Elle's birthday. Lawrence kept telling Elle not to pick a movie theater movie for her birthday present. "We might as well watch something at home and save the money," he said. But, Elle being Elle, she didn't listen. Then, in the theater she promptly fell asleep thirty minutes into the movie. I didn't know Mom had kept her movie ticket, but there it was staring me in the face from the snake's slimy grip.

"Mommies and Daddies share things like money, E."

It all came together for me, just like that. Lawrence was clearly grooming his pure-hearted, tender-loving, never-kissed-a-boy and definitely-isn't-a-whore-like-Olivia, sweet baby girl, Elle, to steal money from her own Mom like it was a fun game. What's a word that means more than mad? More than out-of-this-world enraged? More than so fucking mad I could barely breathe? Whatever it is, that's how I felt.

Elle's face was blank, almost numb-looking; she still wasn't smiling. All I could do was stand there not knowing what to do or say while Lawrence's instructions continued, "hand me the cash there in that main pocket, Honey."

Elle obliged.

"Olivia, come help us find Daddy what he needs," he said, casually and without making eye contact. Lawrence signaled for me to become further complicit in his shameful scheme, he wanted me as close as he had Elle. But, I stayed there in the doorframe watching the two of them steal money from Vivian's purse, and I didn't move.

"Elle, you know a secret is something that only exists between a few people, right?"

"I know, Dad! Duh! I'm not a baby anymore," Elle innocently mocked. I could tell she genuinely wanted a level of reassurance from Lawrence that she was never going to get.

"HA!" He started laughing at her, "You'll always be a baby to me, Ellesha. But, right now, Mommy doesn't know we're taking her money because…" he trailed off stalling to think up an excuse, "Daddy is going to surprise Mom later for her birthday, OK?"

"Ok!"

"Doesn't that sound like fun, baby girl?"

"Yeah, Daddy!"

"OK, so you can't tell Mom about this, OK? Because it's a secret."

"Ok."

"But, you still want to help me surprise Mommy, right?"

"Yeah, Daddy!! Of course!"

"Good. Come on, now, Olivia."

Puke. Vivian's birthday is in February, not in late September. And, I'm pretty sure Vivian wouldn't want to pay for her own birthday surprise, you know? But, sure. Fine. Whatever he says goes. I wanted to help Elle get out of the situation hella badly, so I managed to walk into the room.

"Sure, I can help. How much do you need this time, Dad?" I looked for Lawrence straight in his deep brown eyes when I spoke, but he still kept his head sheepishly downward focused on Elle. He was making his knees replicate the real-life rollercoaster he had us all stuck on, but the irony was completely lost to him because he was locked-in on securing his next fix.

Wow, wait, sidenote: Ms. Walker, would have totally appreciated my "natural and everyday use of the word 'irony'" just now! Legit!

Okay. Anyways, I think that was the first time I actually *saw* Lawrence steal money directly out of Vivian's purse. Vivian had been working double shifts and through the weekends, so I sorta knew she felt financially strapped. But, I never thought Lawrence was at the fucking root of it like that, you know? I had never lost so much respect for someone I cared so deeply about in such a short period of time.

Lawrence took an awkward amount of seconds before responding with, "I don't know whatchu over there rolling your eyes about, Olivia." He was stern and erroneously cocky. A chill immediately ran inside me that forced me to react in compliance -- out of habit rather than respect.

"Sorry, sir. It's nothing. I'll be right back." I'm still not sure how I managed to turn around and walk away at that moment, but I left.

I really wasn't in the mood to start another fight, like I did a couple weeks ago with the whole "boyfriends in the walls" incident. But, my Mom deserved to know what was going on, so I went to disrupt her show. When I walked in the living room I checked the screen to best judge when to interrupt. I waited for Billy's misogynistic hallucination of pips to end before interjecting. Mom was annoyed with the show. She was holding Jasper and staring steadily into the TV set.

"Olivia, come watch with us!" Vivian said, still not breaking eye contact with the screen while extending her arms out to me. Jasper kept his eyes on me while I walked more fully into the room, like he was suspicious. I didn't sit down to join her, and I didn't receive her hug. I just started speaking. I was so mad I could barely breathe, but you'd never know it -- for some reason my face and my tone stayed stale.

"Mom," I said -- quietly.

"Come on! Come join me here on the couch, Olive! They're having a special moment!"

"*Mom,*" I said more strongly, semi-channeling Lawrence. All at once I had gained her full attention.

"What's going on, Olivia?" I sat down close to her on our orange futon folded up in couch posture.

"Dad and Elle are in the bedroom stealing money from your purse right now."

Vivian dared me to a staring contest, and I quickly lost. I looked to my lap for more words that never came. It's like Vivian instinctively knew to spring into action, like moms do, you know? She charged toward the back bedroom, like a superhero on a mission, but Lawrence was already walking out to meet us in the living room.

As far as society, and my life, is concerned, a six-six man with muscles and baritone like Lawrence has always dominated over a petite woman like Vivian who's been trained to always be smaller than the men in her life. Lawrence's disposition was confident, like a peacock, and Elle trailed behind him as Mom backed herself in front of the TV. I'm not 100% sure what happened between Vivian and Lawrence, because I dissociated from reality within the blink of an eye. But, I remember Elle grabbing on to my hand so tightly I became distracted thinking it may fall off.

All of a sudden, I came back down to earth. Lawrence was screaming at me, "Stop! Just fucking stand there!"

I guess I was taking Elle back into the bedroom, and he didn't like it. Lawrence *wanted* me to watch them fight, to see his strength, and to learn to mind his authority at all times... or else. So, Elle and

I became the bugs on the wall he wanted us to be. We watched the horror show as if we had subscribed.

"What, Viv? So you're just going to listen to whatever this little liar says without even *trying* to ask me what really happened?" Then, he turned his attention back to me.

"And you! You think you can just run around running your mouth to your mother and there ain't gon' be no consequences? You think *I* ain't gon' know you came out here just to stir some shit up, huh? Yeah, I know you, little rat! You just think your Pops is a big fucking dummy? Well, I hate to upse*t* you, *Olivia*, but your father is *actually very smart*, young lady." He always over-enunciates when attempting to assert his infinite intelligence or impart his divine wisdom.

"I know, Dad." I never look him even close to directly in the eyes when he's at this level.

"'Dad?!' Who the fuck is 'Dad?'" Now he was being over-exuberant, "it's 'Sir' to you, young lady. You better show some respect."

I licked my lips and broke a sweat before spitting out, "Sir." Vivian's head was on a swivel. Turning back and forth between Lawrence and me like it was a fast basketball game. Even though the music was blaring, the tension throughout our apartment was higher than Lawrence.

"Lawrence, you're being ridiculous!" Both Lawrence and I looked wide-eyed towards Vivian. We were both bewildered, but in very different ways.

My amazing Mom said it again, "don't call her a 'liar' and don't yell at her for coming in here to tell me the truth!"

Lawrence looked crazed whereas I was just wholeheartedly jaw-dropped. I felt a sort of deep rage from Lawrence steaming from his body, sorta like when a person gets out of the hot tub. He was yelling so intensely, and he had actually been standing so close to me, his spit sprayed in my face throughout the whole chastising.

Lawrence continued screaming at Vivian, "I'll call her whatever the fuck I want to! You hear me, Vivian?!"

I guess Vivian had had enough! She literally rolled her eyes and said, "whatever, Lawrence. Olivia isn't the only one in trouble here and you know it. How much did you take?"

"How much of what? I don't know what you're talking about." Lawrence turned and looked at me, nervously kicking my legs back and forth sitting next to Elle who was petting Jazzy. Lawrence swooped down, grabbed my foot up to meet his face, and started pulling me off the futon by my toes. I fell backwards, sorta on my elbows, and Jasper skirted off the futon to our back bedroom. He was the only one who got to wait for the calm safely. Mom lunged to my defense, slapping my foot out from Lawrence's grip. Vivian's reaction made me really think he was gonna hurt me.

"Knock it off, Lawrence!"

"I was just messing around with her, Viv! Damn! Just trying to crack those Hammerhead toes of hers." Lawrence tried to switch gears and make light of the situation, another classic addict manipulation technique.

"For the last time, she doesn't have Hammerhead toes, Lawrence! Stop saying that! You're going to give her a complex about her perfect feet!"

"I'm just saying you know she got those funky things from you." They get distracted with petty stuff like that in the middle of their arguments all the time.

But, Vivian steered them back on course, per usual. "Stop trying to change the subject! How much money did you take?! And were you seriously trying to ask Elle to help you?! *Come on*, Lawrence!" Vivian was stronger than I had ever heard.

I know he thought he was "letting" Vivian be irate. But, in reality he wasn't talking back because he knew he was wrong, he knew he was leaving, and, he knew he took too much money for her to execute any type of exit plan. Plus, he was planning on taking the family car, so he knew we'd be stranded for the night. That's the thing about addicts, they tend to have a hard time holding down a normal job, which leaves the whole providing for the family responsibility on someone else.

Vivian can't afford to call in extra favors or take time off of work in order to drive us to school. She'll risk Lawrence crashing her car again, so long as he promises to get us to school in the morning and she doesn't have to call in late.

Vivian continued, "What are you doing?! What are you trying to do to our family?!" She sat down, just right there on the carpet, crying, and started shaking her head in her hands, "I just don't understand why you're doing this to us. Again."

What was fury dismantled into defeat; but, not just in her. The defeat was within Lawrence, within me, within Elle, and within Jasper too. Even our neighbors must have been feeling pretty fed up at this point, to be honest.

She gathered herself up enough and said, "just go."

"I ain't really tryna go anywhere, Viv," at first Lawrence spoke softly, but when Vivian didn't instantly reply, he screamed.

"I already told you! I don't know whatchu talkin' about!"

Vivian went mute and was virtually unreachable. Lawrence started for his heavy black leather jacket tucked on the back of a kids chair at the kids table.

"All you women are always just too much fucking drama, man! I'm telling you!" After lacing up his shiny black dance shoes he swooped up the keys from the ceramic blue bowl I made when I was little, and yelled "Elle, keep these mothatfuckas in check while I'm out." Then, he slammed the door behind him and was gone.

The apartment expanded instantly, and the whole complex seemed to simultaneously release a heavy-hearted breath. I sat back up on the couch and called for Jasper -- who came timidly creeping back into the living room not fully believing the scene was over.

"Come on over, Jasper, it's okay," I said encouragingly. I couldn't even look at Elle or Vivian. As soon as Jasper jumped up on the couch Vivian stopped crying on the floor and called out for Elle. Vivian looked up and opened her arms, "come on over here, baby!" Elle went to her.

"Mommy isn't mad at you, okay?! It's alright! Everything is all good! You didn't do anything wrong. Okay?" I watched Vivian press Elle into her chest and cradle Elle's head while rocking, nervously, back and forth. The evening had officially started neutralizing.

In the morning, we all hushedly crept around Lawrence, who was sleeping on the floor in the living room wearing the same clothes from last night. Lawrence didn't come home until we were all already asleep squished together on the waterbed in the back bedroom. Nobody heard him. For some reason, Lawrence left the car keys in the cupboard with the fish food and it took us thirty minutes to find them on our way out. The whole time he just laid there on the floor, without so much as a blanket, "sleeping it off, chasing the dragon away," as Vivian calls it.

3

GOOD TIMES (WE WILL NEVER FORGET)

| 9 |

Chapter Nine

September 27th, 2007

It's hard for me to fully conceptualize what's going on at home. You gotta understand that even through all the tumultuous, traumatic bullshit that goes down, my parents are still the *most* in love adults I have ever seen. Their romance is out of this world. When it's going well we all live in an absolute synchronous heaven. But, when it's going badly, we all live in an interconnected, yet asynchronous, hell. It's a beautifully dysfunctional situation that's full of passion. Plus, it's all I've ever known.

My parents met through mutual friends. They were both playing wingman for their friends, but ended up totally hitting it off. The way Vivian tells the story, the two of them danced all night long, just like Justin and me except they were already adults. I've never heard Lawrence tell the story, but Vivian says she got pregnant super early after they met. She chose to have an abortion because Lawrence already had kids and he was still in a relationship. Vivian isn't a traditionalist, but she wanted a planned pregnancy once she felt prepared to raise kids. Sometimes when it's right, it's just right… until it isn't again, I guess.

But, I think for my parents things still really seem right! Like, when we're all driving together in the car, for example. Dad always drives and Mom sits shotgun. I just watch them from the back seat with Elle. If it's been a good day, Lawrence likes to drive with his left hand on the wheel and his right hand stretched out to Vivian. From there he'll either grab on to her hand and periodically kiss and nibble on her fingers. Or, he'll put his hand on the back of her neck giving her a massage and tugging on her ear lobes. Or, he'll glide his right hand up and down her thighs. He can fit them both in one hand. If they're not holding hands, Vivian does the same thing with her left hand, and does her best to match Lawrence's energy.

They make sure the other knows they're taken care of and loved. They're truly each other's best friends. Like, when Lawrence pets Vivian's head and runs his hands all the way down her waist-long "curly" brown hair -- I know they still really love each other. When Vivian lines up Lawrence's hairline with the razor on a Sunday morning before church, I know they still really love each other. When Lawrence is feeling upbeat he has no problem pampering us with foot and back massages. Acts of service are his love language. He'll grab us whatever we want from the kitchen, bathroom, or bedroom while our toes dry from the wet polish.

Then, there are times when Lawrence needs some attention and he wants us to give him a massage. What we'll do is this: Lawrence lays out on the floor in the living room and the rest of us will take turns walking up his body -- from his feet up to his neck, while Jasper licks his face. Vivian's non-verbal love language is communicated when she serves Lawrence his meals throughout the day. That last part honestly makes me a little sick, but sometimes Lawrence will switch things up by cooking dinner for Vivian too. Things aren't always as one-sided as they seem.

It's in all these small, routine moments that I'm reassured -- they still really *really* love each other. In fact, this one time Lawrence picked me and Elle up from school early in order to surprise Vivian with dinner when she got home. It was super random but still super sweet. He was legitimately sweating, plus he was racing up and down the grocery store aisles.

We went to the butcher's block at the back of the store in the meat department to cop some fresh fish. Lawrence told the butcher he was preparing a special fish meal for his "wife and kids," and wanted the highest quality of Halibut (Vivian's favorite). The two bulky men swapped stories about partnership and fatherhood, and then bonded over their mutual devotion for the Seattle Seahawks. They did that male stranger-bonding thing that men do. It's not necessarily weird, but it's just so much more superficial from the way that women connect that it's still hard for me to tolerate.

Either way, we skipped out of the store like we had just hit the loot trick-or-treating, and then we hurried home to get the party started. Dad cranked up the music, he had selected the "Good Times" album by Subway, and we all bopped our heads in the kitchen. Jasper ran between the kitchen and living room, wagging his tail in hopeful anticipation and watching us dig into another fun project together.

Lawrence had delegated tasks out to everyone. Elle was shucking the corn, I was bringing the chopped potatoes to a boil in preparation for mashed potatoes, and Dad was making the green beans and fried fish. Our kitchen was so cramped and stuffed up with bodies that it felt like a million degrees inside, but we surpassed 'making it work' and were comfortably having a hella good time. I was so wrapped up in the fantastic moment we were sharing, I forgot how easily it could all turn on it's head. I nearly knocked the potatoes off the stovetop when I heard Lawrence howl from the sink right next to me.

"What the *fuck* is this?!" Dad exclaimed. From my peripheral view it looked like Lawrence was digging through something -- our food.

"This is fucking disgusting. What the hell?!" He turned towards Elle and me, and held up his right hand, pointing to it with his left.

"Look at this shit!" In his right hand Lawrence was holding a fist full of white fish meat.

Once I looked closer I could see tons of tiny transparent worms squirming between his fingers. My jaw and chin dropped, and I screamed out in unison with Elle, "EW!"

"I fuckin' talked to Pedro for fifteen fucking minutes, and he gives me *this* shit?!" A mean mug took over Lawrence's face and his lips had moved into thizz face position.

"I'm going to *fucking* kill him! He wants to try to trick me into feeding my family this trash?! I will fucking wring his neck until it snaps in half -- I don't give a fuck!" Lawrence's eyes started to widen, and I could tell he was becoming enraged -- he was becoming *that* Lawrence. He swooped up his black leather jacket, slid into his perfectly white tennis shoes, and opened up the door swinging his arms in large circles directing us out the door.

"Come on, girls, let's go!"

In a flash I turned off the stove top and Elle placed her brown paper bag of corn on the yellow kids table. Jasper was the first out the door, Elle and I followed, and Lawrence locked up the apartment behind us.

I'll be honest, I don't actually know 100% of what happened when we returned to the grocery store. Once we got there, Lawrence told me to wait with Elle and Jasper by the registers at the front door. Eventually I heard someone screaming from the back of the store, and I automatically knew it was Lawrence.

"You really wanted me to feed this shit to my fucking kids and wife?! Are you out of your goddamn mind?! Don't fuck with a nigga like me, bitch. A nigga like me will end you, hombre!"

A few moments later security was escorting Lawrence to the front of the store where Elle and I had been waiting. Vivian didn't get a full meal that evening, but she didn't even front after we told her the bullshit story of what had happened with the fish. Instead, she grabbed Lawrence and planted some huge kisses all over his face.

I was a little confused because I kinda felt Lawrence had over-reacted. But, Vivian didn't necessarily hear that version of the story, or if she did, she didn't seem to mind Lawrence's overreaction. So, I just let the criticism fade away and enjoyed the family moment.

| 10 |

Chapter Ten

October 4th, 2007

Yesterday I was called out of class by the school nurse. You know, that's not typically how it's supposed to go unless it's an emergency, but hey. By this point, I'm practically immune to everything abnormal that happens in my life. When I got to the nurse's office she handed me the off-white spiral-chord landline. On the other end of the phone was Lawrence.

"Olivia, I'm coming to pick you up and I don't want to hear another word about it. Your mother's too busy working at her little job to come be a parent, and your little sister is too sick to be at school, so we gotta bring her back home and take care of her." Lawrence's voice was instructional, not functional.

When I hung up the phone I told the nurse that Lawrence was on his way to pick me up from school, but she didn't need it.

"Oh, I know, Honey. Go ahead and grab the rest of your things from your locker, then come on back here and we'll wait for him together." I looked at her and sighed, but I knew I didn't really have a choice. It was the middle of second period, so I was basically going to miss all of my classes for the day.

The nurse continued, "I know. I'll call down to your teacher and mark you absent for the rest of the day again." Our school nurse is chill. She's more like a counselor though. On the days I feel explosive at school because of stuff happening at home she usually lets me rest in her office. So, you can imagine, I'm there pretty often.

Anyway, I gathered up some stuff from my locker and returned to her office. We were both shocked at the short lived wait. Lawrence came flying through the doors, negating any regulations, pointed to me and Elle, and said, "come on, grab your stuff, let's go."

Lawrence gave the nurse a head nod, as if acknowledging she knew who he was would be adequate enough to sign me out. Honestly, Lawrence doesn't typically even enter the building. Normally, he mortifyingly calls the school and makes the nurse walk me outside to his car. So, I guess if I'm getting super technical that was actually a sign he's growing up!

We headed out of the school, then jumped in our family beatdown baby blue 1988 Honda Civic. Everybody stayed silent on the car ride. Elle was sick as a dog in the back seat with Jasper, so I didn't sit shotgun. Instead, I sat in the back and supported her head in my lap for the duration of the ride. Poor girl had a fever, couldn't keep anything down, was shivering, and was completely out of it. I held a brown paper bag nearby with one hand and pet Elle's head laying in my lap with the other hand. I prayed for Elle not to get sick in the back of the car -- both for the smell, and for the issue of upsetting Lawrence.

I had no clue where we were headed. I would have asked Lawrence, but by now I know he'd just say, "you don't need to know where we're going *I* know where we're going, so don't worry about it," like always. All I knew for sure was that we had passed by the exit to our apartment complex a long, long time ago. Headed south to nowhere good.

Eventually we pulled up on some decrepent, seemingly vacant, two-story high, brown chipped-paint apartment building. It looked like it could've been featured on *Cops*. None of the units had their lights on inside, and the units with their blinds open looked empty -- or at least like nobody was home. Elle and I both wondered what the fuck we were doing in a project less appealing than our own, but neither of us asked Lawrence any questions. We just followed him into one of the bottom floor units.

We waltzed into the place like we knew where we were -- but *we* didn't. Or, at the least, Elle and I didn't. As soon as you stepped in you could smell that the place hadn't been cleaned in years. It smelled like the yellow bus *after* school, plus skunk spray, with just a touch of boiled egg fart. I wouldn't need to be convinced that somebody had also recently died in the back of the apartment. I'm not being dramatic, it truly smelled *so* gross.

Nevertheless, Lawrence sat us down on a light pink plastic couch facing an old-school clunky television on the floor. I was surprised when it turned on and real-life, normal ass Cartoon Network started playing. The fucking *Powerpuff Girls*, no less. There were no lights on inside, but the daylight from outside allowed us to see regardless, and everything felt completely still. I couldn't tell you why with 100% clarity, but I didn't feel safe being in that apartment from the second we arrived. Without saying a word Lawrence disappeared somewhere into the black abyss of the apartment.

Elle and I just sat there *not* watching *Powerpuff Girls*. Anyone in the whole world could tell Elle felt like a trainwreck just by looking at her. Elle, who is usually thriving, looked a little like she was dying. Elle, who is usually singing and dancing, or playing with the people she loves, or trying to make people laugh, was completely laid out. I continued cradling her head in my lap so her precious head didn't have to touch the untrustworthy plastic couch. Jasper rested his head at our feet, but I could feel he was listening on alert. Elle was almost lifeless, but then she started talking to me about how she thought she was most like Bubbles.

"I think I look most like Bubbles, Olive." She still does that thing with her voice the little kids do where she accidentally says everything like it's a question. You know what I mean?

"Uh-huh," I reassured.

"But, then I *feel* more like Blossom."

"Yup. I think so too, Elle."

"You can be Buttercup," Elle flatly joked. Even while sick, Elle was cracking jokes and keeping a positive attitude. We kept watching the show until Elle's little legs started trying to run away without her. She looked like Jasper kicking his legs around when he's having an intense nightmare.

"Olivia, I think I have to go potty. Do you know where it is? I don't know where it is, Ollie." Elle's face looked panicked.

"I don't know, Elle. I don't think we've been here before."

"Uh oh," Elle looked scared and tilted her head down, "ok." She slid down from the couch, pulled herself upright, took a deep breath, and said, "I'll go ask," like it was no big deal.

Elle walked down a short dark hallway and opened the first closed door she saw. The room was filled with smoke, it was dark, and it only had a sliver of grey-tinted daylight shining through the closed blinds. Lawrence was sitting on the corner of a bed, holding something to the side of his nose and coughing. There were a bunch of tubes and wires and aluminum foil bits on the floor. The whole thing was sketch.

I couldn't tell you how many people were in the room. Maybe three? The passed out woman was wearing a black fishnet long-sleeved crop top with an orange leather bandeau underneath. I didn't recognize her, but it was hard to fully see her because she was laid out between my Dad and another random guy. Sitting next to Lawrence's side of the bed were a couple guys I'd also never seen. They were on the floor hunched over and dozed off. "Parallel Universe" was playing on a boombox inside my mind.

Lawrence turned around and saw Elle standing in the doorway. Elle had beads of sweat dripping down her face dampening the neckline of her shirt. She stood there frozen with her mouth slightly parted. Elle had only caught a glimpse into the room before Lawrence stumbled over to the door and yelled intermittently between coughs.

"GET THE FUCK OUT OF HERE, ELLESHA! I DONE AL-READY TOLD YOU TO MIND YOUR GODDAMN BUSINESS!" He pushed her out of the room by her feverish forehead, and then slammed the door in her face.

Elle walked back to the plastic couch, slumped over, head hanging low, and blank faced. She hopped back up onto the plastic couch and stared at the TV. Tears were streaming down Elle's face, her breathing became labored, and she started quietly whimpering without saying anything.

Still, I could hear her thoughts.

Elle didn't cradle her head, or wipe her tears, or barely even acknowledge that she was crying at all. Instead, she stared straight into the chunky tv and looked unwaveringly to the *Powerpuff Girls* for the words. Elle gripped the edge of the plastic couch cushions like they were your sand stress balls, and I noticed her knees shaking nervously up and down. Then, I quickly remembered why Elle had gotten up in the first place. I looked at Elle even more intently and noticed the beads of sweat still dripping from her face.

I couldn't tell if Elle was trying to hold it or if she was just scared and crying. I mean, can you imagine the amount of rage that five year old girl was secretly harboring? I can. That's probably why I still feel so protective over Elle, ya know?

It was a silent fart, but Elle's diarrhea shifted the smells in the apartment to a different intensity. It wasn't until the smell hit me that I realized Elle had silently pooped her pants. I didn't know what to do. So, we just kept sitting there watching *Powerpuff Girls* change into *Courage the Cowardly Dog*.

By the time Lawrence came out of the bedroom everything was different. The morning clouds had cleared, the skies were bright blue, and the sun was out raging. When Lawrence realized Elle had an accident he lost it and screamed at her. Really, he chastised her the whole way home, and he probably would have given her a good ass whooping too, but for her pants being full of shit. I don't know why Lawrence was so mad though. Clearly Elle is the one who had been violated, and by him no less.

Either way, we got home hours before Vivian was even on her way. As soon as we got home Lawrence threw Elle's pants away in the complex trash bins outside in the back alley, then ran Elle through a hot bath. By the time Vivian came home from work Elle was already asleep in bed for the night, sweating out her fever. Lawrence never told Vivian what had happened that day. Neither did I, and so neither did Elle.

| 11 |

Chapter Eleven

Do you remember the first time you had your period? Sometimes I wish I could go back to that day and do it all over again. If I could, I might not be as fucked up as I am now, you know? Like in *The Butterfly Effect*, the way you respond to significant moments in your childhood have the potential to change your entire life. I think the first time a crime scene of blood and gushy period plugs took place in my pants was one of those butterfly moments for me.

At first, it was just another normal day. I took the yellow school bus home -- just like I still do. The bus ride was loud, crowded, hot, and smelled of its usual teen spirit funk. It was gross. I mean, let's be honest, the bus -- especially after school -- is always gross. But, if I'm being totally transparent, it also makes me feel awkwardly at home.

Anyway, I sat in the back with the same friends I still kick it with today. Laurie, Charlotte, Nikky, and I sat in the seats like civilians while the boys swung like monkeys from the windows to the standing-grip poles. Justin, Steve, Mark, and Miles used to do this dance routine to "Don't Cha" by the Pussycat Dolls, so they were going off and acting like fools.

Even though they did the same damn dance routine pretty much every day, someone always messed it up, ruined the choreo, and then started an argument with us girls for laughing. We'd go back and forth at each other exchanging yees and yaddameans, speaking in a Bay Area slang that's only familiar to other fast-living street natives. Which was typically when the bus driver would start yelling and threatening to kick "alla us hooligans off the bus." Even back then, the guys could usually smooth talk the bus driver, settle her temper down, and get her to change her mind. The day I started my period was no different.

When I got home I had the entire apartment to myself. I decided to seize the moment, try to freeze it and own it because I consider these moments golden. To get my "me time" started, I closed all our blinds and made sure the doors were locked. The daylight shined through the blinds strong enough that I didn't even have to put lights on. So, I shuck out the covers on my bed, snuck under the covers, and then turned on some music to set the ambiance as background noise. I remember "Sex-o-matic Venus Freak" playing while I slid my hands down into my pants, closed my eyes, and drifted away.

My relaxation session was interrupted by "Still," a Macy Gray ballad sure to make me think of Vivian and Lawrence, and dry me up like a freaking raisin. I sat up to volunteer a hand to the remote control to change the song, but I noticed some gross ass brown grime underneath my nails that stopped me.

When I looked closer, the auburn-looking gunk was all over my fingers too. So, I stuck my hands down my pants and started rubbing around to see if the stuff was coming from me, and it was. Of course I immediately started freaking out. I knew what a period was, but the dark brown blood threw the younger thirteen year old Olivia for a loop, yaddamean? I thought I had some sort of an infection, even though I was still totally virginal at the time.

I leapt up from the bed, sprinted to the bathroom, and called Vivian from the toilet. The phone rang three times before sending me to voicemail, and I nervously rambled through a recording. I think I said something along the lines of:

"Mom? Some thick, gooey, brown gunk is in my underwear and I think it's even coming from me. I don't know what it is and I am really freaking out. I think I must be sick or maybe even dying. I don't know what this is! I'm just hella scared and I don't know what it means! Please call me back ASAP, A-SAP."

I waited for freaking ever. I think it was actually only about five minutes, but whatever, it *felt* like forever. I kept waiting for Vivian to call me back, but I figured she was in a meeting and not available to call back within the foreseeable future, per usual. Semi-earnestly believing I might be dying, and tapped dry of trustworthy sources to lean on, I had to take the risk of calling Lawrence.

The thing about Lawrence is that he is almost always available by phone. Sometimes he runs a little late or he doesn't pick Elle up from daycare like he's supposed to. He's only seen one of my football games where I'm cheerleading. But, nine times out of ten we can reach him by phone. Plus, sometimes he can be the perfect person to talk to in an emergency.

I didn't plan out a way of explaining my peculiar predicament, I just dialed. Lawrence answered after the second ring, "hey Olivia. What's up?"

His voice sounded calm and steady -- it was deep and low like it usually is. Soothing, like a late night smooth jam radio host. I didn't hear any movements in the background, so I figured Lawrence was void of distractions and could lend me his fatherly attention.

"Hey, Dad. Ummm, can you talk? I'm sort of freaking out right now. I think I might be dying or something. I don't know."

"What did you just say, Olivia? You think you're dying? Are you joking?!" He began a fishing expedition.

"No. Well, sorta? No. No, I'm not *dying*. Nevermind."

"What the hell is going on? Are you alright? What are you talking about, Olivia?!"

"I don't know, Dad. I don't want to gross you out, but I've got something wrong happening to my body right now."

"Olivia," he doesn't have a pet name for me, "I'm your Daddy, you hear me? My mother named me 'Lawrence Grove,' you hear me? And *I* created *you*. Well, I guess your mother *and* I created you. Your body comes from me. Do you know that?"

"Uhh, yeah, I do." He'd been filling my head with disturbingly graphic details about where babies come from since I was Elle's age, so he knew I obviously knew what he was talking about. Lawrence made sure I knew.

"Alright, then. I have three other daughters, and I think I can handle whatever it is you called to say to me. Come on now, spit it out."

"Well...." We both stayed on the phone in silence for a few minutes, resisting the reality of the moment upon us, until I started blurting out random phrases.

"There's some nasty stuff in my underwear. I don't know what it is. It's brown and mucusy, and hella gross! I'm trying not to freak out, but *I'm* totally freaking out, you know?"

I stopped myself because Lawrence would consider "hella" a curse word, and I realized I was word vomiting all over the place. Under any other circumstance I would've been scolded, and maybe would've even received a coupon for an ass whooping, for using a curse word. But, under the circumstances of this conversation Lawrence tossed me a get out of jail free card without mention.

All he said was, "Olivia, you started your period," just all calm-like like that.

"No, Dad, it's not blood. Trust me. It's not red at all. Trust me, trust me. It's like brown, sticky, wet stuff! Am I dying?!"

"Olivia," Lawrence's voice shifted from trustworthy to terrifying, "did you hear what I just said?! I said you started your period." I really couldn't even believe what he was saying.

"But, Dad, it's not red. I'm telling you it's dark brown. So that must mean something's wrong, right?"

"Naw. Girl, don't you know when blood dries up it turns brown, and sometimes even black? Your first period just musta took your body a minute to force out, so that's why it's brown. That happens to girls sometimes."

I whispered, "ew," to myself, but Lawrence overheard.

"Yeah, 'ew.' That's right. So, now you know what that means, Olivia? When a woman's period starts?"

"Yeah, it means she's turning into an adult woman."

On the other end of the line I heard Lawrence burst out laughing, but I didn't understand the joke.

"Whew. Girl, you really know how to give your papa a big old laugh, don't you?"

I was confused, and wasn't quite sure where he was going with his line of questioning, so I just silently listened for his Socrates-like investigation to jump to the fucking punchline.

"You won't be an adult until you're in your mid to late 20s. All getting your period means is that now when a guy cums inside of you during sex you might get pregnant."

Even though Elle wasn't home, I felt like she had been punched in the gut by Lawrence just as much as I had.

"Do you hear me?! It means now you have to be more careful with your body when you're out there ripping and running through the streets like you do. Out there fucking all these little boys."

Honestly, his whole response shocked me. I don't know why. He didn't say anything I hadn't heard him say a billion times before. But, I guess I just really didn't think the conversation was going to turn so far left. I wasn't expecting him to be thinking about that as, like, the first thought on his mind, you know? Especially at a time so precious. I also just felt grossed out, if I'm being honest, like my skin had a billion ants crawling all over it. I might just be being delusional, like Lawrence says happens to girls when they're on their period, but I doubt it. The whole thing felt like, ew -- ya know? Why did he have to say it like *that?*

Either way, when we hung up I hopped in the shower A-SAP. Afterwards, I put on some fresh, clean clothes, and microwaved myself some hot honey water like I was Mariah Carey in *Glitter.* I sat at the bar countertop at our kitchen with all the lights out and wished Jasper was home with me instead of out somewhere mysterious with Lawrence. I couldn't even turn the TV back on. I just sat there in silence for a few hours watching the sun dim the shining reflection on the tile floor. Eventually Vivian called me back on her way home from work.

"You're passing over into womanhood, Olive! I'm on my way home now to celebrate my little girl! I can't believe you're just growing up so qui-"

She was switching from the Bart to a SamTrans bus, so we lost connection.

4

GOOD GRIEF

| 12 |

Chapter Twelve

October 18th, 2007

We've all been floating on alright since Lawrence used Elle as a hostage while stealing from Vivian's purse. Additional arguments didn't break out amidst the normalcy of our school week schedules. But, as each weekend inches closer we all start feeling a bit more anxious, waiting for Lawrence's boot to drop. Nevertheless, we continue on.

Last weekend, Mom and I cooked dinner together. Elle colored at the kids table facing into the living room, and Lawrence was sprawled out re-watching *Double Take* for the Nth time. Vivian and I made fried chicken, mashed potatoes, and green peas. I always feel extremely grateful in those soothing moments of subtle serenity. I used to bask in those moments when things felt so effortless, when Jazzy chose to cuddle up close to Dad, and when I actually felt like Lawrence was deserving of the title "Dad," even if only for the time being. I wouldn't dare count on it, but sometimes family time at the Grove's is actually fun and semi-normal.

Once dinner was ready, we gathered in our usual spots to eat. Elle and I sat the yellow kids table together. Mom and Dad on the orange futon -- this time pulled out into the bed. Lawrence laid on his side, using his elbow to hold himself up just enough to hover over his plate. Vivian sat behind Lawrence with her legs on either side of him and right ankle intercepting any spills he may have while transferring the plated food into his mouth. Vivian held her plate of food up to her mouth so as to not spill on the bed and cause Lawrence to flip out. I could tell she didn't want to interrupt the tempo.

The movie was about to end, but Lawrence stopped it pre-emptively. He said, "you see what just happened there, E?"

Elle shook her head "no."

"How often did you hear the women in this movie talking?"

"I don't know," Elle said nervously.

"Right! Exactly! You don't even know because they barely had the women talking. The women were only here in this movie so that men like me would stay interested and keep watching, you see? They were dressed in their underwear, and prancing around the screen like they were prostitutes. But, you know what prostitutes do, don't you?"

Elle shook her head "no" again.

"They prance around the streets in their bras and underwears. So, you see, there's really no difference! The media wants you to think it's normal to act like a hoe, but your Daddy isn't going to let that happen. God watches over everything, E. *Everything.* He's watching to see if you deserve to go to heaven or not, and he's waiting to see if you'll make the same mistakes as everybody else. He wants to know if you'll stay loyal to yourself and to Him, or if you'll be persuaded by the devil."

"Lawrence, chill out a bit, Honey," Vivian soothed.

"It's the truth, Vivian," Lawrence snapped back, "quit playing with her. I'm not lying. The devil wants you to hate yourself. He wants you to doubt yourself and make yourself sick. He wants you to burn in hell with him because he's evil and miserable. You know what they say, right? Misery loves company! The media is evil and miserable too. They profit from controlling you and the way you think, E. They want you to prance around like Orlando Jones' girlfriend, or Vivica Fox in her tight little suit and makeup. You won't ever be wearing something like that into an office, you hear me? Media wants you spending all your money and time trying to please the devil. They're slowly teaching you to hate yourself, so they can do whatever they want to you."

Lawrence kept lecturing to us, "they'll do whatever they want to you because the media is controlled by a bunch of rich, White men; and, men try to do whatever they want with women all the time, E. But, you can't let them. You've got to be ready for the tactics so you don't fall victim to being preyed upon."

"Lawrence," Mom said not quite quietly enough as she ran her hand up Dad's back and on to his shoulder, "come on. Just breathe." She squeezed his shoulder and smiled at him.

"I'm serious, Vivian!" He broke eye contact with her and turned back to Elle and me. "Ellesha, good for nothing guys are going to start wanting to hang out with you now that you're getting older. You know why they want to hang out with you, E?"

My head fell down, to the ground, to get out of the rain like the ant soldiers who march one by one. I knew where this was going, but I couldn't save Elle from being tainted.

"No, Daddy, why?"

"They just want to hang out with you so they can get you alone and then try to cum inside of you."

"*LAWRENCE!*"

"Vivian, now the girl asked. You know what happens after the guy is done cumming in you, Ellesha? Do you know what I'm talking about?" Elle shook her head "no," BECAUSE SHE'S ONLY 5 YEARS OLD.

"After a guy is done cumming inside of you he's going to leave you, and most guys you won't ever hear from again!"

"You're sick, Lawrence," Vivian said as she got up from the bed. She collected all our unfinished dishes, walked into the kitchen, and faced the wall before bowing to pray to the sink disposal.

"It's the truth, Vivian!" He turned his attention back to Elle, "it's the truth. And, God says if you let a guy do that to you it's a sin that you'll burn in hell for for the rest of eternity." It was palpably quiet in this pause. Lawrence hates when Vivian doesn't agree, or doesn't encourage us to agree, with his religious views. He burned holes through the walls and into the back of her head, and then turned his attention back to burn us too.

"Do you know what that means, Elle?"

"No."

"*No*," he said mockingly, "do you, Olivia? Do you know what 'the rest of eternity' means?"

"Yes."

"*Yes*," the mocking continued, "so explain it then! The rest of the group wants to know."

"Elle, 'the rest of eternity' means even longer than people live, it's like, a really really *reallly* reallly long time." I rolled my eyes and nodded my head in fast circles as I spoke to add some levity and encourage Elle to start giggling. "It kind of means 'forever.'"

"That's true, except even Olivia doesn't really understand what it means because she can't really comprehend how long a time 'eternity' really is! Olivia is still too young to really get it like your mother and I do."

According to Lawrence, it doesn't matter how old I get. I'll never have enough experience, knowledge, or years to understand anything at the level *he* does.

"God says, only whores and prostitutes let guys cum inside them before marriage. You girls aren't whores, so I won't let you be running around racking up a reputation for yourselves."

"Lawrence, that's ridiculous! Olivia, don't listen to your Dad." She briefly turned around to lock eyes with me, but then turned back around and continued to bow her head.

"Girl, you better be listenin' to me. I ain't playing with you," now he stood up from the bed, and began patrolling the living room and kitchen jurisdictions like we were his prey. Mom stopped protesting against his insanity instantly.

"You remember how I taught you to hug boys, right?" We nodded. "Get up, you girls show me how I taught you."

Elle and I got up from our seats at the yellow kids table and hugged each other. Lawrence always warns me and Elle about men who "only want to grab on" us. He says, "some guys might ask you to rub or suck on their dicks, or they might not even ask, they'll just force you to do it."

I reached my right arm out to Elle. My entire body stayed facing forward towards Lawrence, until I just barely felt a small warm body next to mine. My left arm stayed down at my side ready to attack if needed -- the correct form. A proper hug means the two involved torsos never actually fully touch. It's not a real hug. It's an awkward pat on the shoulder. Elle's left arm reached out to me, but didn't wrap around. We didn't make eye contact, in fact, our bodies hardly even embraced at all - just like Lawrence taught us.

"Good," he said, "now I know your Mother thinks I'm crazy, but I do know what I'm talking about. I know older men in our family might do that to you girls." His eyes were wide and his mouth fell open slightly. For the briefest second in world history I thought he might cry. But, he continued, "in our own family! So, you really can't trust anyone, girls! You hear me?"

We nodded yes.

"And, if anyone ever touches you, even your Uncle Marlon," Lawrence's brother, "You girls just tell me if he makes a move and I swear to God I'll kill that motherfucker." He was screaming now -- not at us, but to us. Lawrence is just a perpetually passionate man.

"Good hug girls, now sit back down." We obeyed.

Lawrence continued pacing the floor. "No, I know what I'm talking about, Vivian."

"Oh, I'm sure you do," Mom threw in with her back still turned facing the kitchen sink.

"I mean it," Lawrence sounded like a toddler trying to convince the world he wasn't tired.

"I hear you, Lawrence, you mean it." Mom responded utterly fed up. I think she was even sort of mocking him.

"I do." Lawrence's face looked like he wanted to ravage Vivian like Ike Turner, but for Elle and I being there. He was out of this world.

"And Olivia, if you're out there messin' around with little boys, I swear to God I will light a fire up under that ass! You won't be seeing any boys, you won't be sitting down in class, sh*iiiittt*, you might not even make it to school."

"I'm not, Da-"

Lawrence interrupted, "oh, you're not?"

"No, I'm not."

"Yeah, you better not be."

Lawrence settled back down on the orange futon folded out into a bed, and changed channels on the television until deciding upon a basketball game. I eventually got Elle up from the yellow kids table, and we brushed our teeth while Mom procrastinated in the kitchen a little bit longer. Elle cried to me in the bathroom, confused thinking her favorite Uncle Marlon had hurt us in the past but she couldn't remember. Then, we all went to bed without saying another word on the subject.

Lawrence led us all through a prayer on our knees after Vivian turned out all the lights. Elle fell asleep during the sermon, and Lawrence flicked her hard in the back of the head to wake her up. It was so hard we all heard the "click" upon connection. Elle started crying for a bit while rubbing her head, but Lawrence just kept on preaching. Eventually he stopped, then kissed us goodnight before heading out the front door. Mom tucked us into bed, then crawled in with us, and we stayed up singing Christmas songs together until Elle fell asleep.

| 13 |

Chapter Thirteen

October 25th, 2007

Lawrence finally drew Vivian's last straw. I haven't wanted to talk about it over the past couple weeks, the break being so fresh and all, but it's true. I'm confident you've already heard.

The night started like just any other -- something was bound to go wrong. Lawrence was out for the night and Vivian's phone didn't stop ringing. It was obviously Lawrence. He had been calling Vivian incessantly all week even though he'd barely been home. Elle, Vivian, and I had all been walking around sleep deprived from all the disruption and uneasiness. But, who cares?

At the beginning of the evening Vivian answered his calls and excused herself from our presence. It didn't matter, Elle and I could hear both Vivian *and Lawrence* hollering through the phone. When she'd return, Vivian would just continue shuffling Elle and me through our nightly weekday routine. We ate dinner together, we got cleaned up before bed together, and we said our nightly prayer together -- even though Lawrence wasn't there to force us. Vivian's phone kept ringing periodically, but she was starting to ignore his calls. She even climbed into bed with Elle and me after tucking us in, *and* she sang us a lullaby.

Vivian is still just a grown up flower child. Like, the first record she bought for herself was the Tapestry album by Carole King, if you know what I mean... So, she always knows the softest songs to sing us to sleep.

That night she picked "Blossom." Vivian quietly sang to Elle and me, only messing up on some of the words. Vivian reached out and skimmed the outside of her hand down the side of my face while continuing to sing. She smiled at me, as I was barely achieving a semi-conscious state. The consistency of Elle's sound snoring kept Vivian's singing on time. Vivian's phone would ring, and then she'd keep on ignoring it.

I was just starting to nod out when I felt Jasper leap off the water bed and soon heard him start barking out from the living room.

Lawrence had come home -- with Brad and Tinky.

"Wazzup, girls?!" Lawrence shouted from the front living room.

"Wazzup?!" Tinky echoed.

Lawrence's friend Tinky is my favorite of all Lawrence's friends. He's my God father. I used to think Tinky was the best "uncle" out of all of them. But, when I found out that Tinky is Lawrence's drug dealer. It really blew my mind. I was depressed for about two weeks, but I've gotten over it. I think it really tore my heart into bloody pieces because, deep down, I already sorta knew who "Uncle" Tinky *really* was to our family. I just didn't want to actively know it, yaddamean?

Either way -- Tinky always does the funniest imitations of Cartoon Network characters. Plus, whenever we go somewhere random with Lawrence and Tinky, Tinky always stays in the car with Elle and me. He'll ask us about school, talk to us about the weather, and then start making jokes out of our friends and our teachers. Tinky loves Elle and me like we were his own kids -- maybe because he doesn't have any.

Out of all the people I know in the world, Tinky is the only one who makes me think of bright orange. He's goofy, kind, and strange -- my kinda guy. Elle *loves* Tinky, she thinks he's the funniest person on the planet. Tinky has been near--deathly sick with diabetes since

I've known him. The doctors keep telling him he's going to die soon, but that's why I don't listen to doctors. Tinky will never die. He's not human. He's the only invincible human-passing Martian on earth.

Stinky Tinky was there when I was born. As Vivian tells it, she called in sick from work because she knew it was time to give birth, and it was midweek or something. Allegedly, Vivian started calling Lawrence and he didn't answer for a few hours, so she started calling Tinky. Once Tinky got wind of what was going on he tracked Lawrence down and drug him home. The two of them ended up racing Vivian to the hospital just for Lawrence to turn around to them and say, "I'm hungry."

WHAT?!

But, OK, sure.

I guess Tinky stood up and said, "Lawrence, you go drive through McDonald's and grab a burger. I'll get Viv set up in the room with her doctors."

"'Ight cool." They probably did their secret little bro shake, and then Lawrence just bounced - leaving Vivian with his drug dealer while in labor!

I know he actually made it back in time for Vivian giving birth, the contractions, and pushing, and alla that. But, I guess since Lawrence had already had kids, he didn't think it was important to be there for every second... like Vivian had to be.

Men can be infuriating. But Tink is a saving grace. I learned to trust Tinky before Lawrence a long time ago. Between the two of them, Stinky Tink was the most reasonable and the most responsible. A lot of parents will tell you not to trust a drug dealer. But, in my experience the dealers tend to be the most insightful and they look out for the community.

Anyways, when Elle heard Lawrence and Tinky out in the living room she flew out of bed as if she hadn't just been dead ass asleep. Elle frolicked out the back bedroom, up the hallway, and into the living room at the front of our apartment. Mom and I quickly followed after Elle, per usual.

She was charging towards Tinky, "Uncle Tinky! Uncle Tinky" Elle pushed her arms wide open completely ignoring Brad.

"Ellie Bear!" Tinky crouched down, swooped Elle up into his arms, and said, "how you been baby girl?" propping her up on his hip. Elle didn't answer and just squeezed Tinky around his neck with both of her arms and all of her might.

"I told you we were heading for bed a while ago, Lawrence. What are you guys doing here?"

"Ain't this where I live, Viv? Fuck if I'm confused!"

"Naw, you live here, breh breh!" Brad chimed in from the peanut gallery. He's seriously *the biggest* instigator!

Vivian rolled her eyes after breaking a scorching eye contact interchange with Lawrence. "I know you live here, Lawrence, but I thought you'd be out for the rest of the night. You haven't been home all week. The girls and I were just heading to bed. Elle was already asleep."

"I don't give a fuck, Vivian, she's up now!" He motioned his hands over towards Tinky and Elle.

Jasper was jumping up and down on Lawrence. He was just trying to get Lawrence's undivided love and attention -- like most the rest of us in the living room that night. But, Lawrence smacked Jasper across the snout and Jasper let out a singular, reverberating "yelp!" and scurried away.

"You're fucking scratching me, Jazzy. Get down."

"Come on, Lawrence, we're all hella tired. Don't scare the kids before bed and make it so they can't sleep. Where are y'all off to tonight?" Vivian wasn't being combative or anything. I think she was actually just trying to get Lawrence and his cronies to leave.

"We're here, Viv. We were off to make it home, and it looks like we have, so now we're just here kickin' it. You want to see what I got?"

Tinky interrupted while leaning down forward to let Elle out of his arms. "Come on, man. You don't want to go do alla that. Chill out."

Lawrence was clearly going to press onward, "Tink, we came home for the sole purpose of showing Viv and the girls what we picked up along the way."

"Naw, man. Just keep it to yourself. Don't go brangin' that thang out here in frona yuh family. You said you wasn't really finna do that."

Again, Vivian's head was on a swivel. And, Brad was unusually silent. "What did you pick up, Lawrence?" She was cautiously curious, but unintentionally instigating an already high-tension situation.

"Don't worry, I've got this, Vivian." Lawrence snapped. Everybody started shifting around the already too small living room, and we ended up having a good ol' Mexican standoff. We were all essentially trapped in the living room, forced to participate in the moment. Brad stood with his back in front of the patio door leading out to the back alleyway. Tinky stood in the hallway entrance, not knowing he was blocking our exit to the back bedroom. Mom stood next to the yellow kid's table in the kitchen, and Lawrence was in front of the orange futon folded into the couch position with Jasper laying on the ground next to his left foot. Lawrence was closest to the front door -- per usual.

Elle was swirling in circles in front of the television. The TV screen was blue, waiting for one of us to rewind whatever movie we had watched last. But, it was going to have to just keep on waiting. Elle ignored reality and continued spinning her teddy bear in circles. Mr. Teddy Bear is a gift Elle has had since she was born. Vivian's sister that I've talked about before, Aunt Deb, actually got the teddy bear for me when she first found out Vivian was pregnant. But, once Elle arrived I decided it was time I passed it down. You know, onward to the next generation? Each one teach one?

Lawrence made a move towards Vivian and tried to dance with her. He lifted her right hand up into his left hand, then grabbed her by the waist with his right hand and started humming Sade in her ear. Vivian was in her soft blue and purple angel patterned cotton pajamas. Her body moved in unison with Lawrence's even though there wasn't any music playing. But, only momentarily.

"Wait," Vivian said while pushing off from Lawrence's chest. "Don't try to distract me, Lawrence. What did you come home to show me?"

"Aww geez." Tinky said while inhaling and bringing his hands to either side of his head, "just let it be, Viv."

Lawrence's face revealed the insides of his mind were twisting. We could all tell that Lawrence's ego had just been badly bruised by Vivian "rejecting" him -- let alone in front of his friends *and* his kids.

"You really wanna see what I've got, Viv?!" Lawrence grabbed something out from his back pocket and pointed it out straight in front of him with his arms extended forward.

I blinked.

"Lookie, lookie here then, bitch!"

Then, I realized what Lawrence had pulled out from his back pocket. Lawrence was standing there in the living room holding a dark black matte gun. I blinked again, simultaneously swallowing my heart, and realized not only was Lawrence standing there in the living room holding a dark black, matte gun, but that it was also pointed at Elle.

Everything froze and nobody breathed, not even Jasper. My entire life was suspended in space, and only Lawrence could control my fate.

Somebody finally broke the silence by gasping a whispered, "oh my god." Then, Elle hugged Mr. Teddy Bear up tight to her chest for safety and comfort.

"Yo," Brad said aloud, but mostly to himself.

"Come on, dawg. You ain't mean to do alla that." Tinky started trying to talk Lawrence down and de-escalate the situation. Tinky wasn't afraid to look Lawrence dead in his eyes no matter how horrifically Lawrence acted. "Think about that, dawg. Think about that. You don't wanna do that, man. Step back. Step back."

Lawrence's arms stayed extended outward and pointed at Elle. I saw Lawrence's eyes dart from Elle to Tinky, so I think Tinky was actually starting to help. But then Vivian's shock started to wear off.

"WHAT. THE. FUCK LAWRENCE!" Vivian quickly melted into a panic. She looked like a pissed off Sally Field in *Norma Rae*.

Lawrence's attention, and thus his extended arms with a pistol on top, turned towards Vivian. I tried to just focus on my breathing, and my toes in the carpet, and the sound of the fish tank filter bubbling behind us perpendicular to the TV, and the orange couch folded up tight.

"Come on dawg, come on." Tinky didn't lose his temper and start yelling at Lawrence, but he was definitely peacefully protesting for Lawrence to calm the fuck down from the sidelines.

"What, Vivian, you said you wanted to see what I picked up on my way home to you and the girls, right?" Lawrence sounded like a legitimate psychopath.

Let me pause, because I think some extra context might be helpful here. I guess in the past there have been a couple times where Lawrence has threatened to kill Elle and me, then Vivian, and then himself; plus a couple of variations stemming from that same basic premise. There have been times when, in the past, like, before I was born and stuff, when fights between my parents *may* have escalated into being physically violent. More accurately described, there *have* been times, in the past, when Lawrence has escalated into being physically violent towards Vivian after picking a fight with her.

I mean, I guess under any context a father pulling a gun out on his family would be a pretty serious thing. Right? But, I don't know. I just felt like that particular context was important for you to know for some reason. I don't want to go more into all that super darkness though.

Anyways, Vivian and Lawrence carried on going back and forth with each other. "Oh, so this is it? This is *finally* the part where you put us out of our misery, Lawrence?! In my fucking angel pajamas?!" Vivian kept beating her right fist on the heart-side of her chest while yelling.

"Go ahead, Lawrence, do it! Kill all of us here, and then yourself, and let your two best dope fiend friends take care of the rest! Take us out of our fucking misery, Lawrence! *Do it!*"

"She don't mean that, Lawrence." Tinky inserted himself again, and I was thankful. "You don't mean that, Vivian. Come on, man, look at me. Look at your brother, Tink."

Lawrence stood there cocking his head to the right side, contemplating. Lawrence turned towards Tinky, and started blinking his eyes really hard. It was like Lawrence was trying to clear his eyes until he could see a life that he could actually recognize, but it wasn't quite working out.

"Just put down the gadget, man. Ain't nobody in here gon' think you weak or nothin' like that. Just go ahead. Put it down, brother. Put it down. This ain't a game, man. This is real life. This your woman and kids, man. You don't want to do this. This ain't something you can come back from. This a forever thing, man."

"Yeah, you right," Lawrence said faintly, "you right."

"Just go ahead," Tinky soothingly cheered.

Lawrence started lowering the gun down towards his waistband. His focus was on the gun. Lawrence moved one hand off the other, which was still wrapped around the trigger. He placed his hand on top of the barrel, and started wiggling it. The gun raised back up a little bit.

"How you turn this thing on the safety lock again, Tink?"

POP!

Time slowly inched by. But, eventually Elle started coughing. Then, the first thing I remember hearing was Vivian wheezing through her speech.

"Oh my goodness, baby! Are you okay?!" Vivian sprinted to Elle and picked her up with such force that Elle dropped her Mr. Teddy Bear on the floor. Though, to be honest, Elle was pretty much limp. So, it didn't actually take too much effort on Vivian's part.

Lawrence lunged towards Elle in Vivian's arms. "I didn't mean to do that, E! Your Daddy didn't mean to do that!" Elle just curled up in Vivian's chest, and Vivian pulled away from Lawrence to further protect Elle.

"Don't you touch her, Lawrence." Vivian snapped. She frantically patted Elle all over the back and chest. Vivian kept pulling Elle away so Vivian's eyes could meet Elle's, she would watch Elle blink, and then press Elle back to her chest so she could keep burping Elle like a baby.

"Yeah, come on dawg, let's just give the girls some space right now." Tinky walked across enemy lines and used the excuse of Jasper to help guide Lawrence and Brad out the glass sliding door leading out to the back alley. Lawrence was totally flabbergasted. In a daze, he grabbed Jasper's leash from Tinky and followed his lead almost without saying anything.

After the men went outside, Tinky tucked his head in before closing the glass door. "Hey, Vivian, I'm just gonna take him to catch some air and cool down for a bit."

Vivian just nodded in agreement and walked to lock the door behind them. Then, she closed the blinds too. I noticed a copper bead looking thing on the carpet right near where Elle had been standing. So, while Vivian continued securing our lock down I walked over to examine it.

"It was a BB-gun," Vivian said to Elle trying to comfort her, "it wasn't real."

I picked Mr. Teddy Bear up off the ground. Mr. Teddy Bear had a tiny hole in his chest, the exact same size of the copper-looking BB bead.

Once Elle's shock wore off she started wailing out in disbelief, in anger, in sadness, in fear, and in *so* many other emotions. We huddled around Elle, hugging and comforting her with love. Mom rocked Elle back and forth while sitting in one of the kid's chairs at the yellow kid's table in the kitchen. After a while, Elle's weeping reduced to a jagged whimper and she started nodding out. Before she fully knocked out, Vivian walked Elle to the back bedroom and put her to sleep with her pink blankey.

We had been baptized by fire. It was officially the beginning of the end.

| 14 |

Chapter Fourteen

November 1st, 2007

The next thing I remember is waking Elle up later that same night. It must have just been a couple hours after we had laid her down to sleep. A glowing yellow light from the lamp on our bedside table was the only light on in the entire apartment. Well, I guess the only light besides the blue light leaking in from the fish tank out in the living room. I had never seen the blue light look so bright. The olive green suitcase was sitting upright on the ground next to Vivian's feet, and so was our other big white suitcase and a navy one too. Vivian was wearing her long black leather jacket over a white t-shirt and sweatpants -- she had changed her clothes. Elle was groggy, but she went along with everything Vivian said, even without having the full picture.

"Come on, Honey, wake up. Grab your pink blankey, Baby. We're leaving."

Elle looked up at Vivian, sorta blank facedly, and blinked a couple times before reacting. Then, she sat up and got herself out of bed. Elle grabbed her pink blanket, but allowed Mr. Teddy Bear to stay behind. I helped Vivian by carrying the olive green suitcase, and we all headed out. Vivian didn't even lock the door. We just left -- up the stairwell, down the hallway, and through the front glass door of our moldy ass apartment. Just like that.

By the time we exited the front door of our apartment complex we were all running. I think out of instinct, you know? Elle was positioned between Vivian and me. We were both holding one of Elle's hands pulling her along to better match our more grown-up pace. The sky was midnight blue, but it had to have been much later than that, and the road was damn near empty. We followed the stars, all holding hands and looking over our shoulders periodically. I sorta felt like I was Harriet Tubman knowing Lawrence could show up and catch us at any moment.

It felt like we had been running in sticky glue -- not making any progress towards our unknown destination. It was bad enough that it was damn-near Halloween, we didn't need the extra spookiness and fright in the air that night. We didn't want any tricks, or even any treats. With each lonesome car that passed by we stopped and held our breaths as if we could blend into our surroundings like geckos in hiding waiting to attack any predators. I fought the ice cold air permeating my lungs and making my nose run in order to stay in my body fully enough to keep going.

But, finally we reached the nearest intersection, and turned right. We didn't stop running for another half a block until we reached our local Denny's. Mom held the door open for Elle and me and hurried us inside. We sat next to the windows facing the parking lot, not the ones facing the main roads -- for obvious reasons. Elle and I sat opposite Vivian at the table, and patiently waited for our hot chocolates with whipped cream.

Vivian's fingers were crunched up, nails clicking on the table nervously, shoulders uptight and tense. Elle was biting her fingernails while peering out the window. I just kept searching to be sure the restaurant was clear of Lawrence. We were all sitting on the edge of the plushy seats. Our hot chocolates arrived, and even Vivian had ordered one for herself. We sat there in silence drinking our emotional treats. It was the best hot chocolate I've ever had. Between sips Mom would smile at Elle and me, and then look over her shoulder. Vivian inhaled her hot chocolate before it was cool enough for me or Elle to even make a dent in ours.

"Hurry up, girls," Vivian said.

Elle and I weren't able to finish our drinks. Halfway through our hot chocolates Vivian stood up from the table. She pulled her purse up closer to her face and started digging. Soon, her right hand surfaced with some cash. Vivian threw the cash on the table and said, "come on girls, he's here. It's time to go."

Elle and I both took an extra sip of our hot chocolates. Vivian was impatient and grabbed all three suitcases off the ground before starting towards the exit of the Denny's. Elle grabbed her pink blanket and we both hurried after Vivian, who was headed to the parking lot. Vivian let out an explanation to the hostess on our way out.

"I left some money on the table. We have to go now. Thank y'all so much." Vivian turned back, searching for Elle and me. She grabbed Elle's hand, "come on. Let's go!"

Once we were outside I noticed the first thing I actually recognized from the entire night. It was Uncle Mike's car -- a White Rabbit. I told you Uncle Mike is my Aunt Deb's husband, remember? He's also an addict. I guess the story is that he was addicted to Heroin, so he went to rehab. But, the doctors gave him another drug, Methadone, to help him transition from the Heroin. The thing is, now he's addicted to the Methadone and it's messed him up worse than he ever was before.

Vivian had never let us drive in the White Rabbit before, "it's way too fucking unsafe," she'd always say. "There aren't any seatbelts and it's way too old."

But, that night was an emergency situation, and our normal rules of operation went out the window. Mom sat shotgun, and Elle and I piled into the backseat of Uncle Mike's beat down Rabbit. Have you ever seen *Where the Heart is*? You know that scene where Natalie Portman's driving in her baby daddy's car and her shoe falls through a hole in the bottom of the floor? Well, that's exactly what the White Rabbit felt like. Elle and I had to flex our toes to be sure our shoes didn't fall through the holes in the ground. Plus, the car had a certain smell to it that reminded me of the boiled egg fart apartment where Elle got sick.

Somehow we managed, and eventually made it to Aunt Deb's. When we got there, my Aunt Deb had rolled sleeping bags out on her living room floor as if she already knew we were coming. Vivian, Elle, and I just laid out there on the floor. It was easier for some of us to sleep than others. Elle slept through Vivian's vibrating phone as Lawrence continued calling all night, but I didn't.

5

WOODY AND BUZZ (BF4L)

| 15 |

Chapter Fifteen

On top of everything going on, Vivan made me go to school today. I'd give the place a general below average rating. The only reason I even still go around the dump is because of Ms. Walker. She's the only class I'll never skip and the only teacher who gives me assignments I actually care about completing. Being a cheerleader doesn't bring me joy or make me feel any type of extra connection to my high school -- shockingly. I'm probably quitting cheer before next semester anyway. Our biggest game of the year will be in just a couple of weeks, and then I'm out.

I'd much rather hide away from everyone and listen to audiobooks in Ms. Walker's classroom than go to cheer practice. She reminds me of Ms. Frizzle, being in her class is always the most exciting part of my day. Most days that I help Ms. Walker tidy things up and grade papers are funner than hanging out with my friends, anyway. That's just the way I am. Every so often Ms. Walker will give me an upperclassman book to read off the cuff and we'll talk about the story, the characters, and the writing. We've even digressed into talks about how hard high school is and how phony everybody can be.

Ms. Walker is the first Black teacher I've ever had *and* she's a woman. Did you know we spend approximately one thousand four hundred and forty hours in school a year? In California, that's forty hours a week, eight hours a day, one hundred and eighty days a year. In the nine years I've been in school, in all those twelve thousand nine hundred and sixty hours, I have spent ZERO hours sitting in front of anyone that looks even remotely like me. Until Ms. Walker.

I've had female teachers who look like Vivian. White women with long black hair down their backs. I've had teachers who look like the type of men my Grandmother wishes Vivian would have settled down with. Male teachers that don't look anything like Lawrence, if you know what I mean?

I've obviously had teachers who aren't Black. But, I've never had a teacher who smells of Cocoa Butter like my Aunties do; never a teacher who cracks "jokes" full of animosity towards "the system" like Lawrence and my Uncles do; and, definitely never a teacher who pats her wig as frequently as my Grandma Soul does. I haven't been taught in a classroom by a teacher who looks like me until this year, my sophomore year in high school -- and that shit's measurably depressing on its own.

Learning from someone who understands me, *and* looks like me really does one for the culture! Now I finally look forward to coming to school *to learn* -- and probably for the first time ever. It's all because I met Ms. Walker.

She even knows about Lawrence being an addict, but she's really nice about the whole thing, and she doesn't have a big mouth either. I can *really* trust Ms. Walker. One time I even cried in her classroom at lunch. I don't even remember what I was crying about anymore. I just remember Ms. Walker lent me her rose gold highlighter and a mirror, then helped me get cleaned up before classes started back up again. She's a real one.

On the days I can't hang out in Ms. Walker's classroom, I'll kick it with my friends. Not to brag or anything, but we've established ourselves. We're just as popular as we planned we'd be at the beginning of the year. So, everything outside of my home life seems to be going according to plan -- which is great. My social and academic lives are the only ones within my control; and, my investment seems to be paying off.

Nikky and I are the only two Sophomore flyers on the varsity cheerleading team; Mark is a Sophomore grey shirt on the varsity football team; Laurie, Justin and Charlotte are all in journalism writing for our school newspaper. Miles is our school DJ's backup bitch boy, but everybody knows he has better taste than the actual DJ, so he's abnormally cool. Steve is loyal to the soil -- he still just loves to skate.

We always sit on the light tan stone steps, you know, the ones lifted above the entire student body scattered about in the courtyard. You remember, you went there too. Usually only seniors can sit up on those steps, but we've got a corner on the upper left-hand side that's specially reserved for us. There's never any shade, so we always have to dress in layers, and, when it rains we're shit out of luck. But, it's our spot. The ten of us.

I know they don't get it, but I sorta see my friends in colors. Well, if I'm being honest, I actually see most people in color. Take my girlfriend Laurie, for example. Laurie has a marine blue, or better yet, aqua personality. We call Laurie "the Foreigner" of our group because her parents are French. Vivian spent a couple years in France with my grandmother, Grams, as a teenager. So, in a way, I'm sort of distantly French too, and, in a similar way, I'm sort of sisters with Laurie. Laurie and I bond over our Frenchness and she teaches me phrases in French like: *Où est mon argent, Putain.* Laurie cares about the environment and animals, and she loves to wear beaded earrings. Aqua, right?

Laurie also has silky smooth dark brown hair almost identical to Vivian's -- if only it weren't so short. Instead of being long like Mom's, Laurie's hair curls up under the lobes of her ears. Laurie's aqua blue eyes make it impossible for any adult to see her as anything besides innocent. When in reality, she's the most sexually liberal of our entire friend group *and* she was the first to lose her virginity amongst us girls.

Even though Laurie is passionate about politics, and almost all current events happening in the world, she always stays as calm as a clam when talking to an "ignoramus." That's Laurie's word, "ignoramus," not mine. Either way, she's a fantastic writer and friend, like Rory from *Gilmore Girls*!

Anyway, sorry. I know you don't *really* care about my crazy brain and how it functions. You don't really care about how I associate people with colors or about my friends. I'm old enough to know that people don't really talk to one another for the sake of listening. People only tap sound on when they think you're experiencing a public melt-down, or when you're turning your life into a family video in some stellar lighting, or when you've made "it" -- depending on how you define "it."

All I'm trying to say is that lunch with my friends is basically the same every day. Laurie and Justin are the only ones in our group who come with a pre-packed lunch religiously. Both of their parents are married to each other and are all also professionals -- you know, like engineers, lawyers, doctors, and stuff like that. So, I guess it makes sense they always come to school prepared with beautifully packed lunches. To be honest, Laurie and Justin seem to have pretty peachy home lives. I'm not even really sure why they like to party as much as the rest of us misfits do, but whatever. They also usually supply the party favors, and they fit in with us alright -- so we take them in.

Sometimes Miles comes with a pretty little packed lunch too; but, most of the time he just comes with cash like Nikky and me. Nikky's Phillipino parents are barely still married. They spend most days trying to rush out of the house before seeing each other, kissing Nikky on their way out. It hurts her, but she just brags that she gets double the cash. Nikky's got big brown eyes and artificially caramel tan skin that she tanned "until it looked like mine." She loves makeup. Plus, her mom makes the best lumpia I've ever tasted. Nikky's one of those girls who knows the malls with all the best stores, and likes spending her entire Saturday going from one department store to the next hoping to snag the latest trends.

Nikky can be extremely shallow sometimes, but she trusts me enough to open up when she thinks nobody else is looking. I think it's because I'm the only friend she's ever invited over to her grandma's during a big family party. Being around Nikky's family reinforces my friendship with her, plus her grandma reminds me of my Grandma Soul. Really only I know that deep, *deep* down on the inside Nikky is sensitive and kind. Nikky is a bright hot pink, if you couldn't already tell.

Miles' parents are married too. But, his family has been pretty financially strapped since Miles' mom had back surgery earlier this year. Poor Graciella, she's been pretty much wiped out on pain pills ever since, but Miles hates talking about it. Miles' dad is Middle Eastern and Indian, and his mom is a second generation child of immigrants from Sinaloa, Mexico. Miles is a dazzling light cadet blue -- just in case you're wondering -- and my best friend out of all the guys. Miles has spent the most time at my house out of all my friends. Even Lawrence loved Miles when they met a few summers back. During that same visit, Lawrence even gifted Miles the baseball cap off his head. Now Miles keeps the hat safe at his house and hardly ever wears it. The thing is practically ensconced.

Nikky and Miles really get what it feels like to have your parents create a less than ideal home life. At lunch we team up before hitting the lunch lines. We'll scan the cafeteria menu and collaborate on which dishes and snacks to buy so that we get a little bit of everything. Our own little daily smorgasbord.

Typically, the twins and Steve don't come with food or money. Mark and Charlotte's mom died while giving birth to Mark, the younger twin, and their Guardian works graveyard shifts so he's always either sleeping or not home. Mark and Charlotte are two blonde-haired blue-eyed California surfer-looking identical twins who are *super* different from one another spiritually. They remind me of the Olson twins and Hanson brothers.

Charlotte and I are like sisters -- we literally call each other "frister," which stands for "friend who is also my sister." We try not to say it around the whole group, so as not to offend. Charlotte plays on the fact that people stereotype her into being a dumb blonde, and she's got a wildly untamed sense of humor. Ever since Mark started getting into being a habitual badass, Charlotte's really stepped up into filling the tough and tender-loving matriarchal figure her household needs. I really admire her strength, tenacity, and, sometimes, naively positive attitude. Charlotte is for sure for sure a soft lavender purple, like a young Jessica Simpson in "I Think I'm In Love."

Mark, on the other hand, is just untamed. He's like Steve-O from *Jackass* and proud of it. Mark pulls the craziest pranks and, so far, he's broken both his arms, his right leg, his left ankle, and three fingers on his right hand. Mark is a class clown. One time during a test in class Mark drew a picture on his scantron sheet by bubbling in certain answers. It was supposed to be a hamster or something, but I don't remember. At the end of the class when we were all passing our test packets up to the front of the room Mark stood on his desk and started showing off his "masterpiece." Everyone was laughing, but he obviously failed the test and he had to stay for detention. Mark wears big tees three sizes too big or not at all, and when I think of him I see the tint of green that's printed on money.

My friend Steve has a dad just like mine -- ridiculously charismatic and an unpredictable addict. Steve's mom used to be an addict too but I'm pretty sure she's sober and in recovery right now. I honestly thought Steve was going to be the guy I lost my virginity to, since we have so much in common and all, but nope. All through 8th grade every Friday night our whole friend group stirred up in excitement that he would ask me to be his girlfriend, but he never came though. Then, during freshman year, Justin came on my radar. We're all friends, so there was a bit of tension, but Steve just dug into that river in Egypt, you know what it's called? Denial! He acted like he didn't care. When you hear "Build Me Up Buttercup" by the Temptations, you should think of Steve.

Either way, we still speak to each other telepathically like my parents do -- but only in the best way possible. Guess what color hair

Steve has? Yup, it's dirty blonde just like Justin's. Clearly I have a type. Steve is just as tan as Justin, but he has these brilliant blue eyes that absolutely blow my mind -- and, I'm obviously around a lot of blue-eyed people, so, that's really a statement. Steve does these really spot-on impressions of people, and he's just as unreliable as I am. I think I already told you Steve has an older brother in the same grade as one of my sisters? Well, they also have a pitbull dog at home that looks like Jasper. Steve was the first guy I had started having grown-up fantasies about, and he'll probably be the biggest crush of my life until the end of time. Steve is a color of his own -- an impossible color my brain has made up to help fill in all his gaps: like magenta. Steve hardly ever comes to school with money, but one year on my birthday he pulled out some crumpled up dollar bills, out from the bottom of his shoe and gave it to me.

"I have a gift for you," he said, smiling ear to ear, "only for you."

Steve has already mastered the trait of being irresistible -- his father taught him like mine did to me.

The rule at lunch is that nobody will ever have to beg for food. Mark and Steve made a "feed us we're needy" joke once that Nikky ended up taking way too far. After that we all vowed no weird shit like that would ever go down again. So, what we do now is we put the snacks from the lunch lines in with whatever gourmet meal the packed lunch bunch has for the day, and then we'll all feast together. It's funny what lunchtime says about people, right?

When we're not feeling it, we all skip out of school after lunch. We'll spend the day walking around town, talking shit to one another, and skating like we did together in middle school. Lately we've not been feeling a lot of things, independently and collectively. I guess what connects us is a deep-seated bond over our erroneously perceived "rebellion against authority," which is really just our aligned inability to cope with life and the natural order of things. Either way, I fucking love my friends.

| 16 |

Chapter Sixteen

Last Friday was full of fun and games. I hung out with Steve, Miles, and the twins: Mark and Charlotte. They all have daddy issues, which makes me feel more at home with myself and my baggage. Plus, we all like to process the shit in the same way. The anxiety-filled rush of the holidays has been creeping over all of us, and, to be honest, we just wanted to escape.

You'd think being away from Lawrence would set me straight, Lord knows that's what Vivian was aiming for, but, nope. All this freedom just has me reevaluating my past, and reliving the days when things were simpler. I miss them.

Last Friday's fun reminded me of those simpler days. Miles and I rode the bus together after school. We spent the ride exchanging jokes about how miserable our lives were -- just the two of us. Miles, Steve, and I live in the furthest, tucked away side of our tiny ass town. But, Steve wasn't on the bus with us because he was already out with Mark and Charlotte. Nowadays Steve practically lives with Mark and Charlotte. They're his escape away from his crazy family. And, in his absence, Miles and I have grown closer.

Anyway, we hopped off the bus and decided it wasn't time to go home yet. At first he was just talking nonsense, and tripping on his words like he was nervous or something. It was weird, because we were only talking about our plans for the rest of the day. And, turns out, neither of us had any.

"I'm just gonna go home," Miles said pointing in the direction of his house, opposite mine.

"Alright, cool," I responded, "me too. I'll see you later."

I waved, like a lame ass loser, and turned to contemplate my latest decisions. Luckily, Miles didn't let me squirm for too long.

"*Or,*" he hiccuped.

I turned around and took a look at him, unintentionally making eye contact, and said, "or?"

"Um," Miles coughed. In return, I smiled, raised my eyebrows, and tilted my head. I think I may have been flirting with him. But, it was innocent, so don't read too much into it.

Miles smiled and continued, "or, um, yeah, if you want we could try to go find the others. You know they're out here roaming around somewhere. Do you want to go find them?"

"Yeah, fuck it." I was quick with my response, "I don't have anything else going on at home. Elle's been gone for a minute anyways."

"What?"

"Oh," I coughed, "nevermind. Let's just go find everybody else." I told Miles.

We walked on the levee reminiscing about old times. We went back and forth between "the good ol' days" and "damn, we've really grown up." Miles talked about how busy he's been at the radio station, and we corroborated about losing our heads lately. Then, I vented about trying to maintain my status on the cheerleading team in light of my grades slipping. I told him how depressed I'd been feeling, but left out the direct connection to Lawrence and Elle. All I had to do was tell him "I miss my family," and Miles knew exactly what I meant.

Miles' phone rang. It was Mark interrupting, per usual. After a round of shouting over each other, Mark and Miles were finally able to communicate about a meeting spot. In the meantime, I pulled out my headphones and listened to my iPod while the boys barked. I pressed shuffle and "Let Me Love You," by Mario played while I watched a pair of ducks drifting in the levee. Miles hung up the phone, turned back to me, and we continued exchanging after-hours horror stories about our home lives.

"Did you hear my song on the radio this week? It was "Dear Mama," Miles asked, looking at me bullseye so I couldn't escape the moment like my instinct was telling me to.

I shook my head "no," and I could tell Miles was disappointed.

"Last weekend my mom couldn't even recognize me," Miles revealed.

"Damn," I said, restrained and inadequately.

"Yeah, it was booty. She was out of it, man. I played that song for her," Miles said.

"I'm sorry, Miles. I know that sucks." I offered Miles one of my headphone buds. I knew there was nothing I could say to make it better, so I handed him my iPod too so he could choose the music. We walked along with each other barely speaking or making eye contact. Just being there together was enough.

Before I knew it, we were standing in front of Steve and the twins. I had been so wrapped up in the moment with Miles, I almost forgot we were meeting up with the rest of the group. Charlotte officially broke the moment when she screamed, "oh my gosh! Olivia, finally!" She hugged me like we hadn't seen each other in a thousand years.

"Hey," I said, distractedly.

We were standing on a walking trail woven through an apartment complex that none of us live in. One of our favorite random pockets of the world. We love this pocket because it's right on the water, and it's just steps away from the rec. center. So, most adults didn't bother venturing over there. Mark was already smoking a spliff. Steve looked as if I were the drink of cold water he needed. Like, now that I was there he was refreshed. It was everything.

"What took you two so long?" Steve asked, avoiding my eye contact and looking straight to Miles as if flexing. He's always quick to prepare for something that will never go down.

"Nothing, man. What are you talking about? We were just walking trying to get here to y'all." Miles answered, sounding confused even though he wasn't.

"Let's go," I inserted, "what are y'all up to?"

"We were just walking through here to get to the levee so we could finish a joint in peace. Y'all down?" Mark asked.

"Yeah!" Charlotte answered for me, telepathically.

"Yeah!" I echoed.

"Igght, let's go then!" Miles joined in excitedly.

The five of us walked through the white and green apartment complex sharing a joint. The complex was only two stories high but they felt like skyscrapers that could protect us from view. Charlotte and I let the boys walk ahead of us with the spliff as we whispered to each other in the back.

Charlotte started asking me about my walk with Miles, as if something had gone down. But, I set her straight and steered her into a conversation about Steve instead. Miles cocked his head half over his shoulder trying to eavesdrop, but Charlotte and I ignored him.

"You know you two would have the cutest kids, right? Like, we'd all be jealous of you!" Charlotte encouraged.

"I know," I said while blushing.

"Plus, it's your goal for this year!"

"I know," I sighed before covering it with a joke, "but I ain't trying to have babies right now, so slow your muhfuckin' roll, girl!"

"No, for real though," Charlotte replied before we started laughing.

Eventually we reached the break in the complex that led to the levee. There's only one bench, so there wasn't enough room for us to all sit together. Steve and Mark were either trying to skip rocks on the water or intentionally throwing them at the duck couple cruising on the water. Miles sat between me and Charlotte.

We hung out listening to songs like "Boulevard of Broken Dreams," and smoking together. Just taking in the scenery and collectively ignoring the series of messes happening in our independent lives. By the time I got home I was too crossfaded to do my homework, so I just went to bed and skipped dinner. Not that Vivian noticed anyway.

| 17 |

Chapter Seventeen

November 29th, 2007

We stayed at my Aunt Deb's for a couple of weeks. It was just girls because all of us women needed a fucking break from the deadbeat men in our lives, yaddamean?

My Aunt Deb decided to leave her husband too, and definitely for a good reason. A couple months before we left Lawrence and moved in with Aunt Deb, my Uncle Mike had unintentionally started a fire in their old house together. I guess he was getting high and fell asleep while using the lighter, so the carpet caught fire and then spread throughout the rest of the house while my Uncle Mike was zonked out.

My closest cousin in age, Brittney, woke up first. I guess Brittney smelled the smoke and sprang into action. She woke up her older sister, my eldest cousin, Amy, and they split up the responsibilities. Brittney grabbed the fire extinguisher from their basement, and Amy woke my aunt and uncle up from their sleep to usher them out of the house.

I told you it wasn't *just* my life burning down in flames.

The fire was the last straw. It started a chain of events. Ultimately, my Aunt Deb separated from Uncle Mike and told him not to move into her new rental house with my cousins. Within no time, we jammed the rental house full of *Little Women*. We banned together while waiting for the next step in our lives to present itself.

But, shout out to the sisters of the world though, amiright? Or, am I right?

My Aunt Deb is an inspiration to Vivian, and vice versa. It only took a couple weeks before Vivian found us our own spot too. The search was hectic, but my Aunt Deb and my cousins helped the whole time. Watching the two of them felt like watching *Thelma and Louise* in real life. I was starstruck.

Of course there have been some hiccups along the way. Split ups and moves are tricky. We had to go back to our old apartment to grab more of our old clothes and toys. Also, Elle started having nervous breakdowns in her new kindergarten class upon Vivian leaving after drop off in the mornings. I might as well be drawing hamsters on my scantron answer sheets like Mark because my grades are plummeting so quickly. But, I guess that's all to be expected since I've barely been doing any work all semester.

I was even called to help calm Elle down after Vivian dropped her off at daycare. I asked Elle why she was so upset to see Vivian leave, and Elle cried out, "it's because I can't remember what she looks like when she's gone!"

I tried to reassure Elle that Vivian would never abandon us, and that she will always come home to us at the end of the day. But, it didn't really seem to help much. Elle just kept crying, "I don't want to forget her, Ollie! I'm too young. I won't remember her."

"You won't, E. It's not like Mom's going to die or something. We'll just see her a little later today!"

"You don't know that for sure, Olivia. You don't."

I haven't seen Lawrence since we left and I won't lie, I really fucking miss him. But, I also get why Vivian got Elle and me out of that apartment. I'm grateful. I guess it just takes time to adjust to my new normal, and it's been a slowly progressing endeavour, to say the least.

Outside of that, nothing too new has been happening. My love life is still pretty nonexistent since Steve won't ask me to be his wifey already. Charlotte, Nikky, and Laurie keep asking me to have a sleepover or for me to go to one of their houses after school. They don't know shit about what's going on in my head at home right now. So they don't understand why I just want to be left alone. Plus, I think Ms. Walker is starting to get suspicious of me too. She sent me an email asking how I was "holding up," which was sus. Maybe she just really cares about her students though. I don't know. I'm starting to think I can't trust anyone any more. I am disconnecting and it's starting to feel like nothing matters.

| 18 |

Chapter Eighteen

Last weekend we went to my Grandma Soul's house. It was the first time since the split from Lawrence. Even though she's Lawrence's mom, in some ways, she's better friends with Vivian. When my Grandma Soul called Vivian to check on our Sunday dinner plans, she assured Vivian that Lawrence wasn't going to be invited so that we could all come over instead.

"Lord knows imma take the heat for my grandbabies every time, Vivian. You best believe," I heard my Grandma Soul reassured from the phone. Vivian was super hesitant at first, but Elle and I were so excited to see our aunties and cousins that there was no way she was actually going to make us skip out.

My Grandma Soul is called "Grandma Soul" for a reason. When we walked into her house it smelled like soul food. The familiar smell of all sorts of dishes rushed my nose. Fried chicken *and* grilled chicken, mac n cheese, greens, corn bread, black beans, hot dogs, mashed potatoes, yams, pumpkin pie, cheese cake, and a plethora of additional side dishes tingled in my nostrils and made my mouth water.

My uncles and adult male cousins were split between the grill, the card table, and the television set. My aunties and adult female cousins were split between the kitchen, the card table, the living room couches, and the bathroom. There were basically herds of people in every room. In the living room, my older cousin was braiding people's hair. She started with the afro of our most tender headed cousin, and advanced to our toughest headed family member, my Uncle Sean.

"Pull that shit tighter, Keke," Uncle Sean, who had just been released from San Quentin, joked. "I can't feel shit you're doing up there," he kept encouraging her, "get in there!"

"I'm *tryin'*, Cousin, but there ain't nothin' here!"

Everybody broke out howling.

In the bathroom, women of assorted skin tones were helping to press, relax, and or straighten each other's hair. I think the reason we love dressing up and playing with our hair so much is because we've grown up watching scenes like this since before we can even remember. We're constantly trying to learn new ways to style our hair and feel pretty, which can be really hard when you have our texture of hair and don't have the skills. So, while my Grandma Soul stayed stationary in the kitchen, Vivian stayed stationary in the bathroom to make sure Elle and I didn't try anything too crazy. Last summer Elle decided to give herself a haircut without any supervision and came out of the bathroom looking like Michael Jackson in "Rock With You." Babygirl was looking disco jerry curl, mullet fresh.

Someone put down the hair straightener without another person instantly claiming it again, and Elle looked up to Vivian with puppy eyes.

"*Please*, Mom, please!"

Vivian must've really been feeling the holiday spirit because she allowed my Auntie Norma to straighten Elle's hair. It was the first time Elle ever had her hair straightened, and even I was shocked by how long it was. Elle walked around my Grandma Soul's house swinging her hair back and forth for the rest of the night. She became a completely different, brand new person and I was loving it. Elle didn't let Vivian wet her hair down for the next week. Even after Vivian did finally wash Elle's hair and it returned to being all curly, it was too late -- Elle had been reborn.

| 19 |

Chapter Nineteen

December 13th, 2007

Friday is a big social day for me. Unless I'm with Lawrence and Elle, of course. Usually on Fridays my friends and I will walk to Catamaran Park after school and sip on some drank together. Mark brings the ganja and rolls us a few Js that we'll usually smoke under the gazebo or on the swings, depending on if kids are around or not. Last Friday was no different.

After smoking under the gazebo with everybody, Laurie, Miles, and I went to lay in the grass together. I don't know if you remember or not, but it was one of those days that reminds you that real winters don't exist in California. So, Laurie, Miles, and I laid in the grass field together and sang some of the songs playing from Laurie's iPod on shuffle. "All the Things She Said," by t.A.T.u. was playing.

"What the hell do you listen to, Laurie?!" Miles joked.

We laughed and talked about the shapes of the clouds for a few minutes, before I sprang a hidea on the two of them. Yeah, a hidea, do you get it? High idea. I said, "Nikky's birthday is coming up on Tuesday, let's throw her a surprise birthday dinner! What do y'all think?"

They both loved it! We immediately started planning the whole thing, right there in the grass field. Once we had enough details planned out -- the where, Applebees; the when, Tuesday night; and the who, all of our friends, -- we ran back to the rest of our group still sitting under the Gazebo. I took Nikky on a walk with some faked crisis of the heart while Laurie and Miles filled the rest of the group in on the surprise birthday dinner plan. Apparently everybody else quickly jumped aboard.

I pitched our idea to Nikky's mom later that night when Nikky was being picked up. Nikky went to grab her backpack and jacket, and I ran up to her mom's driver-side window to "catch up and say hi," per usual. Nikky's mom agreed to our plan and said she would make sure Nikky arrived on location at the designated time -- 6 PM. By Tuesday night our whole class of sophomores, the cool freshmen, and some of the most down to earth juniors had all been invited. We even considered inviting some of the coolest teachers on campus. Then, reality hit and we thought about how they'd definitely dampen the fun. Either way, Nikky was *totally* clueless the entire time. It was so great!

Nobody ruined the surprise -- Laurie, Miles, and I were all shocked everybody had actually showed up within the half hour window we had allotted. It was great. We told people the dress code was dinner formal, and folks really showed out! Miles and Laurie had gone decor shopping, just for balloons and streamers and stuff, but it wasn't even necessary! Everybody was so dressed to impress they naturally transformed the family dining room area into an elegant, high fashion looking VIP room. That we were at Applebees no doubt helped.

When Nikky arrived in the parking lot she texted me and I screamed at everybody to duck down in their booths. Laurie and Miles held the fort down while I walked Nikky in from the front door talking her ear off so as to add distraction. At the perfect time, when Nikky and I were about two steps away from reaching our section, everybody jumped up from their booths and shouted:

"SURPRISE!!!!"

Nikky's hands jerked up to her mouth, but she screamed through them, "AHH!!!!!!" Her face turned red, which it does often, and she started crying. Then, Nikky started recognizing all the different random people and hugging everybody like she was Princess Diana!

It was like a movie. Pretty much everybody in attendance stayed at the restaurant till closing, so, by definition, I guess the party was lit -- right?

Actually though, if I can be totally *totally* honest, it was all sort of a pain in the ass. Nikky was whining and being ungrateful all week because she thought we had all forgotten about her birthday. I mean, I get she didn't know we were planning her a huge surprise party. But, still. Laurie, Charlotte, and I were planning our Friday night with Nikky so she wouldn't get suspicious. So, it's not like Nikky literally thought her friends weren't planning anything. She knew we hadn't forgotten.

Plus, once Nikky actually arrived and figured out that we *had* planned her a big birthday shindig she was still being snotty. She barely sat with any of us for the whole night. Instead, Nikky spent the majority of her evening talking up this Junior she newly has a crush on. This year she's forgotten all about her original goal to hook up with Mark, and she's moved on to someone colder, older, and "more mature."

I don't remember hearing her ever say "thank you" to me, or Laurie, or Miles, or any of her other guests. Not even a "thank you" to her mom, who was obviously instrumental in helping us execute the vision. Plus, just to top it all off, Laurie, Miles, and I were left with a huge bill at the end of the night. We had anticipated some people would dine and dash, but damn. So, that was pretty stressful and Vivian was pretty upset with me for not being more responsible -- especially on her "single-parent budget."

But, there were also a couple of positives, I won't lie. Remember how I told you Steve and I have a thing? Well, last night Miles and Mark told me that Steve still likes me. I had been wondering if he still liked me or not -- since I'm still not his girlfriend. But, at dinner the guys told me that Steve said for the Nth time that he wants to ask me out. I've been hearing them say that since I was in middle school, so when I hear it again now I don't hold my breath anymore. We'll see if that ends up happening or not. Probably not. I'll keep you posted.

Either way, this super cute thing happened during dinner. It was the type of thing that makes me fall in love with him. I guess another window into the depths of his mysterious soul. I was sitting at one of the tables with my arms crossed and shivering a bit. Honestly, I don't even remember being cold, but whatever. Steve was sitting at the table behind me with some of the other guys and freshmen girls, but I guess he was facing my back. Then, when he saw I was shivering, Steve came over to sit with me. He sat down in the booth next to me and wrapped his black jacket decorated with stars around my shoulders. It's one of those jackets that zip all the way up the face opening at the hood.

"Here you go," Steve said with a subtle little smile and head nod.

I swear, he's *so* smooth. I can't even front, he was making me wet just by staring in my eyes. I just smiled back hella big and said, "thanks," raising my eyebrows to Steve once our eyes connected.

You better believe I held on to that jacket all night! Plus, when Steve was catching a ride home with Charlotte and Mark I tried to give it back. Steve just said, "that's ok. You can hold on to it," and winked like I imagine Ryan Sheckler would have!

"NO PROBLEM!" I thought, but didn't dare say aloud.

So, at the very least, out of all the drama and money spent since Tuesday night, at least I've been able to wear Steve's jacket to sleep all week. Can't put a price tag on that!

Basically, I'm just trying to hold on to the good and let the rest of it go, OK?! Next week I'm supposed to go to a San Jose Sharks game with Elle and Charlotte, and I'm stoked!

6

VIOLENT CRIMES (KARMA)

| **20** |

Chapter Twenty

January 3rd, 2008

I'm not ready to say "Happy New Year" to people yet. I'm too busy praying this year will be better than the last ones. You want to know how my break went? Horrifically. Mostly because Elle and I finally saw Lawrence.

While Vivian worked, Elle and I stayed with my Uncle Marlon and Auntie Bette during break. It sucks that working parents don't get to spend school breaks with their kids. Especially during the holidays. But, my Uncle Marlon and Auntie Bette feel like second parents, and we always have hella fun at their place.

Uncle Marlon has actually been the most consistent, reliable, and trustworthy male figure in my entire life. Uncle Marlon is in security. He's a club bouncer -- which means he kicks the angry people out of the club so they don't ruin everybody else's time. Even at his job he projects "safety."

My Uncle Marlon is the youngest sibling in the family, almost like me. He gives these big ass huge bear hugs that hurt so bad they start feeling good. I've even craved his bear hugs in my loneliest moments. I guess I've grown to love them. Plus, even though my Uncle Marlon is taller and heavier than Lawrence, I've never felt afraid of him in the

132

slightest bit. Not feeling afraid of the adult male in the room has been super refreshing.

My Uncle Marlon's wife, Auntie Bette, pronounced "Bet," is also my absolute idol. Auntie Bette is fierce. She's void of apologies. She's not just beautiful, she's sexy, she's bold, and she's in control of her own body --and any man who would dare to stand in her way. Auntie Bette loves styling Elle's hair in "puff tails," or picked out afro pigtails, plus she loves dancing as much as Elle and I do. In fact, "it's a requirement" if you ask her.

Auntie Bette says accessories are a woman's best friend, and she's not lying either. Elle and I are like Auntie Bette and her best friend, "Crazy Kendra." They're always laughing and whispering to each other. They inspired Elle and me to come up with our own secret way to communicate with one another. Now we're so quick at speaking Pig Latin that we've fooled people into thinking it's a real foreign language.

Plus, Auntie Bette takes the best pictures! When I grow up I want to be Auntie Bette. She's the most confident, appropriately overly-expressive, and yet still put together woman I've ever known. She works with hearing imparied students in schools, so she signs American Sign Language while she speaks and her hands are always in motion.

Auntie Bette is bold. She isn't afraid to interrupt the Target store clerk to ask him to stop staring at her boobs amidst a casual conversation. Auntie Bette is so badass she'll even go to work with Uncle Marlon at the club - working security.

Anyway, Elle and I were staying with them a lot during winter break while Vivian was at work. Then, one day Lawrence showed up at the front door unexpectedly. I think our Uncle Marlon felt extra guilty and bad for his brother, Lawrence, because of the situation. You know, Lawrence not having been allowed to see Elle or me in a few weeks, and Lawrence having missed his first holiday season without his family, that is. So, when Lawrence showed up at their house, crying and begging for Uncle Marlon to let him take Elle and me in his car, my Uncle Marlon caved.

"It's just to sit and talk and catch up without y'all breathing down my back for a bit," Lawrence bargained.

What ended up happening instead is that once Lawrence had Elle and me in his car, he took off. We drove up and down the freeway as Lawrence kept stopping to call Vivian from various phone booths to see if she would answer a number that wasn't his. Poor guy still doesn't know how to *67 his calls. Within no time it got dark outside and Elle fell asleep in the back seat - at least Jasper was there with me.

"How do you get back to your place, Olivia? Give your Daddy some direction so he knows where he's going, please."

I've ironically been referred to as "the Rememberer" in my family since before I can even remember. So, I guess Lawrence just knew I knew where we were and how to get back home. I also knew Vivian didn't want Lawrence to know where our new apartment was, but the third wall existing between the two of them had to break down eventually, and I really wanted to go home. I guess I was just the right contractor to send in to handle the job. As soon as I pointed to our complex directing Lawrence to turn into our parking lot off the side of the road, he started laughing.

"You're kidding," he cackled.

"Nope. This is our new place." I pointed up to our third story balcony out of the corner of my eyes.

"Wow. No shit." Lawrence shook his head. "Here, tell your mother we're downstairs," he said, handing me his cell phone that was already mid-dial to Vivian.

"What do you need, Lawrence?"

"Hey, Mom, it's actually me, Olivia."

"Olivia?! Finally! Are you OK?!"

"Yeah, I'm fine. We're downstairs."

"You're down-" I saw Vivian lean out over the railing of our balcony. "Oh, wow. OK. I'm coming downstairs right now."

Vivian was able to keep our address secret from Lawrence for the past few months - ever since we had left our old apartment. But, I had ruined that secret by telling him how to drive Elle and me home. I'm not 100% sure what the better option was in that scenario, but whatever, that's what happened. I don't think Vivian was mad at me for it or anything. Most of all, she was just glad to know Elle and I were safe and still alive.

As we waited for Vivian to greet us downstairs Lawrence talked shit, "*this* is where y'all been held up, huh? Right here?!"

"Yup." I looked onward into the bushes bordering the small complex parking lot while Lawrence continued laughing like a hyena.

"Just right here, huh? Out of all the places in Seattle, y'all picked *right here*, huh?"

"Yup." I said again.

"Boy, your mother is about to lose her shit, Olivia."

Finally, Vivian appeared from the garage gate.

"Watch this." He nudged my upper arm with his right elbow, upbeatedly, as Vivian approached.

"Hey there, you guys!" Vivian was smiling, waving at all of us, as if she weren't freaking out inside. Once she made it over to Lawrence's car he started in on her,

"So this is the place you decided to hide my kids away from me?"

Vivian rolled her eyes and dipped her head backward, "Olivia, get your stuff and say goodbye to Jasper, OK?" I nodded. "Great," Vivian rolled her head back towards Lawrence.

"Yes, Lawrence, this is where we live. You weren't even supposed to have the kids today. You know you aren't even supposed to be here! You're not allowed to see me or the kids right now, Lawrence. Haven't I already made that more than abundantly clear?"

I had neither seen, nor heard, Vivian and Lawrence talking since the night we ran away to the Denny's and left him. But, it was clear this wasn't the first time they'd spoken. To me it felt good to see Vivian in the same space as Lawrence again, even if they were clearly broken up. They weren't pretending to be married any more, not on a break, and not separating, but broken up and totally donzo. I won't lie, that was sort of tough to feel so palpably. It made me miss the seldom good old times.

"Look, we're not even a five minute drive from the girls' school," Vivian explained, "we have a bunch of friends and family in the area, and you're not that far away. So, yes, this is the place I picked for us to live."

"No shit," Lawrence interjected.

"Right!" Vivian threw her stank face to Lawrence, "Ok. So, what?"

"It's close to family, and to the girls' school, and even to me, you said?"

"Yes! What's wrong? What do you want to complain about now?"

"Nothing, Vivian. I just think it's funny you went through alla this drama and effort to get away from me,"

Vivian started trying to talk over Lawrence, but he didn't stop talking so they were both just sorta talking on top of the other. Vivian said, "Lawrence, you're damn right I spent the effort to get away from you,..."

Lawrence continued calmly, "when you clearly can't stand to stay away from me for more than two seconds."

Vivian's point was the last of the exchange, "after you shot our five year old daughter with your fucking BB gun!" There was silence for a minute and they just stood there looking at each other. Lawrence broke eye contact first, looking down to the asphalt ashamedly while forcing a fake chuckle and flicking his nose.

"Alright, fair enough." he wiped a smile on his face, "I just think it's funny you moved here when I live *literally* just right around the corner, Viv."

"What do you mean?" Vivian tilted her head far to her left side, as if additionally saying, "quit playin'."

"I moved into the Rosewood complex around the corner, like seven buildings down, just a couple weeks ago."

"Fuck," Vivian gasped.

"I know!"

"You're kidding me?" Vivian asked, but she already knew the answer. It was more of a rhetorical question used as a ploy for her to have a bit more time to gather her thoughts.

Lawrence interjected again, "Naw, I don't play."

"Lawrence, you can't afford to live on your own, so what do you mean you live around the corner?"

"I live there with my girlfriend now, Vivian. Looks like I know how to move on too." Lawrence moved his face back and forth in front of Vivian's as if he had just hardcore dissed her on the playground in front of the whole school. "And I'm sober now too," he added as the cherry on top.

Vivian sarcastically smiled at Lawrence and said, "great." Then she turned to me and Elle, who was barely awake or grabbing on to my hand, "hug your father goodbye and let's go upstairs. I'll run a hot bath for you while you tell me about your day."

| 21 |

Chapter Twenty-One

One thing I'll never miss about high school is P.E. I'd happily take three extra classes with Ms. Walker rather than go to *that* class. Shoot, I'd even take two health & wellness classes before I'd opt into taking physical education. Something about forcing a bunch of teenagers to perform athletics in front of one another really gets our hormones ramped. It's like a game of self esteem-themed Russian roulette, and it's terrifying.

I don't love it. Everybody reverts to caricatured performances of gender norms. The girls roll their gym shorts up so short they have raging camel toe, while the boys convert every simple activity into a major ego tournament. During my freshman year of high school I didn't have P.E. with any of my friends. I was pretty much a loner, and the girls in my class used to make fun of me. They would laugh at me when I actually ran the mile, snickering each time I lapped them. Then, one time, when I was on the bleachers trying to catch my breath from the suicide drills, the Regina George of the gang approached me.

"Hi," she was giggling and kept looking at her backups, "um, we were just wondering if we could ask you a question."

"Yeah?" I responded hesitantly.

"Why doesn't your hair move when you run? Is it not real or something?"

Becky ran back to her friends laughing before I could respond. I stood there debating if I should run after Becky and show her how much rage nappy-headed Black girls like me keep in check on a day-to-day basis, or if I should just let it go. My hands were in fists and just as I reached the tip of her backside ponytail, Miles walked over to our class. He worked as an office assistant during third period, so he used to go to all the different classes collecting attendance. On this particular day, Miles showed up to my class at the perfect time. He saw me heading the wrong direction down a one-way street and pulled me out of it.

"What's good, Olivia?!" he hollered to me over the sea of sweaty teenagers, "what's crack-a-lackin?!" Miles held his arms out wide, calling for a hug.

"My brotha! What's good, Timberland?!" I hollered back. I smiled without thinking about it, changed directions, and skipped to go hug Miles.

"I saw what you were just doing, Olivia," Miles egged on, "what was that about?" He asked me what was wrong and why I was about to go after Becky, so I told him straight up.

"She's not even worth it, Olivia, don't listen to silly people like them. Those girls don't have any idea about anything cool in this world. They aren't going to get how bomb you are. That's on them -- not you." Miles reassured me just before my P.E. teacher walked over for the timeless power play of "where are you supposed to be right now."

I intentionally wasn't friends with The Mean Girls, but their bigotry still hurt like hell. Even though I channeled "X Gon Give It To Ya," when I saw any of them for the rest of the year, I took their laughter to heart. Not *right* away right away, but, soon after, I started straightening my hair on Sundays.

To tell you the truth, the way my own friends reinforced my attempted assimilation hurt worse than those silly girls. Charlotte and Laurie started giving me compliments about my hair and how "good" I looked all the time. Nikky started acting jealous and rude more frequently. Especially once she saw how the guys also responded positively. Mark and Steve even stopped calling me "Medusa."

I know everyone was trying to be nice by paying me the extra attention. All of it was flattering, but each compliment felt back handed. I couldn't help but hear my supposed friends saying, "your nappy hair wasn't cute" and "I couldn't relate to you as well with all that stiff, Black, Afro-ready hair blocking me," even though they weren't.

Well, at least not so directly.

I am *the* Black friend in our group. Plus, as Nikky and Mark love to remind me, I'm "only *half* Black." Of course Miles will usually stand up for me, and call them out for making racist "jokes." But, I still think it's safe to say they don't understand the sort of otherness I feel. They definitely don't consider my Blackness as being as deeply rooted in my identity as it is. They don't understand the complexities of needing to use the eyes at the back of your head at all times. They're not busy checking their backs when we're out being teenagers. Sometimes Miles will look over his shoulder before hopping a fence. But, for the most part, they're all too busy looking forward to be looking back.

"They're privileged" in that way, as Lawrence says. He's not wrong, but it's not as big of a bother to me as he makes it out to be. It can definitely be alienating, and can make me want to isolate. But, on the positive side, feeling incessantly misunderstood motivates me to meet new people. Like, I will *if* I make it to college.

Well, actually, there's a new guy at our school this semester named John. I haven't really talked to him too much, but he's in my English class with Ms. Walker, so I see him every other day. We've worked up a friendship enough that I can call him "Doe," since I don't really know him, and we laugh about it.

John is new, but he already has an infamous reputation. Rumor has it John was caught selling edible brownies to students at lunch and the school threatened to expel him. They never even called the cops. It never would've gone down that way if John were Black, but nobody's ready for that conversation. I guess John had the right complexion, and his parents had the right amount of zeros in their checking accounts. He basically just had to transfer schools. One of his friends, Peter, even transferred schools with him "in solidarity."

But, nobody really knows much about John. The fact that he's quiet and super secretive doesn't help. He says the stories I've heard are "just rumors, except the part about Peter." So, I don't know if he's lying, or shy, or what. He's so quiet and super secretive that I can't read his truth.

I've only been able to get a few facts out of him. So far, I know that his parents are legit first-generation immigrants from Russia. Also, he's got sandy blonde curly hair that he keeps short, and grey-blue eyes. I associate John with a solid grey color - both because he's so mysterious and because of his eye color. I think of that light color of grey that's used when people don't upload a photo to their profile. Do you know what I'm talking about?

Every time John tells us a story he blushes. I don't know if he's shy or if he's got a photographic memory accompanying his story-telling. But, he's got this swagger that makes me feel like he's had a new girlfriend every other week since kindergarten. So, I don't really care about the details.

So far, all I know is that John, to me, is grey. If any other juice comes to light, I'll definitely keep you posted.

| **22** |

Chapter Twenty-Two

January 17th, 2008

I did it again. I hung out with Lawrence without Vivian or any other additional supervision. Lawrence is still telling everybody that he's sober now, so Vivian wants Elle and me to bond with him.

"I don't want to keep you away from your father, Olivia," Vivian retorts to my protests. I guess since it's been a few months, and now that Lawrence is our neighbor, Vivian stopped seeing it as a big deal to leave us alone with him again. "He's done it before, he can do it again. Especially now that he's sober," she said.

Big mistake - HUGE.

Lawrence lives on the top floor of his complex. It isn't a big deal or anything, but it gives you some sort of data point to hold on to for your own sake. His apartment complex has a pool, a hot tub, and a basketball court, which is super rare for places up in Washington - unlike here.

When we pulled up, Lawrence dropped his jaw. At first he went up to the back seat window of the car. He pressed his face up against Elle's window, and started making pig noises and blowing raspberries. Elle pressed her face up against the window and returned the favor. Vivian and I looked at each other and cockily rolled our eyes - she went first, and then I returned the favor to her.

After Jasper joined in on the window licking fun, Lawrence pushed his face back from Elle's window. He made his way up towards Vivian and me in the front seat. Lawrence gave Vivian a head nod before quickly shifting his attention to me. He squished up his eyes really tight and rubbed them, as if unsuccessfully trying to rearrange the image of me staring back at him.

"I barely recognized you," Lawrence said while cracking a half-hearted smile like it wasn't already painfully obvious.

"Well," I shrugged and then waved, as if reintroducing myself, "it's me."

"You've just gotten so thick that I didn't quite recognize you there, Olive!" Lawrence grossly cackled.

Calling me thick was Lawrence's most polite way of saying that he thought I was getting fat. It was as if he thought I had, perhaps, indulged in some emotional eating as a way to cope with life. But, he was wrong. Lawrence's alleged expertise in the field of substance abuse was mute at the moment. His subconscious wouldn't allow him to acknowledge the obvious correct answer. The truth behind my weight gain was that I'd been engaging in emotional use of spirits and greens as a way to cope.

"You've just got a real different look when you're chunkier, Olivia!" Lawrence giggled like a little boy, per usual. He looked me up and down, and then turned his eyes towards Vivian and Elle for confirmation the situation was indeed humorous. It felt like I was sitting under an airport security scanner and everyone around could see so deep inside of me they could see my skeleton. But, thankfully, only Lawrence laughed. Jasper started barking and shut him up.

The sound of Lawrence's laugh simultaneously offended and triggered me. So, I just took a deep breath and looked to Vivian for reassurance. She nodded, ever so slightly so as to not alert Lawrence we were speaking telepathically, and gave me permission to continue existing.

"Welp," I said in acceptance, "it *is* me." I stuck my chin out a little bit and kept my lips pressed tightly together. Then, Vivian curled her pointer finger towards herself repeatedly, nonverbally asking Lawrence to come down mouth-level to her driver's side window. I could tell she was yelling at him under her breath, "you sound like an asshole," Vivian said.

Vivian and Lawrence exchanged a few more hushed words at her window. Then, Lawrence casually pushed away in a pushup-like position, trying to flex and play on his Michael Jordan looks. He reached his arms up to the sky and then back in a backward extended standing bend. He spread each finger as far apart from the other as possible and let out a fake-sounding monster yawn. It was clear Lawrence was done engaging with Vivian, and he made it even more abundantly clear by saying, "come on girls, grab your stuff and let's get going."

We walked off, but it ended up that Lawrence didn't take us up to his apartment. Instead, after Vivian drove off, he took us to the basketball court. "You need some exercise little lady," he scolded, "you're getting thick."

Or, was it just puberty?

No other kids were at the basketball court. I guess because it was cold as fuck outside. It was January in Washington afterall. Nevertheless, we just went with it and shot around playing basketball with Lawrence to stay warm.

"Your form is all wrong, Olivia. Here, you gotta hold the ball like *this* when you shoot it. Right up by your face like this." Lawrence started jerking me, and, sure, I guess the basketball too, all around the court. "Now use all your strength, push up from your legs, give a little jump, click your heels in the air, and then shoot it right into the basket."

Lawrence always wanted to have more sons. Really he *only* wanted to have sons, but, instead, he got one son and six daughters. A couple years before meeting Vivian, Lawrence's first daughter died. I guess she was born sick and her health issues didn't go away as she got older. Eventually those complications killed her. Lawrence was in the Marines at the time, and they wouldn't release him to go to the funeral. They said there was nothing he could do anyway. So, I guess he started a fight with one of his superiors in hopes of being discharged.

The Marines still wouldn't release Lawrence, so he broke his own leg and started drinking. It was just a few months after his dishonorable discharge that Lawrence first started smoking crack.

For the next few years, he tried to get it together. He moved back in with my Grandma Soul and started helping her with her estate sales business. Along the line he reconnected with his high school girlfriend and they got married. Everything was starting to get better. If you want to know my opinion I think Lawrence got "triggered" after having his second child, but he's not ready for that conversation. The *real* problem was that he was still using and abusing. He says he "didn't see it as that big of a deal." Anyway, he met my Mom and "finally settled down." Or, at least that's how *he* tells the story.

Lawrence may have daughters, but he thinks he can protect us from all mankind *and* train us to be his boys at the same time. Unfortunately for Elle and me, that's just not how it works. We stayed at the basketball court shooting hoops and playing chase with Jasper for an hour or so. Lawrence kept checking his watch the whole time, and eventually he instructed that it was time to leave.

Once in the car, Elle made the mistake of asking where we were going, "that's for me to know, Ellesha, you don't need to worry about that." Lawrence predictably said in response.

Soon he had transitioned into talking about Vivian, "your mother is the love of my life, girls. She's absolutely the love of my life. I'd take her back today in a heartbeat if that's what she wanted." I rolled my eyes, but Elle perked up and hung on to Lawrence's every word, "I really would. What would you girls think about that?"

Elle became so excited she peed - spiritually, not physically. Elle was animated and encouraged the idea, "yes, Daddy! I want you to get back together with Mommy!"

"You should tell her that's what you want, E. What about you, Olivia?" Lawrence looked for me to meet his eyes in the rearview mirror, but I was purposefully avoiding him. I didn't want to share my opinion - which is that the idea of Lawrence and Vivian getting back together reminds me of the idea of trying the cinnamon challenge: fucking horrible.

"Elle, are you going to tell your Mother you want her to give your Daddy another shot?"

"Yes," Elle enabled.

"Good, that's my little girl! Go on and put in a good word for your Dad. Your Daddy just wants us to be a family again."

"I'm gonna tell her, Dad! I'm gonna tell her you still love her and that you want to be a family forever."

I just rolled my eyes, and looked out the car window watching the trees pass us by while listening to the hope in Lawrence's voice diminish. "Good, Elle. That's good." His anguish was cracking through.

"Mmhm," Elle said innocently. She was looking down, combing through her doll's hair with her fingers, while silently plotting the reunion of our parents. I think Lawrence knew Elle was already begging Vivian to take him back, and that it wasn't going to work. Nothing was going to bring Vivian back after the hell he'd put us all through, and he knew it. I watched this reality continue to sink in for Lawrence. The denial being written all over his face told me he was about to get defensive and turn on Vivian again.

"You girls know she's done drugs with me too, right?"

Elle and I both looked up at Lawrence, and then to each other. We had no words, and in the silence Lawrence took it upon himself to take up more space.

"Yeah, well she did. Your mother was there one of the first times I ever did cocaine, and *she did it too*! Oh yeah, she used to be the one encouraging *me* to get high. Back before you girls were born your mother used to do all the same partying that I did. She used to stay out at the club with me. She used to like getting high and drinking with me all night. The only difference is that she had you girls and wanted to stop, but I wanted to keep going. You see? That ain't nothing different, she's just the same as I am. That's why we got together in the first place, you see?"

Elle and I both just sorta stared at him. I guess we didn't know what to say. The idea Vivian would ever do drugs seemed so insanely out of this world I could barely even stand the accusation. But I was quickly distracted from his insult by his next assertion. At this point, he was just pushing.

"And I know she's already fucking somebody else."

I don't even remember what happened next. I think Elle and I both just sorta started zoning out at that point. Eventually, Lawrence allowed the radio to fill the space, and before I knew it, we had pulled up in the rec center parking lot.

There are only a few activities Lawrence brings Elle and I along for. My least favorite is going to NA meetings. The meetings are like Alcoholics Anonymous, but more customized for drug users. I've been a handful of times now, and each meeting has been just as boring as the last. Lawrence usually leaves Jasper, Elle and me in the car, twiddling our thumbs for a few hours while we wait for him to come out of the rec center. Other times, Lawrence wants Elle and me to "learn something," so he makes us join him inside.

The people in Lawrence's NA meeting say the most fucked up things I've ever heard. Things like, "I knew it was wrong, but I sold this guy my wedding ring so I could score another bag of dope and get high." Things like, "I was so strung out that I went to work and beat the shit out of my best friend. He almost died." Things like, "I fell asleep at the wheel with my five year old daughter in the back seat and she *was* killed. I wish I could just take it back."

Yeah? Well, you can't, asshole.

That's honestly the type of thing I want to scream back to half of these people when I hear them- but I don't. I know it would be totally disruptive to their recovery processes. I'd be displacing my emotion, as you people always tell me anyway. Plus, I wouldn't ever want to be the reason someone relapsed. I mean, the 12-Step Program seems to be the program that got Lawrence sober, right? So, I know it's helpful for *them* to have this space, the addicts; but, it's not at all helpful to *me* to be in that space.

When I hear these stories, I can't help thinking sarcastically. Something about the whole conversation makes me feel defensive. Like: *aw, you poor addict. I'm so sorry you ruined the lives of everyone nearby who loves you. Sounds rough. For you, personally. Please take your time. Pour on and on about it for us. Please!*

Geez. Instead of venting to other addicts, why don't they ask the actual people who they fucked over for forgiveness? I know that's one of the steps. I'm fifteen years old and I'm still waiting on my apology from Lawrence. Plus, it's not even like he's living up to the principles! You're supposed to humble yourself, let go of trying to control everything, and take moral inventory of yourself. I haven't seen Lawrence doing any of that; and, the damn tenants are written all over the walls, so I don't know how he's still missing it. I've even memorized the rules! Maybe I just don't understand because I'm not an addict like Lawrence. But, from this vantage point, I'd change the whole freakin' system if I could. Honestly, I'd change just about everything if I could.

Lawrence has a specific drug counselor he's supposed to check in with before his NA meetings. The drug counselor is this geeky, four-eyed, totally straight-edge looking white guy with strawberry blonde hair with freckles who sits behind a desk and wears one of those preacher collars. The dude looks super serious and square, but both his arms are tattooed all the way up. Lawrence tells him about the last time he did drugs; his "triggers," meaning Vivian, Elle, and me; and, the consequences of having used drugs in the first place. But, according to Lawrence, that's none of my business. My job is to just sit there. It's not my job to listen or form opinions about his life anyway - not like it affects me or anything.

The only thing Elle and I enjoy about these damn meetings is the candy. In the large group meetings Lawrence will grab handfuls of candy and then share some with us in the car after he leaves. I don't really eat the candy because I don't trust that it's not laced with drugs or something, but Elle does. I just give my candy to her so she at least gets double the goods. I'll only eat the candy when we get it from Lawrence's drug counselor directly - he's the only semi-trustworthy one of the entire bunch *and* he gives out Dum-Dum suckers.

After Lawrence's NA meeting, he took us to Ivers for lunch. I liked the time we spent together at Ivers because Lawrence was finally at ease. He tolerated ten knock-knock jokes from Elle, fed Jasper some of his fish and chips under the table, and he even asked me about how I've been doing in school. I may hate the NA meetings, but it seems like they're pretty helpful to Lawrence, so I guess I'll just keep tolerating them and support his recovery process. Hanging out together directly after his meetings is guaranteed fun.

I guess my only real beef with going to the meetings is that I don't like lying to Vivian about how we spent the afternoon. I don't know... I just think, good, bad, or ugly, he's still Lawrence. You know? Out of everything that's gone down, he's still my Dad. Plus, even if I had to sit through another NA meeting, I still got to hang out with Jasper again. That alone made the visit to see Lawrence worthwhile.

| 23 |

Chapter Twenty-Three

January 24th, 2008

Did I ever tell you Elle and I decided to gift our entire bedroom to our toys? When Vivian, Elle, and I moved into our new apartment, sans Lawrence, we deemed it the "apartment of female independence." Community developers that we are, Elle and I saw the empty master's bedroom and were so inspired with ideas for Barbie Bratz storylines and interior design, we gifted the entire master's bedroom to our creativity. Now, whenever we go to Lawrence's house Elle has a little meltdown before we leave. She finds it extremely difficult to part ways with the alternate utopia Barbie Bratz world we've created at Vivian's. So, she fills her suitcase with as many toys as possible. I usually make fun of Elle for being such a baby when she's packing, but on Saturday it actually came in handy.

On Saturday, Elle and I spent the day at Lawrence's. Elle had been bugging Vivian, Lawrence, and pretty much anybody else who would listen about going to the hot tub since she first saw it at his complex. So, Lawrence finally told Vivian he would let us visit this past weekend, since it was so nice outside. It was the first time we met his new girlfriend named Emilia. Even Vivian exchanged a few pleasantries with her in the parking lot. But, once we walked upstairs and

Lawrence got us acquainted with Emilia, he left without any indication as to when, or if, he'd return.

"I'll be back," was all he said right before softly slamming the door behind him. A few minutes later we heard "skrrttt" cry out from the parking lot, and we knew he was officially gone.

Emilia, Elle, and I were all just sort of stuck uncomfortably waiting for Lawrence's return. For the first half hour, the apartment was a stalemate. Nobody spoke or barely even moved. Emilia, Elle, and I were all sort of sitting there just staring at each other. We all sort of spaced out while sitting together in silence and wondering what to do next, and for how long. We had no idea. For the first time, Lawrence's notoriously loud home felt deathly quiet.

Eventually Elle unzipped her wheelie backpack, and started pulling out her dolls. She set each one in the middle of the living room floor in an almost-perfect lineup.

"What are their names?" Emilia asked, pointing to Elle's dolls. Emilia looks like a short haired Natalie Portman. She's petite, and bubbly, and upbeat from what I can tell so far. I don't know what color Emilia is yet, but I noticed she likes to wear pastels.

"This one is named 'Loreli,' and this one is named 'Rory.'" Elle said, "they're best friends," continuing to introduce them. She had named her dolls after characters from one of my favorite cable TV shows.

Elle's alternate hybrid doll-drama world filled Lawrence's void, and mended our collective saltiness over having let down expectations. Soon, the alternate world even presented a super serious issue for us to dissociate into: Elle had forgotten to pack a wardrobe for her dolls.

Then, Emilia stepped up to save the day. She continued to engage Elle, "tell me more about them. How old are they? Who are their boyfriends?"

Elle hesitantly smiled up at Emilia, took a deep breath, and then started explaining the basic plot of *Gilmore Girls* up until Rory and Dean broke up for the second time. She only veered off path a little bit. Elle likes to add her own twists to stories. "They're going to prom to decide who Rory should *really love*. It's going to be Jess," Elle said.

"Oh, yeah! That makes sense. Do they have their outfits for prom picked out already?" Emilia asked.

Elle looked down to the carpet and shook her head "yeah." Elle had been begging Vivian to either buy her new dolls so she could use their outfits, or make her some custom outfits for her dolls so they could go to prom. But, Vivian was too busy holding down the fort, and it's not like there's been a stash of extra cash waiting around for doll proms, so neither happened. The consequence was Elle didn't have any dresses.

"Are the outfits here?" Emilia asked.

"No," Elle ashamedly responded, "I forgot."

Emilia immediately hopped up from the couch and ran into the kitchen. Elle and I looked at each other curiously before turning our attention towards Emilia to see what she was doing. As we waited for her to reappear, we telepathically questioned the sounds of her rummaging through the cabinets. Soon we heard Emilia scream, "ah ha, here we go!"

Our eyes widened when Emilia came flying in from the kitchen waving aluminum foil. She was waving it above her head as if it were an Oscar award, clearly celebrating. Elle and I nodded in agreement towards Emilia, in an effort to instill her with confidence, even though we actually had no idea what we were agreeing to. Emilia sat down on the floor in the living room next to Elle.

"Here, hand Rory to me, please." Emilia said while curling her fingers towards herself in an attempt to entice Elle, who took the bait and handed her doll to Emilia. Emilia stretched out yards upon yards of aluminum foil, and then started fervorously wrapping the dolls up like it was Christmas. Elle and I were concerned, and communicated that message to one another in our secret language, pig latin.

"What theme is this prom dance, girls?" Emilia asked while only making the effort to make eye contact with Elle, who just looked up to me and we continued to shrug to ourselves curiously. "I gotchu. A basic prom. Just gimme a second," Emilia confirmed.

Elle and I played Roe Sham Bow while Emilia wrapped Elle's dolls. Elle won, per usual, and she was starting to get overly confident - extending her laugh into a villainous cackle and shoving her head backwards. Emilia interrupted us when she shouted, "look," overtly proud that she had successfully plastered custom aluminum foil outfits to both Rory *and* Loreli. Rory was dressed in a tight-fitting flared pant suit, and Loreli was in a multi-layered midi dress. Each doll was also wearing custom shoes. Before we knew it, the Gilmore Girls were shining bright like diamonds.

Just when we thought Emilia had finished, she opened her palm up and said, "here, now hand me the guys." Halfway through Emilia making custom outfits for the guy dolls, Lawrence rushed into the apartment.

"Come on girls, grab your stuff. Let's go," Lawrence ordered while walking across the living room into his and Emilia's bedroom. He was acting like we were all already in the middle of a conversation with him - not like he had just busted in out of nowhere. This time he was only in the bedroom for a few seconds, and then he flew through the apartment saying, "I'll be downstairs waiting for you girls. If you want to get in that hot tub, let's go!"

Lawrence was short and snappish with everybody. Plus, he was unnecessarily loud - which made all of us jumpy, including Jasper. We packed the dolls away quickly, but carefully, grabbed our pre-packed pool bags still waiting by the front door, and headed down the pebbled stairs to meet him.

The hot tub was perfect. Steam was coming off the water as we walked up, so you just knew it was going to feel fantastic. The anticipation built while we waited for Emilia to blow up Elle's floaties, and Lawrence picked out the right music. I just played with Jasper and tried to help Elle contain her excitement as we waited.

Finally, Lawrence settled on Mary J. Blige's *My Life* album. We descended into the steamy pool, and we let our unapologetically Black nappy hair dunk under the water. Elle kept tilting her head back so her hair would stick to her shoulders and we could tell how long it "really" was.

Lawrence wouldn't get in the water, which was lame. I knew Elle was looking forward to climbing all over him like a jungle gym. I used to do that as a kid too, but whatever. He just sat at a nearby table and sang along to the music. Emilia splashed around with Elle and me while Jasper laid out on the concrete next to us. The sky was so bright that I could feel the sun resting only a few thin layers behind the grey clouds. When my favorite song from the album "All Night Long" played, I asked Lawrence to repeat it a few times and he actually did. He bopped along to the beat like it was nothing.

I should've known that was a bad sign. Lawrence suddenly stood up from the table and started towards the exit. Emilia looked at him, questioning his movement. After he said he was "going to play some basketball," she levitated out of the hot tub and protested. Elle and I stayed in the water, only a tiny bit in the distance, and waited for them to finish arguing. It was as if we didn't exist. I heard Lawrence say something like, "alla you look like fucking prositutes with your little bikinis all out. I don't want to be around all that," and, sure enough, he stormed off.

Emilia turned back towards Elle and me with a fake smile, and said, "whatever, let's just keep having our own fun."

Elle was resentfully wearing her floaties while Emilia and I haphazardly relied on either side of an inflatable donut hole. Of course, Jasper just lay around without a worry in the world now that Lawrence was gone. Lawrence had wrapped his bluetooth speaker in Emilia's pool bag using two plastic freezer baggies. So, I think at some point he was planning to actually take us to the hot tub himself, but I don't know. After he left, I tried not to miss him or worry about where he went.

Emilia grabbed the speaker off the nearby table, stuffed it in the cupholder of her donut floatie, and changed the album. We radiated in the chilly sun and floated around for the afternoon, rebelliously enjoying our day while the new *The Writing's On The Wall* album played in the background.

| 24 |

Chapter Twenty-Four

January 31st, 2008

On Monday, Laurie asked me about Vivian and Lawrence. Laurie and I were going through some of my baby photos, and she got curious. She wanted to know more about the days when we all lived together, and asked a bunch of random questions.

"Wow," Laurie pointed out, "your Dad is extremely good looking, Olivia!"

I rolled my eyes and said, "yeah, so I've heard."

"No," Laurie grabbed my hand looking serious, "I mean it. Like, he's *extremely* good looking. Like, that's baby daddy goals right there." She started flipping through pages and pointing out his face, "do you see this?" I'd nod, and then Laurie would continue fangirling, "is this even real life? I can't." She feigned a faint.

My friends stay drooling over Lawrence. Any time I show my friends pictures they go crazy. When Charlotte met him she was blushing the whole time. But, Lawrence knew how to handle it - that wasn't his first time being fanned over. He started calling Charlotte "Wonder Bread" as a way to poke fun at her Whiteness. It was all out of love, I swear. We were even laughing and stuff. It was fun.

But, for real though, memories of Lawrence smooth-talking random people are integral to my consciousness. Back when I was a kid in the '90s, Michael Jordan was a big deal, and people mistook Lawrence for him all the time. It didn't matter if we were at the movies, a carnival, or a stadium, Lawrence was getting us free tickets. People of all ages and styles just love him, and they want him to love them right back.

"Even your mom is hot, Olivia," Laurie celebrated while looking at our family pictures, "they're *such* a good-looking couple!"

"Yup," I didn't have much to say for obvious reasons.

"So, do you ever wish they would get back together? Should we try to *Parent Trap* them?" Laurie asked.

It's a question everyone asks, especially people like you. Do I wish my parents would get back together? Well, nine hundred and ninety-nine times out of one thousand, I'd say, "hell no." But, if I'm being honest, there's at least one time *out of a thousand* that I *might* say "yes." Mostly when I'm looking through old photos - the only factual evidence that good times actually existed throughout the years.

Like this one series I saw when I was looking at the photos with Laurie. It was a series of photos from the day Jasper came into my life. We were at Carkeek Park in Seattle with Lawrence's side of the family. Grandma Soul was there, running between the different cohorts of cousins making sure everybody had what they needed. Some of my cousins were playing double dutch, and the others were prepping the food on the grill. My Uncle Marlon and Auntie Bette were there too. Uncle Marlon was with some of the other guys, and a few of his bouncer friends, playing with a frisbee.

Auntie Bette was with Mom and baby Elle in the shade. All the elders were with the new moms and their babies on the grass under the big weeping tree. They switched off watching each other's kids and rubbing grease into each other's scalps. They cooed at the babies and braided while catching up on whatever had been going down in the other's lives and homes. Lawrence's absence was the fat elephant at the park nobody wanted to acknowledge. Trying to stick up for Lawrence, per usual, my Aunt Norma kept trying to steer the conversation away from anything Lawrence related, and it was starting to become painful to hear. We were all simultaneously hoping he would hurry up and get here.

Then, just like magic, Lawrence showed up. He sported khaki pants and his famous salmon pink polo that made him look like an everyday family guy. Lawrence's hair was parted to the right side, like Eddie Murphy, and you could tell someone had just cleaned up his lines. He smelled good, subtle, and was wearing a bright white smile across his face.

Plus, he was holding baby Jasper!

At the time, Jasper was just a puppy. He was only like four or five months old, so he had some substance, but it was also still obvious he was just a pup. Lawrence had Jasper wrapped in his right arm, and attempted to wave at us with his left, even though Jasper was attacking Lawrence with kisses.

"What does he have there, Vivian? Is that a *dog*?" Grandma Soul asked judgmentally. She pronounced "dog" like "dawg," and pointed in Lawrence's direction.

Vivian looked over and froze with her mouth open.

"Quick, someone give a titty to Vivian! She's ready, y'all!" My Aunt Norma joked to break the tension. Everybody laughed and waited in anticipation for Vivian's response. But, Lawrence made it to our grass patch before she had to figure out something to say.

"Look, Vivian, I bought us a dog!"

"I see," Vivian finally responded, poorly faking excitement.

"Yeah! He's going to be Elle's best friend. They'll get to grow up with each other, Viv."

Lawrence acted like he couldn't see that he was adding an additional responsibility to her already-full plate, even though he'd had dogs all his life. "It'll be great. She needs a best friend to grow up with, Viv," Lawrence erroneously reassured.

"Yeah," Vivian said without enthusiasm. Everybody knew Lawrence had already made the decision. He was keeping Jasper and that was it. Besides, Jasper was love at first sight for all of us. An immediate part of our family.

Jasper and Elle connected immediately. He jumped on her, and she let him lick all over her face - their new normal. My Aunt Osie got nervous and screamed, "grab the baby, Vivian. Protect her." She got up and shooed Jasper back to Lawrence.

"Wow, look at his eyes, " Grandma Soul interrupted. "I don't know what you're going to do with this dog, Son. But, he does have some gorgeous jasper eyes."

"Yes, Ma'am," Lawrence responded after he finished kissing her on the cheek.

"So, what's his name?" my Aunt Norma asked.

"Well, to be honest, I haven't picked one yet. I was just at my buddy Tinky's house and he was selling the puppies for five hundred dollars a pop. I wasn't even looking for a dog," Lawrence said, playing up his innocence. "We had a little connection goin', so Tink said I could take him for free! He's so cute, I just couldn't turn away. Look at him, Viv!"

"I know," Vivian said, "he's really cute, Lawrence. But-"

Lawrence interrupted Vivian to ask for Grandma Soul's approval, "Mama, what do you think about the name 'Jasper?'"

"That's nice," Grandma Soul said indifferently before getting up to check the food on the grill, "I'm just gon' be right back. That's a nice dog, Lorenzo," Grandma Soul grabbed Lawrence, hugged him, and then said out loud in his ear, "but you ought to have checked with your lady before doing something like that." Grandma Soul patted Lawrence on the back, then wobbled over to the barbeque.

It only took a few minutes of Elle and Jasper playing together before Vivian was also in love with him. We all spent the rest of the day together, laughing, rolling around in the grass, and chasing each other around the park picnic benches. Lawrence didn't lose his cool and Vivian didn't cry. It was blissful.

Jasper spent the afternoon following Elle around. They even took naps together at the same time; and, damn near in the same belly up, feet kicked out, careless position.

But, there were only a few more months of blissful moments after that day. I can only remember the good times when I see them happening. And, when I see them, I secretly still wish my parents would get back together.

7

YEE

| 25 |

Chapter Twenty-Five

February 7th, 2008

Nikky won't stop complaining about her body. Ever since she started dating that junior guy, she's been nit picking every detail about herself. This week, she found out her good-for-nothing-but-his-Chandler-Bing-hair boyfriend cheated on her again. They've been dating like .2 seconds, and he's already being a douchebag. All week Nikky's been spiraling. All she does is talk about her imperfect body, whether we're at school, in the girls bathroom, or hanging out at her house. She's acting like she's not perfectly aware that practically every guy on the planet wants to date her. Nikky is like a Fillipina version of Kate Hudson in *How to Lose A Guy in Ten Days*, she could barf all over a guy and he'd just say, "do it again."

"I think my thighs are getting completely out of control. Why didn't you warn me, Olivia?! You're supposed to be my main bitch!" Nikky "jokingly" yelled at me yesterday.

I was sitting on Nikky's bed sorting her CD collection from her bootleg DVD collection. I was trying to distract myself from Nikky self-harming. She was ransacking through her closet and talking about how unpretty she looked and how heavily she weighed.

"Also, I don't know if my period is about to come or something, but, in general, I just *feel* wider, you know? Like I can *tell* I'm taking up more space lately."

Nikky was *so* right, but *so* wrong. Sometimes being Nikky's friend means you'll be suffocated by a lack of space frequently, but it's never ever because she's "wider." It's because Nikky's narcissism can be totally and utterly exhausting. She can be the most down to earth person, and then, take up all the space in the room, unapologetically. Sometimes I admire it, but most times I'm just triggered. I can't stop being Nikky's friend, though. Being her friend makes me better appreciate Vivian, and I really need that in my life right now. Take yesterday, for example. While Nikky complained about her body and her wardrobe instead of her scumbag boyfriend, I mentally channeled Vivian in my head.

Vivian always says, "nooo, no, no, no, no! Don't complain about your body right now! Your body right now is fantastic! Your body right now is spectacular! Your body right now is beautiful ba-bay, and don't you forget it! This is the time where you're really reaching your prime. You can do anything!"

She becomes even more impassioned.

"This period of life you're in right now is the most precious time in a woman's entire life. It's such a short, short, seemingly microscopic, time - this window of unabashed flourishment. You have to seize it, Olivia! Don't you waste a single second of this time in your life talking down to yourself and diminishing your light. Don't fall into that trend when you get bored with your friends and have nothing or nobody better to talk about but yourselves. No! Not my daughter. You are the sun. You shine bright!"

I'll nod my head in agreement the entire way through the lecture. If I'm feeling real manic, I'll even raise my hand to Her, as if she is the Lord sending me a Word. It's a signal to let Her know I have received the message in my soul. But, it's not enough. Eleven out of ten times Vivian continues on with her lecture until it's complete.

"If you don't like your body at this age, then you're probably never really going to like your body, Olivia. And, guess what, YOU ONLY GET ONE BODY, BABY!!!" She cackles to herself as if it's a new discovery. It's in these speeches that I understand Vivian and Lawrence's once *not* Avril Lavigne "Complicated" compatibility.

"You've got to love yourself, Olivia. That includes your whole physical body too, baby. I expect you to live a long life full of love and happiness, and that shit just isn't going to happen if you're over here thinking it's cute to start giving yourself a dysmorphic complex, ok? Your body is the one thing in this world that is always going to be yours - no matter who might try to steal it from you. You gotta own it, and nobody else. Not your friends, not your feelings of inadequacy, not the media, not your father or any boyfriend - *you*. Teach yourself to love your body now and you will be further ahead than all of your friends in twenty years, I promise. Not only is that shit toxic, but it's also distracting and time-consuming. So, stop it! You have a ton of other things you need to be thinking about."

There's a sense of fear mixed with anger because as Vivian repeats this speech, she begins remembering that she can't *actually* control my mind or the way my brain dysfunctions. Vivian pulls out her work briefcase and hecticly shuffles through her papers.

"Do I need to give you an assignment to keep your brain moving? Is that what you're trying to tell me? Here. Come here. Try this," eventually she'll find a blank business visualization exercise or ten-year financial planning document and shove it between my fingers.

"Here you go. Go ahead and see if you can fill that out. There's a good exercise for you to think about if you want to think so much, little missy. How do you like that? Let me know when you have questions and we'll walk through it together."

Then, Vivian trails off murmuring to herself still processing whatever comment I made to her that revealed I was feeling 1/4th ounce self-conscious, "talking about how you don't think you're cute.

You know you're cute! Don't worry if you're too this, or not enough that, Olivia. Don't waste time worrying about shallow stuff like that."

To be honest, I don't know if it's the automatic fear of not wanting to plan out the next ten years of my life or if it's the "you shine bright" part of the lecture that actually gets to me. All I know is that it works. Especially when I hear Nikky, or any of my girl friends, going on and on and on talking about themselves. I try to give them the Vivian speech - sometimes it works, sometimes it doesn't. Other times I don't have the energy, like this week with Nikky.

"I'll give you your flowers because you deserve them, Nikky," I told her for the Nth time yesterday, "but it's on you to water them or not."

| 26 |

Chapter Twenty-Six

February 14th, 2008

Have I mentioned that John has been giving me rides to school a lot lately? He noticed I was wearing this Kingdom Hearts shirt a couple weeks ago and complimented it. Then, we started talking more and more in class which totally pissed Ms. Walker off. So, we exchanged numbers and he offered to start driving me to and from school, "so I don't have to take the smelly bus any more." We've also been texting a lot at night, and he's always checking in on me throughout the day. He's been continually flirting with me, but he's only just stopped dating this older girl named Susie. It's hella weird. This week he told me he was "sick of her," and then last night he called me asking if I had a boyfriend. I don't wanna sound cocky, but, come on!

This morning John showed up with flowers. On the ride to school he kept asking about my plans for Valentines - especially after I told him I was busy. It was cute. John was acting all jealous, asking me if I was going to be hanging out with Steve or Justin for the special day. I had to keep telling John that I was "busy, but not because I'm hanging out with either of them."

"Oh, no?" John questioned in return, "you're not even going to go see Miles?"

"No!" I sang, naturally exuding my charming self. John laughed in response. For the rest of the ride to school we listened to the *Stadium Arcadium* album pretty much in silence. But, every now and again John would look over at me from the corner of his eye and raise his eyebrow, pretending to be mischievous.

I really like John. He's way more mature than Steve or Justin ever was. He's quiet, and calm, and he doesn't really do much. To some people that may sound boring. But, at least John isn't always getting my hopes up like Steve or Justin did. He's easy. Predictable.

At lunch he kissed me so everyone could see. We were all sitting on the stone steps in the courtyard like we always do - all sort of doing our own things. Mark and Steve were standing off to the corner goofing around talking shit to each other. Miles was sitting down next to Laurie writing something, probably a poem or some lyrics, in his notebook. The rest of us, Justin, Charlotte, Nikky, and me, were standing around talking and taking bites off each other's food. I heard someone coming up the steps from behind, but barely thought anything of it.

I knew it was John when I felt his hands wrap around my waist. Seconds later his chin rested upon my shoulder and chest pressed up against my back - like it was just normal. Nikky and Charlotte's eyes got big and they closed in together snickering and whispering, "oh my gosh," like two toddlers. Laurie, Miles, and Justin minded their business, while Steve acted like he didn't notice and Mark continued to crack jokes. I spun around in John's arms as his hands remained clasped around me. I hugged him like adults do, with my hands cupping his neck and shoulders, as we kissed in front of everybody.

It felt like it was supposed to happen.

Even before today, I noticed my relationship dynamics have been shifting. I miss my friends. I obviously still see them, of course. I was just with Nikky last week. But, things have been different since I started hanging out with John. Not everything, but small things. Like, I'm starting to miss out on some of their inside jokes and horror stories. Laurie has to "catch me up" during first period, so Nikky doesn't chastise me or distance me from the group. It's sort of crazy how different things are now. It's nothing like what we all planned.

I'm also starting to feel like I don't know what's going on with anybody any more. Like, I don't remember the last time Miles talked to me about his mom. Or, Steve about his dad - the few times he actually opened up. I have no idea how home life for Charlotte and Mark is right now, or if Nikky's parents are still together or not. I literally haven't been to Laurie's for a safe, happy, loving, home cooked meal since 2007. I'm sure her parents miss having me over.

Plus, on the romantic front, I miss Steve and Justin. I miss taking things slow. I miss really getting to know the other person, and building a strong friendship. I miss daydreaming of all the different ways our first kiss will happen. I miss the other person having the same sense of humor as me and laughing at each others' funny jokes. I even miss wondering if they would call me at the end of the day. Now I know that neither of them is calling, and if I don't call John by 9 o'clock he'll start blowing up my phone.

A lot of the guessing has gone out the window, even though I feel like I still barely know him. Sure, the mystery is sexy. But, at the end of the day, I miss the comfort my friends brought to my life. It's sort of crazy how different things are now. It's funny how nothing turns out the way you predict it to. I guess growing apart really *is* part of growing up, huh? And starting relationships with near total strangers is part of it too. I mean, not that John and I are in a "relationship" yet or anything like that. But, like, yaddamean?

| **27** |

Chapter Twenty-Seven

February 21st, 2008

Vivian's birthday was on Valentine's Day. The Valentine's Day tradition in my family is to focus all of our love and attention towards Vivian. Grandma Soul used to say: "love is the opposite of capitalism and we sure ain't celebrating that." So, the Grove family never celebrated Valentine's Day. Then Vivian was introduced. My Grandma Soul quickly went back on her word, per usual, and started throwing Vivian yearly birthday parties on V-day.

To be honest, I was a little worried about what the family was going to do this year. But, turns out the plans were the exact same. My parents were together for like five or six years before they even had me. So, I guess that's why Vivian's relationships with my Grandma Soul and my Aunties have lasted with or without Lawrence.

Anyway, Grandma Soul and Uncle Marlon are the only two in the family who live in actual houses, so we usually have parties at one of their places. This year we had the party at my Uncle Marlon and Auntie Bette's house. Everybody was there - even Lawrence and his girlfriend, Emilia. It actually helped that so many people showed because it forced my parents to just go ahead and get along. Except for the part when I heard Auntie Bette and Vivian whispering about Emilia.

"She's so young! She's practically the girls' age," Vivian tossed in.

"I mean, she definitely looks like she's barely twenty," Auntie Bette returned.

I think Vivian was just being jealous. Emilia is really nice. She's like an older sister instead of a parent, and I'm cool with it. I don't need another parent at this stage of my life.

Vivian's party was poppin'! It was one of those Seattle days where the skies are still, and the sun is out, but there are stubborn grey clouds that keep trying to interrupt the moment. You know it won't rain, but you're not out sunbathing either, and the touch of warm wind breezing through the air is just right. We had a bunch of BBQ going on the grill, per usual, and we played hella rounds of Backgammon. The adults talked a ton of shit to each other while the kids responded with better game strategy. Older cousins, who already knew better than to play with the adults, jumped on the triple XL trampoline in the backyard. The babies who couldn't play at all, like Elle and the other younger cousins, exercised their imaginations by pretending to be *The Lion King* in the front yard. A mix of the Whispers, Joe, Eryka Badu, the Temptations and the Supremes, and Anita Baker extended from inside the living room to clear beyond the property lines.

I don't really have much to say about it beyond "I gotta say it was a good day." We just straight up enjoyed each other's company. There was no drama, and nobody went off on one another. The food came out pretty fucking perfectly - thank you to my Grandma Soul; and, Vivian was smiling almost all day long. I guess the only semi-weird thing was that Lawrence announced he volunteered to be the assistant basketball coach at my school. He did seem perfectly fine, if not totally sober, the entire party, so I bet it'll all turn out alright if he starts coaching.

The party progressed nicely. Some of my grand aunties put aside their rummy cards and came together long enough during the party to bake an assortment of cakes for Vivian. My Aunt Norma, with a scalp-length side-parted wig and hazel freckles across her cheeks, baked Vivian a lemon poppy bundt cake from scratch. My Aunt Ossie, with the curled high top ("non-wig") and similar freckles to my Auntie Norma, baked Vivian a square chocolate cake with a white glaze frosting - also from scratch. Then, my Aunt Margaret, who just straight up doesn't have any more time for wigs and rocks her natural curls, baked Vivian a box of yellow cake with chocolate frosting that my Grandma Soul helped to make. Grandma Soul, the middle sister like me, has shaved and bleached hair like Sisqo. She made Vivian her famous "Black Princess Cake," which is really just a normal princess cake but with a black marzipan top. We sang Stevie Wonder's "Happy Birthday" to Vivian a billion times, and everybody's heart walked away full. Elle was so full she even fell asleep in the car.

I know there's still a lot more to be worked out with my parents, and, yeah sure, with my school work too. But, for now, it was really nice to just have a normal ass week without any dramatic situation going down. It was nice to not feel the stress of an emergency, and to not need to reach out for help. You know what I mean? I didn't have to worry about Vivian or Lawrence, because I knew the elders were holding everybody down. I finally felt like I could just breathe, let loose, be vulnerable, and actually be a kid. Or, I mean a teenager.

It was fucking great!

| 28 |

Chapter Twenty-Eight

One of the best results of Vivian leaving Lawrence is that I've been able to engage with having a more lively social life. Remember how I've been missing my friends? Well, I talked to John about it, and he's been inviting my girls out with us.

Well, Laurie is actually doing a ton of Pre-SAT work with a private tutor. So, her parents have her on "lockdown," as Laurie explains it, and she hasn't been hanging out with us. I'm not taking the pre-SAT because, at this point, I'm not even sure if I'm taking the big kid SAT or going to college. Plus, nobody besides Laurie is even talking about it. Planning for the future right now feels so irrelevant it's not even funny. But, Charlotte, Nikky, John, Peter, and I have become quite the little lunch bunch lately! So, that's something!

I don't know. I haven't really been sticking to my goals this year - as can be expected given my circumstances, right? School sucks, obviously beyond Ms. Walker's class, and lately I haven't been seeing my future in sight. It's almost like there's no light at the end of the endless tunnel. I'm trying to keep it together even though I feel completely crazy. But, I guess that's why I'm here, right?

Anyway, I hacked Vivian's email over the weekend. She was acting fucked up all weekend, and it was weird - especially since her birthday was damn near perfect. So, I read her email inbox. Hidden in page three of her infiltrated inbox was an email stream from Ms. Walker. Ms. Walker wrote Vivian and told her I was seeing John - or something of the sort. She told Vivian that I've been distracted in class, slipping in my school work, and talking to John a lot lately. Ms. Walker even told Vivian that I was "becoming a distraction to others" due to my "blatant refusal to acknowledge the rules."

It's bogus. Hella annoying.

Either way, Vivian's been cleaning the apartment a lot lately. She sat me down recently and asked me to "slow down." Whatever that means. I felt sorta "defensive" as you might say, but I guess I haven't really cared about my school work at all lately. So, *that* part is fair. The thing I'm really mad about is Vivian talking to Lawrence about the whole ordeal. It feels like she'll do anything to give him a wide-open ass window of opportunity to show up as a parent. Vivian says she's "tired, and exhausted, and running out of options," but I don't know what she is talking about. It's all just typical teenage behavior, right? I told her to stop scrubbing things and take a nap.

Then, Lawrence called me up last night and left me this bogus ass message. He started the voicemail as he usually does, helplessly from two states north, but with a distinct tone of everlasting authority, "Olivia, this is your father," he said on the recording.

"You know that."

Then, Lawrence told me that Vivian had filled him in on "what's been going on." He said he knew "all about" my academic down-fall, social spiral, and overall "phase of acting out typical to teenagers," as he called it. He was leaving me a message to get me back on track and coach me to the path of righteousness or whatever, but I wasn't really having it.

"Your mother's been telling me what's going on with you Olivia," Lawrence almost threatened, "and I hope you know you have a family to turn to in this crazy life. I'm glad to know you think you have friends who are there for you, Olivia, but I want you to remember this: nobody will ever understand you like your family does. Your Mother told me you've been acting out and your teacher's been emailing her for help to calm you down in her class, and you know that ain't right, Olivia. You know you're a leader," he continued repeating. I've heard the same lecture since I was a pup riding along with Jasper in Lawrence's window washing equipment van.

"They gon' follow you naturally. So, don't make everybody beg for you to show up. Eventually they gon' stop begging to see you. They'll just be looking for the next person to take your spot - and you can take that from me. Step up and set an example. Make it easier for people to like you, not more difficult. Learn to be comfortable with yourself, E, and know that you're a LEADER. You set the tone for yourself and your friend group, even on the days when you feel like life is one big "I Wish It Would Rain," Temptations song. Demand the respect you want to reap from the world, Babygirl. Remember that nothing would make your Daddy happier than for you to continue to grow and challenge yourself with all sorts of things and experiences."

Lawrence shifted from instructor to comrade, as he does, and ended the message upbeat. He said, "Take the stars from the crowns ahead of you. Allow your skin to shine in the moonlight that it craves. I am wishing more successes to you, Baby. I'm very proud of you. Keep striving for the best. You are the sun, the stars, and the sky, so swallow the moon and behave as you wish, my Dear. I love you."

| 29 |

Chapter Twenty-Nine

March 6th, 2008

Lawrence has been consistently participating in coaching my basketball team ever since Vivian's birthday BBQ. So, she allowed Elle and me to sleep over at his apartment on the weekend. Last weekend was our first sleepover, and this really funny thing happened.

First, Lawrence took us to his second girlfriend's house. Let's just call her "Lucy" for the sake of clarity, because I honestly don't remember her name. So, Lucy's house is sort of in this grassy, long dirt road, Santa Cruz-y type of area, and her house has a bunch of big tall windows all around it. I think some people find that sort of style super gourmet and fancy, but, to me it just felt like a giant fish bowl with meticulously planned blind spots.

Lawrence and his- "Lucy" disappeared into her back bedroom for a few hours. So, to kill the time, I played dolls with Elle on the living room floor. It was daytime, but you could feel the sun was starting to go down - especially since Lucy had decided to keep her blinds wide open. I'm not going to lie, the sun shining on the long green grass outside was actually really gorgeous, so I didn't mind having the blinds open. I took a casual glance over my right shoulder and out the front window amidst playing dolls with Elle.

To my surprise, I noticed two huge White dudes with long ass beards creeping up the dirt driveway. I knew Lawrence would've ran his mouth at Elle or me if we disturbed him in the back room without the house being already halfway engulfed in flames. So, I just left him alone and kept my eyes on the situation. The White dudes were dressed in these super nice looking black suits, and they came walking straight up to the house with such confidence I knew they were there on a super sketchy mission. I could just feel it. Plus, with them being pretty big White dudes in suits and all, you know… I just kinda thought they could be hitmen or maybe even the FBI or something!

I really just don't think either of those extreme options were *so* out-of-line, given Lawrence's history! But, whatever. So, I still didn't want to alert him or Elle, who hadn't noticed the men, right? So I told Elle, "Hey, let's pretend we're on a high-risk mission and we have to get some special potion from the kitchen, and then bring it back here to the couch without being seen by the outside world!"

It obviously wasn't the best excuse in the world, but it worked. Elle eagerly agreed to the terms of the game, dropped her dolls on the floor, and started slugging herself into the kitchen without even looking out the window. I went first and showed her how to do the army crawl where you only use the forearms on the ground to get you from point A to point B. I call it "slugging" because that's what your body starts looking like when you do the crawl for a long time.

Anyways, we slugged our way quickly into the kitchen and hid in the blockade created by the L-shaped counter space just in time. I turned back around to peek out towards the front door after Elle had made it into our safety base. The two strange men held their hands up to the windows and peered inside.

They started scouring "Lucy's" home looking for any indication of life - and there were plenty of them. Elle's dolls were left laid out on the living room carpet floor. The cable television was still powered on and playing *The Jungle Book*. Lawrence's jacket still tossed over the largest chair in the living room. Jasper started barking in the dudes' faces at the front door. Then, the White guys left without even knocking. I guess the big black pitbull must've scared them off, what do you say?

Then, much later, when it was already dark outside, Lawrence and "Lucy" emerged. After reading the tempo of the room for a while, which seemed pretty solidly upbeat, I decided to tell Lawrence what happened when Jasper had been barking. Lawrence was sitting with "Lucy" on her yellow knit couch and they were half watching a standup Richard Pryor skit, and half watching Elle and me play with her dolls on the floor.

"Hey, Dad, these two really intense looking guys came up here to the house peering in the windows when y'all were in the back room."

"WHAT?" Lawrence's eyes almost popped out of his eye sockets, per usual. He was immediately off the couch, pacing the living room, and on the prowl. He looked out the window towards the front door and said, "what did they look like, Olivia?"

"I don't know. They were White, had hella long beards, were wearing really nice suits, sorta big." I put my arms out to the side like bended wings and faked a flex to indicate to Lawrence that I was talking about the dudes' muscular shapes - not their tummies.

"Oh, no way." I could tell Lawrence had started to relax, but he was still trying to play it off as if he was hyped up. He walked over to the front door, "tell me more, Olivia. What happened next?"

"Well, I don't really know much more, Dad. I was sorta thinking you would know who they were since they were probably here for you." Elle and "Lucy" didn't move their bodies, but both of them turned their eyes brightly on me like headlights.

Lawrence opened the front door, looked around protectively, and picked something up from the floor. "They were here for me, huh?"

"I don't know. I think so," I shrugged.

"No, Olivia," Lawrence tossed a small pamphlet into my lap and continued, "they were here for *all* of us!" Lawrence sat back down on the couch and started laughing his deep barrel belly laugh. So, Elle, "Lucy," and I all started cautiously laughing too - even though I don't think any of us understood what was going on or why we were laughing. Finally I turned the pamphlet over and saw it was a Jehovah's Witness believer's guide.

The whole situation ended up being something that made all of us laugh. I was over here thinking these dudes were straight up drug dealers or FBI, but Lawrence didn't even get mad at me for assuming the worst. Of course the guys weren't actual drug dealers or hitmen! They were just devout Jahova's Witness believers trying to spread the word and convert folks. It's been refreshing for something as trivial as that little incident to be the scariest thing that has happened to me all week!

Plus, as a super bonus, Lawrence cooked all of us breakfast in the morning. Lawrence, Elle, and I all slept at his apartment between Vivian's and the school... you know, the place he has with his *real* girlfriend, Emilia? Well, Lawrence woke up early and started blasting Christian music through the apartment to wake us all up. It was Dr. Seuss' birthday, you know that guy who wrote those *Oh, the Places You'll Go* books? So, Lawrence wanted to celebrate by making us green scrambled eggs and blue bacon for breakfast.

Honestly, I think he just colored the food by adding in some food coloring; and, I'm not sure why he felt the need to smear blue food coloring on all the strips of bacon, but I appreciate the effort. To be real with you, I don't even think the book said anything about the ham being blue, but, again, I *so* appreciated Lawrence's effort! Elle had the time of her life, and refused to brush her teeth after breakfast or even after we got home back with Vivian. Instead, she preferred to run around with her dark blue tongue hanging out for the rest of the day. She was so proud she kept repeating the story of how her "Daddy" had made *her* green eggs and blue bacon for Dr. Seuss' birthday.

8

THE LINE OF FIRE

| 30 |

Chapter Thirty

March 13th, 2008

On Saturday, when Elle and I went to Lawrence's house, everything went smoothly. It was actually sort of fun! We played Rummy 5000, Speed, and Backgammon with Lawrence and Emilia pretty much all night. Lawrence even asked us to walk on his back for a massage like back in the day when we all used to live together.

Lawrence sprawled out horizontally across the living room floor laying on his belly. He widened his legs far enough that Elle and I could each walk up one leg at a time, but close enough for us to reach out and hold on each other's hands too. Once we got to Lawrence's butt, Elle went first. She walked up Lawrence's back, pausing to "squish the knots" on the sides of his neck, and then jumped off. I walked up Lawrence's spine second, I didn't pause to squish, and I didn't jump off. Instead, I controllably lowered myself to make sure I didn't hurt him.

While we were playing cards, Lawrence sat out for a few rounds to drink a few beers and eat his spicy Doritos and sour cream. He listened to us girls smack talk each other and kept hyping each of us up at different times - switching alliances like he did sidechicks. Emilia was sitting in between Lawrence's legs at his feet. Elle and I tried to warn her. We kept making a bunch of "line of fire" jokes, and even Lawrence would be doing his deep barrel belly laugh like, "HA HA HA!"

-- it sorta sounds like a hyena howling -- but Emilia didn't understand what was going on until Lawrence farted. It was one of those silent but deadly farts. All of a sudden Elle and I noticed Jasper get up from his sleeping position near Lawrence and go sit in the hallway away from all of us. We started cracking up and waited for it to hit Emilia - we knew we'd still have a few seconds to cover up before it hit us.

"OH MY GOD! WHAT THE HELL IS THAT SMELL?!" At first she looked scared, like maybe there was a dead animal, but then she turned to look at Lawrence and was hit full force. "UHH LAW-RENCE!" She started waving the air, like *that* was going to really help, and stood up. "GROSS, DUDE!!!!! THAT'S NOT NATURAL!" Emilia ran far away from the line of fire into the kitchen and started laughing. "Is that what you meant," she was trying to speak through choking on the remnant smells, "when you said 'line of fire'?!"

Lawrence, Elle, and me were all cracking up in the living room. Elle and I didn't even evacuate - we were both just so happy to be having the moment that we stayed as fully entrenched in it as we could. Jasper came back to the living room too, and you know how sensitive dogs' noses are! But, even he started trying to get in on all the action. He attacked us with licks and his violently wagging tail that Elle complained about. It was hilarious.

Lawrence had had a few beers and a couple mixed drinks throughout the night. I could tell he had smoked when he took Jasper out to potty too. But, he said he was still fine to drive Elle and me home since we live just a few blocks away. Emilia and Lawrence argued about it for a bit, but you know he's going to do what he wants to do 110% of the time. So, she just said, "fine, well I'm not getting in the car with you."

I should've expected Lawrence wasn't just going to drive us home. As soon as we hit the freeway I knew we were taking a detour. Lawrence rolled all our windows down and smoked a blunt while we drove up the highway. Usher's "U Make Me Wanna" blasted through the speakers over the sound of the passing wind. Then "Sweet Thing," by Mary J. Blige, then "Area Codes" by Ludacris and Nate Dogg, and so on and so forth. Just another mixtape on another night.

Eventually, Lawrence said, "come on up here, Elle. Unclick your belt and climb up here to the front."

Elle followed the directions given to her with a cocktail of hesitation, fear, and excitement. Neither of us 100% fully trusted Lawrence at that moment, but what other choice did we have besides to go along? Elle climbed up to the front seat and sat on my lap in the passenger seat also known as "shotgun." Then, I unbuckled my seat belt so I could stretch it out far enough to lock in Elle and me at the same time, but Lawrence interrupted me.

"Na, Olivia, she's coming over on this side with me."

"She is?" I begged the question.

"Oh yeah." Lawrence stretched out his right arm and held Elle really tight in his hand like he would a basketball. "Come here, Elle, you're going to drive us for a little bit now."

We were driving south, an opposite direction from Vivian's. Even though it was dark outside there were a ton of cars on the road with us - any one of which could have easily noticed the five year old driver that, at least to me, stuck out like a fucking sore thumb. After Elle got settled on his lap, Lawrence laid his seat back, and told Elle, "tell me when I need to hit the brakes."

"Ok!" Elle smiled ear to ear, but I could tell she was also secretly freaking out. Elle is young, but she's not literally still a baby, ya know? She understood enough in the moment to know that if she didn't take driving seriously we could all be severely injured. I'm the one studying to take my driver's license test this May - not Elle. But sure, let's give *her* the extra practice.

She had one hand on either side of the steering wheel and kept us going straight until Lawrence interrupted. "This is boring," he said. "Come on. Let's do something. Turn this way when it's clear." Lawrence tugged the back of Elle's jacket at her right elbow.

"Here, pull this down," he instructed while tapping the blinker.

Elle pulled, and the car started clicking. Lawrence and I both looked over our right shoulders to check for cars. There were none.

"You should start getting over now, Elle, it's clear." I told her.

"Ok!" Elle was still smiling ear to ear, "like this?" she said.

"Yup, and then turn right up here." Lawrence pointed to the next light at some random intersection. Upon approaching the light, Lawrence started excitedly shouting instructions to Elle.

"Crank it! Crank it, Elle! You gotta turn the wheel, girl!" Lawrence started laughing out loud.

Elle shuffled her little hands around the wheel as fast as she could to turn the car to the right. It looked like she was working some huge machine, but, I mean, I guess she was - right?

Well, the damn near twenty minutes Lawrence "allowed" Elle to drive was pretty fucking terrifying. It was actually about thirty nine minutes, but still. He kept nudging me with his hand and laughing. He was boasting because he was proud of Elle's driving skills, and he was having the time of his life. I was super nervous because I thought Lawrence was going to have Elle drive us all the way back home. But, instead he instructed Elle to pull over a block before Vivian's. Elle tucked herself back into her booster seat, and we continued home like nothing out of the ordinary had even happened.

| 31 |

Chapter Thirty-One

March 20th, 2008

This week I thought I'd be able to come back in here and hesitantly report to you that things still seemed to be going alright. I really wanted to tell you that I've still been cheering and that Lawrence has still been sober. I wanted to tell you that he had been showing up to basketball practices twice a week like he's supposed to; that he's been respecting his role as an *assistant* to the real coach; and, that he's been respecting my unspoken boundaries. Plus he hadn't had any public meltdowns in front of my peers, yet, - which has been pretty awesome! I might have even come in here and said "it's been fun," and maybe even that it's been some of the proudest weeks of my whole life. But, now that's all gone to shit.

I had basketball practice with Lawrence again. Elle typically just sits on the sidelines watching and cheering us all on, and yesterday was no different. The coach of our basketball team. Mr. Adams - he's pretty chill. Mr. Adams is a White dude with long blonde hair, and he's always either wearing sandals or tennis shoes. Mr. Adams is a total tree hugger. But, I guess he used to play basketball in high school and college, so he's actually got some skills.

Yesterday, Mr. Adams stopped me while we were doing drills. He was trying to teach me how to shoot from inside the paint, just a quick and simple layup, but when there are a bunch of people on defense blocking me. Mr. Adams was giving me a small pointer about my form when I noticed Lawrence heading towards us from the opposite side of the court. I tried to hurry Mr. Adams along, "ok, cool. I think I got it now. Thanks." I said.

Of course Lawrence felt so threatened that he had to come interfere. He stepped in and started correcting Mr. Adams - in front of everybody. Mr. Adams was uberly polite towards Lawrence the entire time. At first Mr. Adams let Lawrence correct him. Mr. Adams blew the whistle to run the play, and I was blocked at the net again, so I wasn't able to make the basket. Both Lawrence and Mr. Adams stepped in again. By this time everybody had stopped playing ball and had started watching Lawrence and Mr. Adams coach me. Then, to break the increasing tension, Mr. Adams even tried to include Lawrence in the coaching moment.

"No, see? I still think her form is just a little bit off. If she squares up to the net and then goes directly at her opponent, she'll be able to drive straight to the net, right?" Mr. Adams *was* being a little patronizing towards Lawrence, and he was obviously trying to tell Lawrence, "look, dude, I may be White but I know what I'm talking about," in the most polite way. But, also, Lawrence was the one who put Mr. Adams in the awkward position anyway, so... it was a jump ball.

Either way, the situation escalated way out of hand - Lawrence started cursing Mr. Adams out right there on the basketball court in front of everybody. All of a sudden, this little thing had become a huge scene. I saw some girls laughing in the corner. It was mortifying. Lawrence walked all the way up in Mr. Adams' face practically begging for Mr. Adams to throw the first punch. Luckily, because it was clear Lawrence's ego was having a complete meltdown, Mr. Adams remained compassionate and didn't budge. It also probably had something to do with the fact that Lawrence would've totally smashed Mr. Adams in a brawl, but, you know, I'm not really trying to give

Lawrence any gas like that. The whole situation just felt wrong. It was the epitome of every reason I knew he shouldn't have joined the team in the first place.

"Sober" whatever.

The tantrum didn't end until Lawrence realized it was mute because Mr. Adams wasn't engaging. Then, out of a combination of immaturity and embarrassment, he flicked Mr. Adams' baseball cap off Mr. Adams' head. He said, "come on, grab your stuff and let's go," and then stormed out of the gym without waiting.

Elle and I trailed behind while Lawrence hid out in his car in the parking lot. He sped off as soon as we jumped inside his ride. Once officially off school premises and on the road, Lawrence immediately started talking about how he was going to quit being an assistant coach. The only blessing of the entire day.

It was *so* stupid, but even more, it was so, *so* embarrassing. So mortifying it feels like it literally happened yesterday. Don't forget, I still had to go to school with all of those people every day, you know? As soon as we left the gym I knew the story was probably spreading across town through the grapevine.

So, I called the cheer coach and told him I quit that too, just to speed the news up. Nobody has asked me about quitting the basketball team yet. But, Nikky called and nearly cussed me out for quitting the cheer team immediately after it happened.

"I can't believe you'd just quit the team without even talking to me about it! What's been going on with you lately? You've been acting completely different." She finally fit in, "now I don't have any real friends on the team. We were supposed to be doing this together!"

I didn't know what to say to Nikky. And, I don't know what to say about Lawrence. Those are his demons - not mine.

| **32** |

Chapter Thirty-Two

March 27th, 2008

Do you remember hella long ago I told you Lawrence made a dumbass comment about Vivian seeing someone else? Well, it turns out Lawrence wasn't lying. Apparently Vivian really *has* been seeing someone new! She only just told us about the whole thing last week, and only because she was going on vacation with him. I think his name is Roger or something? It's a super appropriate name for him since, from the few pictures I've seen, he's got silver Mr. Rogers lookin-locks and an old man sweater wearing style.

The plan was that Vivian was going to go on vacation with a few of her "girlfriends." So, Elle and I were going to stay at my Uncle Marlon and Auntie Bette's house while Vivian was gone. We were supposed to go to our after school program last Friday as usual, and get picked up by my aunt or uncle later in the day. But, Lawrence had other plans for us.

Instead, Lawrence picked Elle and me up right after school, knowing all the other responsible adults in our lives were still working. We basically just drove around with Lawrence to his various window washing jobs for the rest of the day. Finally, later that evening, we went back to Lawrence's apartment with Emilia. Vivian didn't know

187

Lawrence had us until much later in the night. It must've been hours after picking us up from after school that Lawrence actually called Uncle Marlon.

"Aye, man. I picked the girls up from their lil daycare this afternoon and I'm just going to have them stay with me until Vivian gets back from her lil fucking vacay, iight?"

What was my Uncle Marlon really supposed to say to Lawrence after that? You know? I mean, sure, some type of "naw, *man*, you know that wasn't the plan. Let me come get the girls," or "I'll be downstairs to get them in five minutes," would've worked. But, my Uncle Marlon is the baby of his family, so I understand why he wasn't necessarily prepared to do all that. Instead, Uncle Marlon pretty much just said, "Alright. Cool, man. Just holler if you need anything, or if you want a break, or something like that."

Lawrence had Uncle Marlon on speaker phone and he was rolling his eyes towards Elle and me to make fun. I didn't pay Lawrence attention because Uncle Marlon was saying some really important stuff. "I've got Nelly here with me this weekend. I know she'd love to see the girls and play and do alla that." Nelly is my cousin who lives in Yakima. The fact that she was here from the other side of the mountains was a big deal because she lives so far away. But, Lawrence didn't even seem to notice.

"Gotcha, man. 'Igght I'll talk to you later," Lawrence said before hanging up without thinking a thing about it. He didn't even wait for my Uncle Marlon to respond. Just click.

Once Vivian found out, about an hour or so after Uncle Marlon called, she lost it. She, like the rest of us, was fed up with Lawrence switching around plans without collaborating with the rest of the village. She was sick of his spontaneity.

Elle and I were at Lawrence's apartment having dinner with Emilia, and Lawrence was on the phone with Vivian. We could hear him screaming from inside the bedroom even though the door was closed. Emilia kept trying to distract us so we didn't have to listen to the details.

Emilia tried a whole gang of things to keep Elle and me entertained during dinner. Her initial stories and knock-knock jokes fell short, even for Elle. She eventually won Elle over by making spaghetti with a meat sauce for dinner - Elle's favorite. But, just when I was about to project my feelings of helplessness into disdain towards Emilia, she flipped me too.

While Elle and I were in the kitchen helping Emilia cook dinner she taught us a trick. She said she had a special way to test when spaghetti noodles were finished. Then, without notice, she just threw a couple noodles at the wall. Some stuck and others snapped straight back off the wall and down to the floor. "It's not quite ready yet" Emilia said nonchalantly, and then just kept on cooking with a big smile on her face. Elle thought it was awesome, and so funny. I'm not going to lie, so did I, but, hell if I was going to show it to her, though - you know? It would have felt like fraternizing with the enemy or something. Even though nobody else was blaming life's woes on Emilia, I was.

Later, when we sat down for dinner, Emilia shared even more tricks. She leaned in towards the middle of the dinner table and whispered, "did you know I can do another trick with my spaghetti noodles?!"

We were intrigued. Elle and I looked at each other, shrugged our shoulders, and then looked back to Emilia without directly answering her question.

"OK. Check this out." Emilia tilted her head and seat backwards while remaining fully in her chair and balancing on the tips of her toes under the table. I swear I thought Emilia was going to fall backwards like Vivian always warns will happen, but she didn't. Emilia raised her right arm up above her face, pinching a single spaghetti noodle between her thumb and pointer finger. The noodle hung down towards Emilia's nose, and she lowered her hand in a way so the end of the spaghetti noodle started going down her nostril. Elle and I looked at each other and started shrieking. The spaghetti noodle dove deeper and deeper down Emilia's nostril.

"Emilia, it's in your nose!!!" Elle pointed out while giggling hysterically, as if Emilia wasn't already fully aware.

Emilia's head and chair started returning back to the upright position. The spaghetti noodle, on the other hand, was jetting everywhere. It was stuffed down Emilia's nose and coming out her mouth. THE. SAME. NOODLE. She looked at Elle and me with her eyes wide, and in a muffled shriek she said, "See?!?!?" letting out a huge smile. Emilia started flossing the noodle back and forth between her nose and her mouth, excitedly, "look!"

"EWW!!!" Our curiosity developed into disgust; but it wasn't such a totally overwhelming sight that we had to look away. We both just sorta cringed to ourselves and didn't take our eyes off Emilia for a single second. We held each other's hands as tightly as we could. Even Jasper started barking at Emilia a little bit - understandable, you know, it was a pretty shocking sight to see!

Emilia shouted over to Elle and me, "look!!!"

As if we weren't already drooling out the mouth with astonishment. Honestly, as much as I hate to admit it, I thought that shit was so cool! Emilia *immediately* collected all the points and coins I could've ever given her. She was the medication of innocent laughter we needed.

Elle and I both started trying to make our spaghetti noodles go down *our* noses and out of *our* mouths. But, it didn't work - well, not that latter part anyway. Emilia pulled her spaghetti noodle out of her mouth by pulling it from her nose, and she started coaching us on how to master the skill.

"No, no, no! Don't force it down your nose!" Emilia laughed, "that's not how you do it! Here, look!"

Emilia tilted her head back to start demonstrating the proper form to Elle and me again, but then she suddenly stopped. Before you knew it none of us were eating at all any more, let alone joking or laughing. We all just sorta softened out and settled down, trying to casually put our spaghetti noodles back down to our plates. Lawrence looked at us like he was surprised when he opened the door and came to the table to join us. He looked at us like we were crazy and the visual evidence in front of him was pissing him off even more than the fact itself being true. Emilia made eye contact with Lawrence while her head was still leaning all the way back from her seat, and then she quickly sat back upright and pulled the noodle from her nose. I wanted to laugh out loud, but I didn't dare.

"I was just showing off a little trick while we waited for you. I didn't think you'd want us to start eating without you." Emilia's eyes followed Lawrence around the dining room table and into his seat across from her.

Lawrence yanked his chair out and sat down, then stuck his middle finger to the bottom middle of the plate, through his bundle of spaghetti noodles, like he was a prince. "Yeah, well, while y'all were playing your little games this food got cold. So, now you want my kids to eat *this* cold food for dinner, Emilia? You really think they're going to like this shit?"

"No, I can warm it up for them. We just didn't know when you'd be ready to eat with us, Lawrence."

"They still have school they have to get to in the morning, Emilia. If you were a *real* parent you woulda already been thinking about that and you would know it's damn near 9 PM. The girls need to hurry up and eat, bathe, and then get to bed." Lawrence looked at Emilia with devil eyes, and he looked like he actually wanted to hit her, but was being polite or something because Elle and I were there. Emilia confirmed my assumptions by the way her body quivered in her seat. She didn't move from the table to heat up our food until explicitly directed to by Lawrence. She pretty much stared down at her plate through the rest of dinner.

Elle and I cleaned our plates off in the sink, thanked Emilia and Lawrence for the food, and then shuffled through the shower. When Elle was in the shower washing herself she dropped a bottle of conditioner on the bathtub floor, and it made a loud crashing sound in unison with Elle screaming. I checked on Elle, which made her snap out of it, but it was too late. Lawrence started pounding on the bathroom door and wiggling the locked door knob trying to force his way in.

"Girls!!! What's going on?! Open the door right now!" I was honestly more scared of Lawrence potentially getting into the bathroom than I was of Elle having potentially hurt herself.

"We're fine Dad, Elle just dropped a conditioner bottle." I called from inside the bathroom with Elle.

The tension throughout Lawrence's apartment was so tangible you could feel it anywhere you went. It didn't matter if we were sitting in the dining room eating dinner, hanging out in the living room watching tv, or hiding out in the bathroom trying to wash up before bed. All night it felt like we were all waiting to see how much worse the present situation would deteriorate.

I heard Elle sniffle in the shower after Lawrence stopped pounding on the door. I turned back the curtain a bit and saw Elle was crying, so I asked her what was wrong.

"I just really miss Mommy," she said while wiping the tears, snot, and shower droplets from her cheeks.

"Me too, Elle. Me too."

9

PROJECT MAYHEM

| 33 |

Chapter Thirty-Three

April 3rd, 2008

I didn't tell any of my friends what happened last week. Miles was pretty much the only one who noticed that I was acting differently, and he tried to ask me what was up during class, but I fully ignored him. My hope is that people won't get suspicious. So, I've pretty much just been staying out of sight.

My whole friend group looks different now, and that's helped me stay under radar. John is sort of friends with Miles, and Mark. But, he's so different from my group of friends. The misfit guys are badass, and artistic, and misunderstood, and I love them. John is just a little too careless for them, you know?

Take John and his friend Peter, from John's old school, for example. They like to do drugs together. Not just smoking the reefer every now and then, but actually taking pills and stuff too. I've been hanging out with him, and let me tell you, John stays high all day. I don't even know if he has passion for anything besides smoking weed, honestly. John would much rather kick it with people who smoke 24/7 like him. So, that's why he's always around Peter.

There's been so much going on that I haven't really been in the mood to see my friends. Normally we would've spent every day of spring break together. But, so far the only real socializing I've done outside of Saturday was when I went to Nikky's house with Laurie to make curtains. Nikky's been wanting more privacy from her family now that she's having sex, so she wanted to add curtains to her bedroom window. Laurie, being the creative that she is, knew exactly how to execute. So, we linked up, went to the craft store for materials, and then got to work. Nikky picked out materials to make white curtains. True to character, she grabbed hot pink Cheetah Girls-like material for the borders.

It only took us about an hour to make the curtains. We used a hot iron and fusing strips, my Aunties and Grandma Soul call it "witches magic," to stick the materials together. Then we sewed the borders down. Laurie was very pleased with herself, but as usual, nothing much impresses me right now. I tried not to spoil the mood though. We sang our hearts out to "Into You," by Tamia, and then just talked about boys. Nikky talked about her emotionally abusive, chronically cheating boyfriend who she recently lost her virginity to, and Laurie talked about Miles. I felt defensive whenever Laurie started talking, but I think it's just because I'm so close with Miles. I know they're actually good for each other at the end of the day, so I made myself let it go. Nikky just continued on and on, mostly rambling to herself, obliviously.

I mean, I guess everything's been going pretty smoothly. But, I don't know. It's all still just been a lot. You know? Like, what a fucking year.

I'm super thankful that Elle exists though. She brings so much light and silliness into my world. In spite of all the craziness going on at home, she still manages to convince me to put together a costume and meet her on stage in the center of the living room every now and then. Yesterday Elle had arranged a playlist for us to have a mock concert, and it was epic. She dressed up in a black sequin crop top that only had one lasagna-sized strap, and denim blue velvet bell bottoms. Elle picked my outfit out too, and she did our makeup. It's as if she's grown up three years over the last few months.

For Christmas, Vivian bought Elle this purple karaoke set with two semi-functional microphones. The microphones are connected to this small, battery-operated, super amateur DJ set. The set has background music and buttons for instruments you can mix in with the music if you press them. There are also two disco balls that light up and spin around - you can choose to have them on or not. Elle's favorite setting is to turn the microphones on at the highest volume and to turn the disco balls on full blast. She didn't really buy the shotty DJ set, so she usually kept the music and instruments off. But, who doesn't love a built in cheering crowd button though, amiright?

Or, am I right?

Elle turned down the lights and let the disco balls run. The playlist was top notch. It featured "I'm Like A Bird," by Nelly Furtado; "Bring it All to Me" by Blaque, "Something Real," by Phoebe Snow, "I'm Not Missing You," by Stacy Orrico, and much more. Elle sang the shit out of "Fat Boy," even though she couldn't be further from the character, and we both sang "Life Uncommon," by Jewel.

Elle had planned out choreography for a string of Jennifer Lopez songs, including "All I Have." Have you ever seen a little girl sing along to a song with so much passion it makes you a little concerned? Well, I started feeling that way when Elle started belting out J-Lo.

"Ok, Elle. Go ahead and let them know! Sing it girl!" I encouraged from behind while waving my hands side-to-side in unison with the beat.

Then, she let me take the floor for "Thinkin' About You," by Brittney Spears, and "Stan," by Eminem. At some point Vivian walked in while Elle was doing a solo to "Underneath it All," by No Doubt, and she shut the whole production down. It was a shame because we were truly gigging. But, whatever.

"Oh, *hell* no," Vivian half joked.

I don't even know why Vivian was so shocked. *All* humans have a sense of sexuality that needs to be expressed. What does she think Elle's doing when we play Barbies and Bratz? Honestly, for a five year old, Elle has fantastic taste in music. It sounds lame as fuck, but these concerts at home have been saving my troubled mind lately. They bring so much light and fun and escapism into my life, and honestly, I need that sort of escape right now.

I got in a fight with Vivian later in the night though, and things took a turn for the worse. That guy she's been dating, Roger, he showed up in our parking lot last night, and I caught them hooking up.

What happened was that my intuition woke me up, and I knew something major was missing. I went looking around our apartment, and found that Vivian was missing from her bed. Then, when I peeked outside, I recognized Roger's car outside. Elle was deadass asleep, so I grabbed a copy of the security door key, and journeyed downstairs. When I got there, I saw Vivian and Roger hooking up in the back seat. I picked my jaw up from the floor and hurried back inside before Vivian or Roger could notice me. By the time I had levitated upstairs I could barely even focus on anything. I just saw red and wanted to fucking smash everything in sight. Instead I decided to write Vivian a bunch of notes. Most of the notes just read "I fucking hate you you dirty slut" and "I saw you fucking Roger with his daughter asleep in her back seat booster chair" - stuff like that.

I taped my notes to Vivian's bedroom door, so when she came back upstairs she saw them and "woke" me up out of bed. We argued in the living room so Elle wouldn't be woken up, but it was short lived. After I said "God, Mom, you're such a slut," for the second or third time she slapped me and brought us both back to reality.

I went into the nearby bathroom and grabbed the bottle of Advil. I poured out enough pills to cover up all the wrinkles in my cupped hand, and waited for Vivian to look at me. Once I watched her eyes bounce from my cupped hand full of pills back up to my eyes a few times, I quickly swallowed them - only using my accumulated spit to help them go down.

"What the fuck, Olivia," Vivian said sounding fed up and turned off, but not concerned.

"Did you just swallow a handful of pills?" I just looked at her, trying my very best to channel Lawrence, and didn't answer. "Did you?!"

"I don't know," I said walking upstairs towards Elle, sleeping in the bed we made up in the middle of the floor. Vivian followed me. I laid down next to Elle, still with my back towards Vivian, and waited to fall asleep for the rest of my life. I didn't look back. But, I heard Vivian let out a loud over-exaggerated sigh as she turned out the lights, "you want to hurt yourself and self-destruct like your Dad, Olivia? I won't stop you."

Obviously nothing happened, right? I mean, I'm sitting right here in front of you today. So that means the pills must not have worked. Next time I ought to just try more.

If you really want to dig into the juicy stuff I could tell you about last weekend. Shit got a little crazy when I went out with my girlfriends. It was on Saturday, Vivian's own National Various House Chores Day - laundry included. I needed to scratch my wild oats, or however the saying goes, after the whole mini-trafficking experience with Lawrence. So, I decided to go ahead and spice things up in my current real life. I knew Vivian wouldn't miss me or her car keys, so I went ahead and took them off her hands.

At first, I just drove around the apartment complex solobolo. But, after I started getting comfortable, I wandered out into the main roads. The first person I picked up was Nikky. I knew her energy would match mine and she'd be down to get just as crazy as I wanted. Nikky was only a hop, skip, and a bridge away, so it didn't feel like a big deal when I randomly called her from outside. She answered her phone and I semi-screamed back at her, "bitch, come outside *right now*! I got a brand new whip for you!"

The car was actually Vivian's new '92 purple-gold Toyota Camry that we call Rosey. I was hella just trying to flex. But, honestly, it didn't even matter. Any sort of wheels feel like a fucking limited edition spaceship to us at this point in life. Nikky came skipping out of her house with a huge smile slapped across her face. Almost within the same breath of settling into the passenger seat Nikky took over controlling the stereo. She chose Lil Jon and the Eastside Boyz, "Get Low."

We rolled all the windows down as far as they would go, and debated on who we should pick up first. We agreed it just made the most geographical sense to pick up Laurie first and then Charlotte. After we swooped Charlotte, I parked the car down the road so her guardian didn't see us while we plotted out our plans for the rest of the day.

Want to know the brilliant idea we came up with? To drive thru McDonalds to get some food. Of course. I should've known the best idea we could collectively agree upon would somehow involve food. But, it was a great choice. McDonald's fries are probably the most reliable thing on this earth. After we inhaled our food in the parking lot, almost entirely avoiding any suspicion, we had to think up our next plan.

I turned the car on and "Ghost Ride the Whip" was playing. Laurie pitched the wild idea to go to the Spirit Halloween store and buy some out of line face masks, and we all agreed. After grabbing an assortment of Jabbawockeez-looking, Ronald Reagan-looking, and Michael Jackson-looking masks, we returned to the parking lot to think up a few more bright ideas. Driving down the main roads with a ride full of my best girl friends felt cool. But, I won't even lie, I was scared as fuck. So, I drove us back to the McDonald's parking lot to waste time.

Lawrence, Grandma Soul, Vivian, and pretty much everyone else in my family has stressed the meaning behind my skin color since before I can even remember. Being Black, specifically driving while Black, means a lot of things. Most importantly, it means that I am to stay away from trouble. More explicitly speaking, it means I need to avoid interacting with the police - on any level. Living with that type of pressure as a child feels outlandish and unfathomable. It almost makes me want to act out even more, but for being afraid of losing my life or endangering my family.

Mark and Nikky still poke jokes at me for being "on edge." Mark will obnoxiously sneak up on me and shout things like "freeze" if we're out somewhere public, or "stop" if we're out walking around. Whenever one of them proposes a scheme that's too risky I'll respond by saying, "I can't be doing that, y'all, I'm Black," and try to conclude with "y'all probably wouldn't even get in trouble if we got caught." But, they think I'm being dramatic. As if they automatically think they know better than me.

My friends like to focus a lot of time and energy telling me they don't see my color. But, we all know that's a lie. What they really means is that they're ignoring my skin color, my hair texture, and all my other subconsciously perceived inadequacies. In truth, I wish they saw all the complex melanin shades of my skin. I wish they saw and encouraged the real, full me. But, as isolating as it is to switch between personas, there's also a huge amount of exciting exhilaration that I want to hold on to for forever. There's a feeling that no one knows the real me - and that can be sort of fun. As if I'm holding on to a secret between me and me.

Anyway, by the time we went back to the McDonalds parking lot we were really feeling ourselves. "Ghost Ride the Whip" played on the radio again, and Laurie and Nikky hopped out the car to start going dumb in the parking lot. Each of them left their car doors open, and danced within the doorframe for their pleasure. I sat in the driver's seat while Charlotte pulled her phone out and pressed "record."

Nikky was pinching the right shoulder of her big-T and moving it in small circular motions. She was thizz facing and held her left arm out - faking like she was trying to stabilize from actively riding an imaginary whip. Laurie's face was up to the sky, she was sorta hopping back on her left foot, and her arms were down by her hips as if she was holding a weight in each hand. She bobbed her head back and forth, putting in serious neck work, while Charlotte and I cheered from inside the car.

Before we knew it, it was twilight. John kept calling on the hour, as if it was his job to alarm us with the time. So, in the name of safety, we decided to call it a night early. I drove the girls home one by one, and then decided to take the long route back to Vivian's. When I got home she was still so busy scrubbing out the inside of the bathtub to notice that I had even left - let alone that I had taken her car for a little joy ride for the day.

So, yeah, that's been my spring break so far.

| 34 |

Chapter Thirty-Four

April 10th, 2008

On Tuesday, I had to leave early from school again. Elle was sick, and since Vivian was at work, Lawrence had to take care of her. Then, since Lawrence can't really take care of Elle alone, I had to be pulled out of class too - per usual.

Every visit with Lawrence seems to have an element of surprise. But, this wasn't actually too bad. Lawrence drove Elle and me straight to his house, and let us cuddle in his bedroom. Emilia and Lawrence share a king-sized bed, with a huge comforter and a ton of pillows. It's way different from the water bed we used to have growing up. Now, Lawrence has a grown up, king sized throne that sits so high up off the ground I have to hop up on to it. It reminds me of *The Princess and the Pea.*

Anyways, Lawrence tucked Elle and me into his throne. In his bedroom he turned on the cartoon show where dragons go on adventures with a brother and sister duo. Lawrence was being peculiarly paternal, "do you want some soup, Elle? I can make you some right now."

Elle took Lawrence up on the offer.

"Ok, Baby. What kind of soup do you want? We have chicken noodle, we have some black bean soup, we have some veggie soup, and we have spaghettios too, but you probably shouldn't eat that."

"I want chicken noodle, please, Daddy!"

"You don't have to say 'please' to me, E, I'm your Daddy. It's my job to serve you. You just stay here and I'll be right back with your soup." Lawrence smiled at Elle with ease..

"Ok." Elle responded.

"Alright now. Do you need anything else, Honey?" Elle shook her head, "Ok, sweetie, don't leave. I'll be right back with your soup."

Lawrence gently closed the door behind him, as if he were actually concerned about being too loud. Then, Elle and I cuddled in the bed together and watched TV. Elle was sort of fading in and out - she wasn't massively sick and puking or anything, but she did have a fever. Jasper laid at the bottom of the bed keeping our feet warm.

After the show switched to *Osmosis Jones*, Lawrence ventured back into the bedroom. "Here you go, Elle," Lawrence said while setting a standing leg tray across Elle's lap. Once the tray met the bed successfully Lawrence released a huge sigh, like he was half relieved, half surprised, but I'm not sure.

"You girls need anything else," he asked us.

We shook our heads "no," but Lawrence kept trying to probe, "are you sure? You don't want any crackers or soda or anything?" Elle was too busy guzzling down her soup to answer. I just shook my head again and said, "I think it's good, Dad. Thanks."

He said, "ok, good. Good." Then he gave Elle the head nod and said, "how long do you think it will take you to finish that bowl of soup and glass of water?"

She just shrugged. I don't think Elle was trying to be smart with Lawrence or anything, she just genuinely didn't know. I don't think Vivian has ever served Elle as many liquids in one sitting as Lawrence did. Literally, probably never. But *for sure* not when coaxing Elle to sweat out her fever in a nap. Elle didn't answer Lawrence, so he repeated his question.

"Huh? I don't know what that means, Ellesha." Just when I thought he was completely fed up, Lawrence cracked a smile. "Do you think you can finish the soup in ten minutes? Fifteen? There's no way it could take you twenty minutes, right?"

I could tell Elle was starting to feel stressed out and inadequate by the way her eyebrows crunched together. She said, "I don't know. I'm just starting to get a little full, so I might need to take a break?"

"Ok, well, don't rush, Baby. Just take your time and eat up. Take a break when you need to, and I'll come back to check on you in about thirty minutes, okay? We'll see if you've finished by then or if you still need more time, ok?"

"Ok," Elle agreed, "but I might finish before thirty minutes, Daddy."

"Didn't you just say you needed to take a break?"

"Yeah"

"Ok, then take your break, Ellesha. Just stay in here for thirty minutes and when I come back I'll see how much you were able to get down, ok?"

"Ok."

"Alright, then. Enjoy." Lawrence backed out of the room again, and softly closed the door behind him.

Elle looked up at me and said, "does he think I eat too slow because I'm still so little, Ollie?"

"What?! No, Ellie Bug. I don't know why he kept asking you that question. He's being weird."

I could tell Elle didn't believe me because she started shoveling food into her mouth faster than I'd ever seen before. Not even fifteen minutes later, Elle had gulped down the entire bowl of chicken noodle soup *and* her glass full of water. Once she had finished, Elle slid down her pillows so she was laying flat on her back, and lifted up her long sleeved lavender cotton pajama shirt. Elle poked her stomach out as far as she possibly could and looked like a pregnant five year old, if you can imagine.

Elle started patting all over her tummy like she was drumming, and proudly said, "Ollie, look!"

She smiled at me once we made eye contact, and said, "I finished everything!" as if I hadn't heard her sucking, slurping, and burping her way through.

I laughed to appease Elle, and said, "great, now you just have to wait for Dad to come back."

"It's cool. I can do it." Elle said, sounding too grown up for her own good, "I'm not a baby anymore. I can put my own dishes away. I want to help Dad!"

Then, just like that, Elle bounced out of bed. She picked her tray of dishes up off the bed and headed out the bedroom - leaving the door open behind her. I followed Elle, and stood in the doorframe so I could watch over her rites of passage journey. I stayed out of sight from Lawrence, but I could hear him coughing from the living room. Lawrence interrupted Elle in the hallway by jumping out from in front of the fireplace. Elle stopped in her tracks, and Lawrence started yelling.

"WHAT THE FUCK ARE YOU DOING OUT HERE?" There was a pipe, some aluminum foil, and a small clear plastic baggie atop the mantle that Lawrence had had his fingers wrapped up in.

Elle didn't budge a millimeter.

"WHAT?" Lawrence popped his eyes out at Elle, "ARE YOU TRYING TO FUCKING SPY ON ME OR SOMETHING?"

Elle shook her head "no," and looked down at her little toes.

"GET THE FUCK OUT OF HERE, THEN." Lawrence shooed Elle away in a really dehumanizing sort of way, snapping his fingers to capture her attention. Elle scooted away from him accordingly, food tray still in hand, holding her breath. When Elle was back in the bedroom she immediately closed the door behind her and set her tray of dishes down on the floor near her side of the bed. She flopped her torso over the bed and sobbed into the blankets with her arms at either side.

Lawrence followed behind Elle, and pounded on the bedroom door, "I SAID 'DON'T LEAVE AND WAIT FOR ME TO COME

BACK,' DIDN'T I, ELLESHA?!" It was a rhetorical question, he didn't really want either of us to answer.

"NOW STAY IN THERE UNTIL I COME BACK LIKE I SAID THE FIRST TIME."

Lawrence punched on the door one more time and shouted, "NOW," as he trailed off.

I wanted to lock the door, but I knew Lawrence could have kicked it down if he wanted to and it would've just made him more agitated. So, I didn't. Instead I went to stand beside Elle. I stood there and just rubbed her back while she sobbed. It wasn't just a casual cry, like when Vivian says "no" to Elle when Elle holds up a bag of Mother's Cookies in the grocery store. This was a sob, where I could tell Elle was having difficulty even breathing. It fucking sucked.

After about five minutes I could tell she was starting to stabilize, so I ducked down to sweep her feet off the ground. Elle's body was limp - like, she poured zero effort into helping me lift her weight. So, getting her up onto Lawrence's throne became a bit more of a task than I initially anticipated. Nevertheless, the emotion of the moment motivated my inner Hulk to shine.

Once I managed to lift Elle's feet to the top of Lawrence's throne, I jumped on myself and rolled the blankets down. I tucked Elle, Jasper, and myself deep into the covers before cradling her in my arms. I pet the hair on the top of Elle's head and kissed her forehead occasionally, whispering "shhh shhh shhh, it's okay, Elle. It'll all be ok. Just go to bed." Elle cried herself to sleep in mine and Jasper's paws.

After it turned dark outside Emilia came home and woke everybody up. Elle jolted up into a panic because she had to pee, so we braved leaving the bedroom together. Elle and I snuck into the bathroom, and Jasper ran out to Lawrence and Emilia in the living room to distract them. I heard Lawrence greet Jasper with a sound of cheer, so I knew the coast was clear.

Elle released her demons, and then used the cheesy butterfly painted stool so she could wash her hands in the sink "all on her own" afterwards. When we went out to the living room I could see Lawrence sprawled out on the couch with Emilia sitting super glued in a criss-cross applesauce position at his side. Emilia and Lawrence plastered smiles across their faces, and in unison said, "hey!"

Emilia continued further, "how are you feeling Elle?"

Emilia opened her arms so Elle would come sit on her lap. Elle didn't answer Emilia, but she ran over and sat atop Emilia's lap all the same.

"Are you hungry," Emilia asked.

Elle and I shook our heads "no," even though, truth being told, I was actually really hungry. Lawrence sat up from the couch and went into his bedroom. Everybody tracked him with their eyes. The mess on the mantle from earlier had been cleaned up. He emerged from the bedroom with Elle's tray of dishes and carried them into the kitchen. We heard some shuffling, and then Lawrence emerged for the final time - now with the spicy Doritos and sour cream. He walked back over to the living room and sat back down on the couch in his same spot. The sour cream was already sorta pink, instead of white, from the cheese spice no doubt.

"Okay," Emilia continued, "well, who wants to play Monopoly then?"

"Oooh! I do!" Elle broke out of her scared shell and started bouncing up and down waving her hand in the sky. Monopoly does that to her every time.

"Sure, I'll play." I said, looking towards Lawrence who was eating a handful of freshly dipped chips.

"Let's go! Y'all ain't ready for Papa Bear to whoop on you again. Come on, bust it out," Lawrence said excitedly.

Emilia shuffled through the games and decks of cards in the chestnut cabinet from our old apartment until she found Monopoly. Elle dug the board out of the box. We all called out our preferred playing pieces while I sorted the beginning playing money out from there. I was the cautious curious cat, Elle was the always loves you no matter what dog, Emilia was the fancy car, and Lawrence was the consistently kicks you when you're already down boot. Appropriate, right?

Well, we all played Monopoly copacetically for a while. Emilia was winning and I was trailing shortly behind. Elle and Lawrence were tied in last place. So, of course Lawrence tripped Elle up when she couldn't count how much money she was supposed to give him. Lawrence owned Marvin Gardens and he had a house and a hotel on the property.

"I own it, so that's $24 rent, and then I have two houses on it, so that's $24 times $15. What does that equal, Ellesha?"

"Hmm, let me count," Elle said, beginning to count her tiny little fingers.

It was ridiculous. Ella had barely even started learning subtraction. Plus, it wasn't supposed to be a multiplication equation, it was an addition equation. Lawrence was too fucked up to notice the difference, and nobody said anything. Instead, the room fell tensely quiet, as Elle looked up to the ceiling.

"Don't look up there. God ain't gon' save you! He can't give you the answers to life!"

A tear fell down Elle's left cheek, and she looked vacantly past the side of Lawrence to the wall behind him. I could feel her boiling with a veggie soup level mix of emotions. Emilia tried to change the conversation and progress the game forward, but Lawrence stopped her.

"No, no, no. Don't try to give her an out. She knows all the words to all her favorite little rap songs," maybe because they're her *favorite* songs, "but she don't know how to do the most basic stuff like her ABCs and 123s?!"

"Lawrence," Emilia tried to rationalize with him, but her efforts were futile.

"'Lawrence' *what?*" he mocked. "My girls ain't gon' be a stereotype, Emilia. They're gonna know how to do all the other shit the other kids know, *and then some* - you hear me?"

"Yeah," Emilia said, giving up any fight she thought she had left over from her day.

The night pretty much continued on with everybody walking on eggshells. Somebody eventually won the game, probably Lawrence, and then he dropped us off at Vivian's for the night.

When we first came home Vivian asked Elle and I how the trip went. But, we could both tell

Vivian was too busy transferring us through the bathtub process to really hear either of our responses. So, we just kept it short.

| 35 |

Chapter Thirty-Five

April 17th, 2008

Now that we're back in school things are a little different. I'm going to turn sixteen soon, then soon after that I'll be a Junior, and before I know it I'll be out of this hellish high school for forever. I can't wait to be far far away from here. But, for now, I'll have to just keep on coasting.

I started the year thinking my high school experience was going to have a major turn around. Boy was I wrong.

I think the general public, and especially my parents, are pretty clueless about what goes on in high schools. Take my health and wellness class for example. In the back of the room there is literally a group of people who smoke, drink, and even sometimes hook up. The teacher is a total pushover who is completely checked out.

It's that class where pretty much anything goes. After fighting her way through attendance, the teacher basically just gives up and sits at her desk shopping online. To fill the time, some people make spitballs and lug them across the room. Others share a handle of whatever they could get their hands on for the day. Hennessey is the most popular. The lonely hearts club keeps their heads down. At the beginning of the school year I sat at the front of the class and kept my head down too. But, lately, I've been sitting in the back with John and the other stoners smoking joints. I know Ms. Walker would be upset if she saw me indulging in the marijuana smog like I have been. But, hey. What can you do? I can't focus on anything school related right now anyway. Not after Vivian told me that Lawrence has officially relapsed - as if I didn't already know.

Honestly, it's pretty amazing what happens in my life on a week-to-week basis. On Monday, Emilia was in a car accident. She's alright. But, her car is totaled. I guess she tried to speed through a yellow light that was turning red, to keep up with Lawrence, and someone t-boned the rear-part of her ride. Emilia's car spun around in the street a few times and she rode the ambulance to the hospital; but, she was released the same day. At first Emilia was pretty shaken up, even though it seems like she's alright now. She even makes jokes about how she looks - "as if" she had been beaten up.

"Not this time," she awkwardly laughed, "now we *really* have to wait to get married," she jokes while rubbing her hand over her neck brace.

Vivian is so gracious she decided to lend Emilia her car while Emilia's car is still in the shop. So, for the past couple of days Vivian's been walking Elle and me to school, and then taking the bus to work. We all have to wake up earlier, which is particularly difficult for Elle, but it's been nice to spend the time together. Plus, now on Fridays Vivian sings the "It's Friday Night" song again, which has been really comforting to hear.

Meanwhile, John and I have still been hanging out. We were hanging out a ton at first, but now things have sort of started to cool down. I'm not sure if it's because we had sex or not though. Who knows? We had sex on a whim over spring break. It was nothing special, so that's why I never mentioned it. I guess once you've already had sex with someone it's *really* hard not to have sex again. Maybe that's why parents always tell kids to wait.

You know? Like, now that I know what it feels like to do it it's hard for me to only want to stick to making out. I'm always thinking like, "no, come on, let's just fuck," and I feel like it's expected of the situation. Maybe that's only with John though, since he's the only guy I've been with outside of Justin. But, I don't know. I felt sorta bad about sleeping with John after we did it. But yeah, after you do it you can't go back; and that's the truth. In the moment, I didn't think too much about it beyond, "I swear to God you better have a condom."

We didn't plan it or anything. It was just another day I skipped school to hang out with John at his house. We were making out, rolling around John's bed, and not watching some random movie. We had both been panting pretty heavily for some time and feeling each other up. John used one arm to tether me to his body, and another to rub his fingers over my nipple. We were underneath his thick ass blue plaid comforter, which both made time disappear and the two of us super sweaty.

I was dripping wet, and what was once dry humping soon turned into near penetration. I untangled my fingers from his hair and scooped my spine to make room for my hand to unbutton my pants. John looked down and knew what was up. We were for sure about to have sex. But, instead of savoring the moment and taking his time to fully feel me up properly, John rushed through to home base.

We were in contact for a good couple of minutes, maybe four. All of a sudden he sorta pulled out, hunched over, and started groaning. I thought it was weird as hell, but I just laid there with John collapsed over me humping into the air. I figured he didn't know what he was doing. After a few seconds John extended his arms straight, lifting his torso from mine, and looked me in the eyes smiling proudly.

I was still confused, so I said, "what? I think you fell out."

John sat back on the heels of his feet between my legs. He grabbed me by the thighs and pulled me down on the bed, which I thought was sexy as hell until I felt a big wet spot on my back. I looked up to John with my face resembling the dishevelment my mind was sorting through: *what the hell is that?*

"I already finished," John said, still annoyingly smiling.

The wet spot I was feeling on the comforter beneath me was a pile of John's sloodge. It was wet, mucusy, and disappointing. The sloodge on my back symbolized that John was one of those guys who erroneously thought that sex ends when the guy finishes. Whereas some guys obsess over if they made you orgasm, John didn't even ask if I had enjoyed myself or if I felt satisfied at all - which I didn't.

I was equally disappointed with the girth of his packaging. John has an excessively small dick. I was so sad when I finally felt it and there was almost nothing there. Like, come on now. All that work, and stress, and secrecy, and self-betrayal for nothing.

10

THE ORIGINAL MS. JACKSON

| 36 |

Chapter Thirty-Six

April 24th, 2008

Today has been a total fucking fog, man. I'll be honest. I know what happened this morning, but I basically have no idea where I am or what I'm saying. I'm barely even here. I pretty much just don't exist and we should skip over me today.

All I remember is waking up this morning. You can really tell we're fully moving into the heart of spring now, huh? I can. When I wake up the sunshine has a distinct tint of yellow. You know that song "Misty Blue" by Dorothy Moore?

Well, when I woke up this morning it felt like misty yellow. It was so bright it sort of felt like the blinds didn't matter, but for them blocking the rest of the world from view. I had this off putting feeling deep in my spiritual core before I even opened my eyes, like I had just woken up from a horrible dream - you know?

Elle was passed out right beside me, snoring her ass off, drool dried up on the side of her mouth and all. I didn't want to wake her, but I could hear Vivian crying in the bathroom.

"He finally did it. I can't believe he finally did it." It sounded like Vivian was mad, but it was contradictory to the amount of sadness I heard from her weeps. I knew I needed to get out of bed to check on Vivian. The tone of her voice told me she was talking to someone about Lawrence.

You have to remember, Vivian's always talking about how Lawrence is either going to "wind up in jail, kill himself, or get murdered." I honestly feel like she's being a little dramatic when she says that, but I only say that from experience. Like, when we all used to live together, for example, Lawrence never really went to jail.

There were a couple times Vivian actually decided she needed to call the cops on Lawrence for domestic abuse. Like, the very first time he threatened to kill Elle and me. Lawrence was out for a night of partying, but he kept calling all night to "check in," per usual. I think it was like every eight minutes, or some random, unpredictable thing like that. He would purposefully call Vivian to keep her from sleeping.

In turn, that led to Elle and me not sleeping either. Eventually Vivian stopped answering. But, then Lawrence would leave these really horrible messages that blared through the voicemail box. He would say things about how he had people following Vivian, and about how he knew she was cheating on him. Then, out of left field, he called saying he was going to kill Elle and me if Vivian ever tried to leave him. The last voicemail he left before she called the police was about how he was on his way over "to check up on" her.

Every single time the cops responded to a domestic violence related call they shat the bed - pardon my french. But, seriously, they would question Vivian and Lawrence in separate corners of the living room - barely allowing any privacy to the alleged victim in the situation, you know? Just like total morons. Then, the officers would either wait around until Lawrence left "for the night," or take him to jail for the night. Most frequently, they wouldn't do anything at all - besides blame Vivian with their "what did you expect" attitudes.

So, sure, I guess technically he "wound up in jail" before. But, it never even lasted more than twenty four hours. Lawrence would usually just come home the next day, between eleven AM and two PM, even more broke and pissed off than the night before. It sucked for everybody involved. Granted, that only happened on a couple occasions, but yeah. It's still enough to tell me Lawrence will probably never *seriously* "wind up in jail, kill himself, or be murdered," as Vivian always says.

Anyway, as I crept towards the bathroom silently, I heard Vivian. She was repeating her questions like, "how many times? HOW MANY TIMES?!" and "where? TELL ME WHERE!" which I thought was all pretty confusing.

When I reached the door frame of the bathroom I saw the total state of devastation Vivian was in. I hadn't seen her so down and defeated since when we all lived together in the gross ass ground apartment. But, this morning she was sitting on top of our dirty lime green shag carpet toilet seat cover, and she was hunched over with her elbows on her knees and her head in her hands.

Vivian's left hand was holding our curly stringed landline to the left side of her face, and her knees were shivering up and down. The bathroom lights were on, which I thought was strange given the excess sunlight illuminating our apartment. It was like Vivian needed the innate comfort from the artificial light to ground her steadily in reality. The whole scene felt *completely* eerie. It was all so unreal and felt dangerous. I didn't even want to cross the bathroom threshold, to be honest.

I just stood there watching Vivian cry for what felt like an eternity. She didn't ever seem to notice me - which was weird. Then, all of a sudden, Vivian sprang upwards, dropped the phone, and screamed, "OH MY GOD! HE'S FUCKING DEAD!"

Just as she started to melt down to the floor I blacked out.

Now I'm here. Wherever the fuck "here" is.

| 37 |

Chapter Thirty-Seven

May 1st, 2008

I don't want to talk about what you want right now. First, I want to tell you about this repeating nightmarish dream I keep having. It's scary as hell, but, artistically speaking, it's a seriously beautiful nightmare. The kind you almost want to have again because you *know* you can change the outcome, yaddamean? It sorta felt like that thing... what's it called again? Déjà vu? Like I had been there before, even though I hadn't.

The room was on fire. Like, completely lit up. But, not in some beautiful Baz Luhrrmann *Romeo + Juliet* death scene type of way. Instead, it was more like - there's so much black smoke it's basically impossible to see and it's unpleasant, type of way. Like a coal mine.

The room was hellishly hot, and sweat beaded up in pearl-shaped water drops on my nose while my head rattled on like a snake. I couldn't see my feet below - let alone in which direction I was clumsily walking toward with my arms, hands, and each finger reaching out to anything they could hold on to. I was hoping to find some sort of safe room, maybe a medical tent with medical angels - like they have at Burning Man.

Instead, the smoke cleared and I was in Heaven with Jesus Christ. Jesus was at the end of the room down a long archway of pink clouds, and Satan was sleeping on the ground, unpretentiously. Jesus and Satan were lovers who wound up on different sides of the track. I don't know how I knew that just off the bat like that, but I did. Satan seemed to be happy, smirking even, and drool was pouring out of his mouth. As I walked closer, I realized Jesus was picking red, black, and pink pills up off His heavenly ground. I also realized Jesus was a She. It was Vivian.

On the ground to Her right, sleeping happily beside Her, was Satan - and he looked like a lifeless version of Lawrence. I told myself to stop listening to so much Destiny's Child and started walking backwards towards the black smoke I had just barely survived previously. Clearly, I would have chosen struggling with the Black Lung over anything that was going down in that fucked up moment. That's how twisted a scene it was.

Then, I saw Ellie. She was playing Barbies and Bratz on the ground next to passed out Satan and female-Jesus. It felt so real that I knew I couldn't just walk away and leave her there, you know? As annoying as she gets, Elle *is* my little sister. It's my number one job in life to protect her. It's crucial to my existence.

While Satan was ambien-style knocked out I tried to get Mama Jesus and sweet baby Elle to escape with me. I tried to tell them we were living in hell and that it was only dressed up as heaven in this nightmare. They refused to listen. Vivian and Elle didn't want to leave because they actually thought they were living in Heaven. "No, Olivia," they said, "we like it here," they said.

They were actively choosing to ignore reality: that we were living, and slowly dying, in hell. Vivian actually sang out "oh, what a life," in my dream, like Sade does in "Paradise." They were completely mesmerized by the devil. Slow dancing in a burning room or not, I knew we wouldn't be able to survive living this way. So, I just started screaming, which of course woke Satan up! But, he didn't just "wake up" in a normal way like you'd expect. Instead, he sat up, laughing his ass off as if he had been awake the whole time.

"It wasn't me," the Satanic version of Lawrence said while staring into my third eye. His tone was sarcastic, almost condescending, like Shaggy.

"It wasn't me!"

I responded by screaming again. Except this time it sounded more like a vicious, rageful roar - like I was angry, like I was really fucking pissed.

Then, all of a sudden, I was screaming in real life. Vivian and Elle surrounded me, and they both had the word "terrified" tattooed across their faces reflecting back at me. My tank top was damp with sweat, so, after I gathered my shit, I excused myself to go shower off in the bathroom. The day didn't slow down, though, and nobody expected any less of me.

Anyway, I guess I have some good news. Lawrence didn't die. Turns out he was only shot through the back a few times. Symbolic, eh? Vivian always says Lawrence has fucked the entire state of Washington, which means he must have gained a ton of enemies. Still, I wonder who in the world could have shot him.

I pretty much blacked out after that phone call where Vivian broke down crying. The one I told you about last week? Well, yeah. When I came to, basically halfway through third period a few days ago, the dust had settled - which was ideal. On the walk home that afternoon, I kept trying to complete the puzzle made up from bits and pieces of my memory.

But, eventually Elle put it together for me. You know how Black men are always being accused of doing shit they didn't do? Like, stealing backpacks, running away from the scene of a crime, waving around a pistol at a park, etc? Well, I guess that's what happened to Lawrence.

It was another typical case of one Black man being mistaken for the identity of another Black man. I don't know the race of Lawrence's shooter, so I don't want to get crazy and call it a hate crime or anything.

But, yeah. It's pretty fucked up. Apparently some guy thought Lawrence was someone who he wasn't. When Lawrence tried to get away from the perpetrator, the shooter let out three shots towards Lawrence's back. I guess the guy didn't even wait to see if Lawrence went down. He just kept it moving while Lawrence crawled away on the cold wet pavement to find some help.

Now that Lawrence is out of critical condition we can finally go visit him, and maybe Elle will start being able to tolerate ballads again. As of right now she breaks down any time she hears anything even remotely sad. We don't mention Tracy Chapman, and we can't listen to Luther Vandross any more because it'll fuck up the rest of the whole day. We were hanging out at our cousin's house listening to Christina Aguilere's namesake album, and when "Reflection" came on Elle had to leave the room and sit glued to our Auntie Bette for the remainder of the day.

Anyway, Vivian took us to visit Lawrence in the hospital. It was a big bag of flaming shit. Or, to say it more politely, it sucked. Lawrence barely even looked like his Michael Jordan doppelganger self. There were tubes crawling out of every entry point of his body. Even the most unlikely spots - like his fingers and his nose and his neck.

To visit, we had to venture to some hospital downtown. We parked underneath the loud ass, windy ass highway overpass. It was annoyingly sunny outside, with these fat fucking white clouds floating around the blue sky everywhere. It was annoying as hell, and I was anxious about seeing Lawrence for the first time post-shooting. Cars flew by Vivian, Elle, and me as we walked from the parking lot to the hospital. I felt like each car was just on it's own emergency journey with zero respect, or thought, towards what we were going through. So, I stared each driver down and tried to look them in their eyes. Whatever.

Elle was carrying her stuffed Simba and Nala dolls, and had to hurry her feet along in order to keep up with Vivian. There were plenty of intersections to get through before we reached Lawrence. At some point, Vivian grabbed Elle by her elbow in an effort to drag Elle up to speed. I'm not quite sure what the rush was. Maybe Vivian just wanted to get the visit over with as quickly as I did, and Elle didn't mind taking her time? Maybe Elle was just as anxious as the rest of us, but had a different way of showing it?

It took forty minutes to make our way through the police officers playing "security," outside my dad's hospital room. When we finally got inside, Lawrence was barely recognizable. I would've thought we were in the wrong room but for the television set being turned on to Comedy Central. Lawrence was wearing one of those white hospital patient gowns with the little blue dots. The whole thing felt sketch.

Lawrence was laid out in the hospital bed hardly conscious. But you could tell he was trying to act all upbeat, you know? He kept feigning a smile, or even a little chuckle, to Elle every so often trying to lighten the mood. But, nothing could distract me from the two chairs sitting at his bedside. The chairs served as an elephant-sized reminder that Lawrence has other families outside of our special little unit, and that they had beaten us to the hospital. I sat down next to Vivian and stewed silently in my powerlessness. The more I stared at Lawrence the more the feeling of guilt overwhelmed me. So, I looked onward to the window.

On the opposite side of Lawrence's bed were a couple of bouquets of pink, white, purple, and yellow flowers. There was also one brown teddy bear and balloons with weights on the bottoms that lined up on the windowsill. The bear was identical to Elle's Mr. Teddy Bear, who had been shot years earlier with the BB-gun. We hadn't seen that bear since Elle left it behind at our old apartment with Lawrence. I think that extra touch of nostalgia made us all a bit more emotional.

At first sight, Elle was scared to go near Lawrence. Instead, she preferred to sit on Vivian's lap. But, once Lawrence recognized we were in his room for real and not just in his morphine-induced dreams, he opened his palm up toward Elle and said, "come here."

"Careful, Elle, move slow, hun," Vivian said.

Elle climbed up to Lawrence's bed with elegance. She was quick to bring her Simba and Nala dolls center stage on Lawrence's upper chest. The dolls have magnets in their noses, so they kiss when brought close enough together. Elle kept pulling the dolls apart and then tritty trotting them back together in an effort to entertain Lawrence.

"Look," the dolls would kiss, "they love each other, Dad." Elle repeated a couple times before Vivian interrupted.

"Let me see it," she said.

Lawrence struggled to scrunch up his tracing-paper-thin gown, and Vivian let him struggle rather than reaching out to help. She kept her arms crossed and stayed seated in the chair with her head tilted to the side as if she were unconcerned and unamused. Vivian didn't have any more time left to give to Lawrence. She was impatient, and angry, but I didn't quite understand why at the time.

Now I do.

Under Lawrence's gown he had been hiding his entirely swollen body. Lawrence had been shot three times: one bullet barely missed his spine and exploded in his belly, another bullet went straight through his bottom lower hip, and the third bullet went in Lawrence's right shoulder and exploded halfway in his chest. The collateral of being "seconds away from dying" was clear. There was a large strip of oozing gauze stretching from the top of his abdomen to down below his belly button. The gnarly looking stitches wrapped around his hip *and* arched around his shoulder blade. The tubes and machines were everywhere and a high-pitched "beep" sound went off every few seconds. Elle sat between Lawrence's legs near his calves next to Jasper, while Mom and I collectively examined Lawrence's body and all of the attached equipment.

"It's alright, Viv," Lawrence struggled to get out, "I can handle her." Elle played pretend with her lions on Lawrence's torso. At first she was imagining they were "a happy family going somewhere to-gether," but then she turned. Elle pretended Simba got hurt and Nala was sad about it.

"She's crying, Daddy," Elle updated, "she's scared about the daddy lion being hurt so we have to take care of her, ok?" Elle didn't look up or ask for a real response. It was a rhetorical question with deep emotional value. Elle continued playing with her stuffed animals, allowing them to prance about as Lawrence started professing his sorrows.

"Your Daddy has a lot of thoughts running through his mind right now, Honey. A lot of memories are flooding me right now," he started crying, "and I'm just so sorry, Elle."

He evolved to weeping, "Daddy doesn't want you to be sad for me, E. He wants you to be happy, be full of joy, be lovely, be beautiful, be gracious. Be as awesome and as bold as you have always been. You're a blessing, Elle, and God will always bless you and the rest of this family."

Vivian sat down in one of the family chairs next to Lawrence's bedside. I just hugged the wall and tried to blend in like a chameleon. Elle was playing with her Lion King dolls, pretending she didn't understand what was happening and couldn't hear Lawrence. Loyal ol' Jazzy boy stayed calm and neutral at the foot of the bed.

"I promise to do better next year if God allows me to live until then. I'm just glad you're OK after all of this, E. You're so special to me, and everyone else in the family too. You're my flower, Babygirl, and I could not have wished for anything better. I don't know why I keep on messing up like this. Your Daddy just has a lot of things to work on, you know?"

Vivian reached out to Lawrence and grabbed his hand, interlocking with every one of his fingers. But, she wouldn't make eye contact. She seemed to squeeze him, pat the top palm of his hand, and hold on again as if they were to engage in a thumb war. Lawrence looked over to Vivian, who was crying.

"You never doubted me, Viv. Look at where we started and where we are now. I'm so proud of you, and I just want you to know how precious these girls are, and this life is to me."

"I know," Vivian gifted.

"You've come a long way and I just want you to know how proud of you I am. I couldn't be more proud, Viv. Thank you for the great family we have. You're a superhero."

"I know," Vivian responded.

"I love you so much," Lawrence continued.

"I know," Vivian smiled and looked at Lawrence, "I love you too, L."

"God has blessed us with so much, Vivian. So much. Just look." Lawrence said as Vivian slowly slid her hand out from his grip.

"I hope you get to have a great Summer, Olivia," He said without looking at me and while wiping his tears. "I'm sorry I haven't been there for you when you needed me," he said, "I haven't been absent, I've just been busy; and money has been tight." Tears continued falling down his John Q-like face, and Lawrence didn't fight it - fighting would've been futile.

The room was pretty much silent, but I think Elle was sorta playing to herself. Lawrence kept his focus on her. Elle, his babygirl, was always a safe place to confide in. Vivian had stopped making eye contact, crying into the hospital bed sheets in front of her. Jasper was asleep and Elle was "absent," so to speak. I tried sinking into the wall, but Lawrence kept confessing.

"I just need to get right with God again, girls. Then everything will get better. I'll get clean again. I know I can get clean again." He took a deep inhale, almost like he was counting to ten - just like you always tell me to.

"Here, Daddy," Elle said right before we left, "I'm leaving Simba here for you." She tucked one of the little lion dolls into the armpit of Lawrence, who was completely knocked out on the morphine by this point.

The whole scene was completely unreal. I'm still pretty much in shock and trying to crystallize what happened. Mostly I'm trying to figure out how I feel now that we're all clear on the fact that he's going to survive. I think I feel really irritated, but I don't understand why.

| 38 |

Chapter Thirty-Eight

May 8th, 2008

On Tuesday I went to Hollywood Video Store with Vivian. We were there to rent our weekly batch of VHSs. She picked out an Idris Elba movie, per usual, called *Daddy's Little Girls*. We weren't even half-way home when Vivian started breaking down in the car. The picture on the DVD box had kicked her over the edge. She started crying, "I'm so mad at your damned Dad, Olivia! "

I asked her what happened, and she responded with some out of this world bullshit.

"I told your dad about your behavior lately. I wanted him to give me some advice about how I should bring it up and talk to you about the whole thing. But, instead he just started blaming me and saying that I was a bad mom. He said that it was my fault you've been acting out." Vivian continued crying while driving.

"I'm so sorry, but I think I want to turn around and return this damn video. I'm just so mad at your dad, I can't watch something like this right now. Is that OK?"

"Totally fine, Mom. Don't even trip." I patted her on the back and stuffed the rage boiling beneath me.

When we got home, I went to my room and called Justin on the phone - just for old time's sake. We hadn't talked one on one in a long time, but Justin will always be my special friend. Somewhere along the sidelines we implicitly took a vow to be there for each other through thick and thin. So, we can vent to each other no matter how long we go without talking.

On Tuesday I needed him more than ever. I called him up and started venting about my childhood, and Lawrence. I was telling him about the shooting, which, at this point, was pretty much top secret news nobody else knew about. I was describing to Justin how Lawrence's shooting had gone down.

"So, I guess he was out super late at night trying to find his way back to his car. Then, he said outta nowhere some dude stopped him and started questioning him."

"No way," Justin responded.

"Yeah, forreal. He started questioning my Dad and thought he was someone who he wasn't. My dad could tell that the guy was sorta sketch, so he turned the opposite direction, and started running as fast as he could. But, I guess the guy with the gun still had a clear shot, so-"

Vivian popped her head in my bedroom, interrupting our conversation, "what are you talking about?" she asked.

"Nothing, Mom. What's up?"

"Really? You're talking about nothing?" I just looked at Vivian blankly because I didn't know what to say. Plus, I knew Justin could hear everything, "are you sure you're not talking about your dad getting shot? I can hear you down the hall."

She was half in the doorway, half out, and had clearly been eavesdropping, "well, that's not what happened you know?" Vivian was leaning in through the doorway.

"Yes it is." I looked as annoyed as I possibly could and challenged her, "what happened then?"

"Olivia, come on." Vivian smirked and nodded her hair towards me, "he was on Catfish corner at three o'clock in the morning. What do you think he was doing?"

I shrugged, and shook my head "no," indicating that I had no idea what she was trying to imply.

"He was buying drugs!" Vivian shook her head in return, rolled her eyes, and then closed the door - leaving me to spiral all on my own.

"Hey, I gotta go, Justin," I said, hanging up before he could respond.

All this time I was going around thinking Lawrence was shot for the pure truth that he's a Black man. I actually felt bad for him and defended him against Vivian like a naive little child. When, in fact, he was shot while buying drugs - just like any other stereotypical "nigga."

I immediately dialed Lawrence's number without even thinking. He answered casually after about three or four rings and said, "hey, Olivia, I'm just catching up with your oldest brother right now. What's up?"

With all the confidence he'd taught me to feign, I said, "I want to say some tough things to you right now, but I don't want to hear how you're going to react. So, I'm gonna call back and leave you a voice message - OK?"

He waited on the line silently for a minute to see if I had anything left. I said nothing so he continued, "well, I don't know why you're acting like you got some big ol' secret, Olivia."

"But, if you think you wanna go ahead and be big and bad then imma let you go ahead and say what you wanna say, OK? Go ahead and get it all off your little chest, 'iight?"

I could tell by Lawrence's tone that he was challenging me to take the bait. To his surprise, though, I was finally ready for that type of heat.

"Cool, thanks." I said flatly before hanging up. I called Lawrence back immediately, and he let the phone ring through to his voicemail like he said he would.

"This is Lawrence," his voicemail recording repeated back to me, "leave me a message." I could tell Lawrence was pissed off when he had recorded the voice memo, and it's rhetorical impact was hitting just as intended. I was extra intimidated to leave the message. But, I forged forward in my convictions regardless. Like, Tia and Tamera Mowry telling Roger to 'go home,' I was going to do this, you know?

"Aye, Lawrence," I said. It was the first time I had the courage to call Lawrence by his first name to his face over voicemail. "It's your daughter, Olivia," I continued, as if he didn't already know, "and I just wanna leave you a message so you can hear me saying on playback that you're a fucking fraud."

I think the gulp that I took was audible, but I continued on anyway. "I know that you were shot while trying to buy drugs, not because of some bullshit mistaken identity story like you've been telling me for years. You were shot trying to buy drugs. You probably didn't pay the guy enough, like a typical fucking crack addict, and your drug dealer shot you while you were happily walking away, right?"

I couldn't even believe my words. Even though I knew Lawrence wasn't on the other line to answer me directly, I felt like I was looking right through his soul, and I was shaking.

"Right, well, I just want to let you know that I know how big of a fucking phony you really are and I want nothing to do with you. Ever."

I hadn't confirmed that any of what I was saying would be alright with Vivian, but I was just on one - you know? I couldn't stop. I kept going in on him. "I'm so sick of you always making someone cry, or yell, or scream, or fight. You have absolutely no right to say that Vivian is a shit mother, you know? Like, who do you think you are? You've barely even been fully conscious, let alone present, for over half our lives. Maybe beating people down is your way of trying to handle things, but it's definitely not the way my mother does things. And, it's not the way I want to learn to handle things in my life either."

I was more openly heated towards Lawrence than I had ever seen myself, and I was loving it.

"Also, you want to try to call me out for having the very attitude towards my mother that you taught me to have? Seriously? You really have the audacity to tell me how to act, or treat her, when you're the very person who taught me how to disrespect her in the ways that matter most in the first place? I may get mad, but at least I've never shot at her baby. At least I've never stolen her money, or her faith, or her sleep for no reason."

I started laughing like a whole ass psychopath. I knew I sounded crazy, but also, he sounded fucking crazy too, right? Like, to what degree was he actually planning to assert his fatherness? You know? Was he really thinking he was going to drive over and lend a loving helping hand? Was he seriously trying to help discipline me? It's not as if he's ever been consistent in first fucking place.

"Naw, naw, Daddy-o, That's not how it's about to go-" I continued.

BEEP. Lawrence's answering machine cut me off like I was at the Grammys.

A few minutes later Lawrence started calling me back, he even left me a voicemail in response. But, I didn't listen to it, and I definitely didn't answer any of his calls. So, sayonara, try tomorrow, nice to know ya. You know? I pretty much just left it at that, and we haven't talked since.

IT'S ONLY LOVE THAT GETS YOU THROUGH

| 39 |

Chapter Thirty-Nine

May 15th, 2008

I'm finally sixteen!! Yaddamean?! Ayyye! I *finally* have my license!! Can you imagine how hard it'd be to wait to drive if you'd already been driving since you were four or five years old? Damn I've had to be patient.

But, I did it! I have my license! The law says I'm still not allowed to drive my friends around or anything. You're supposed to wait a year, unless you have a note from your parents and you're driving to, or from, a school-related activity. Something like that. As if I'm actually going to follow that rule. As if *anyone* ever follows it. All it means is that I'll have to lie to Vivian about where I'll be going, what I'll be doing, and who I'll be doing it with. Oh well. At least Laurie, Nikky, Charlotte, and I won't have to walk through to McDonald's anymore! So, that's an improvement.

Want to know what though? I almost didn't get my license! The instructor said I was "speeding practically the whole time," and that I didn't stop long enough at the cross walks. But, beyond those couple of things I didn't get anything else wrong. So, she couldn't fail me.

After my driver's test I dropped Vivian off at work. She made me promise I was going to drive straight back to school. But, John had purposefully played hooky so I could go to his house. So, instead I went straight to John's. I didn't stay there for too long. Especially since Peter was there playing Call of Duty with John when I showed up. I mostly just went there to prove that I passed and to show off that I could drive *myself* around now. I probably only stayed for thirty minutes. The guys were distracted, and John didn't show the appropriate amount of excitement, so I left for school to gloat with *my* friends.

During my drive back to school I rolled all of my windows down and blasted the music. The sun was out, but you could feel the morning in the air even in spite of the hot-day energy floating around. I was singing along to my jams. I had made my way through an acapella solo concert of "Makes Me Wonder," "U + Ur Hand," and "Sexyback" when I noticed the cars on the road going snail speed.

In my zone, and in the midst of the achieving Ludacris' part in "Lovers & Friends," I glanced in my rear view mirror. Then, back to the clear open road of opportunities ahead of me. Then, I did a double take, and looked back up in my rear view mirror again. It took me a minute to process what I was seeing - a triple sized fire truck with the lights blaring. Of course the sirens were having their own little drive-by community concert. But, I didn't even hear those until the truck passed by my driver's side window. I pulled over right before being run down by the emergency truck. I had to stay at the side of the road for a minute just catching my breath and praying my aloofness didn't prolong the emergency.

It's like I turned sixteen, and instead of being able to celebrate, the world wants to teach me a lesson. To teach me to listen to Vivian when I think she's just lecturing about some unrealistic, parent-based safety fears. It's like life is trying to tell me to be humble, or to teach me that I don't actually have my shit together like I think I do.

I swear I hate the whole system. But, oh well. At least I have my license!

Last weekend I had a hella fun time for my birthday - minus the fact that I had to work. On Saturday we all stuffed in John's Buick like it was a clown car, and he took us to the beach. The drive out to the ocean looked wild to try to drive. I guess I hadn't noticed it before, but now all roads look like car arcade fantasies to me. I spent the whole ride looking out the window being semi-sad I wasn't driving, and semi-grateful to have a solid DD like John. Nikky and Charlotte kept screeching at John, trying to get him to stop at one of the flower shops at the side of the road.

"It's her sixteenth birthday, John!" Nikky pressured.

"Yeah," Charlotte encouraged, "come on! You haven't even gotten her a gift yet!"

"Oh shoot," John joked while passing shop, after shop, after shop, "I just missed it! Maybe on the next one!"

I never got flowers, or anything special from John, but my birthday was fun. Even if nothing really happened. At the beach, we all got so drunk that we were fully swimming in the ocean without wet-suits. I guess that's the sort of freedom parents worry about when their kids get their license. But, I swear it was just some harmless fun. We splashed around in the water, ran around on the beach for a few hours, and ate some fat ass sandwiches to sober up before heading back home. It was pretty much just another typical day hanging out together, but at the beach.

John was our designated drunk driver, and he safely carried us back to town. After the beach we went back to the pool at Vivian's apartment complex and swam some more. John and I made out in the hot tub in front of everyone for a bit. And, my sixteenth birthday ended up being an all around great time. I'll be honest though, a soft yellow voice in my head kept me wondering about Lawrence the whole week-end. I haven't heard from him since I told him off over the answering machine last week, which makes me anxious.

Especially since I've been on edge about him relapsing all year. I mean, Lawrence has been "crack clean" for almost ten years, ever since he was shot, but he started missing our "daddy-daughter phone dates" last summer, so I immediately knew something was up. By July, Vivian was reluctantly telling me that Lawrence had stopped calling to check in with her too. We all knew it was sus. There's no way to control or cure an addict - *I know.* But, I still thought he would at least call me for my birthday, ya know?

Every year he calls at dawn and sings a traditional 3-rounds of birthday song renditions: the one from my childhood church, the traditional Stevie Wonder version, and then the one from church again. He also always sends me a card promising that next time he'll visit us in California "for sure," even though he doesn't. But this year he didn't call me to sing. He just sent me another late birthday card that only arrived today.

You want to know what it said? 'Cause I kept it so I could I tell you. He said:

"My Dearest Olivia, always know that your father ALWAYS Loves U. As I marvel at your strength, I can't help but smile, cry, and smile again. I am so proud of you. You're blessed with a drive and determination that is accompanied by the willingness to have compassion for those who do not have the same confidence as you do. You have my respect because I am always challenged to grow with you. Yes, you can be a bit brash, I know all about that. For the life of me, I have 'NO clue' where you got that from. :) Just remember to be careful who you direct all of that energy towards. Others do not know or understand you like your family does. 16 is a very special birthday and I'm sorry I could not be there on your special day, but I will try next year. As you journey on to the next phase of life I will continue to ask God to bless you and protect you, and to guide your footsteps. Many individuals have been praying for you and this family and shall continue to. I know I speak for all of our family, present and absent, when I say we love you and that you make us very proud of you Olivia. There is only one you, and you are very very precious to me and everyone else! You have not been a little girl for a long time, but you have been

and will always remain my lil baby, the youngest of your clan:
Mom + I. As you continue to develop into a young woman you
remember to always carry yourself with the highest respect,"

That part was underlined a bunch. And, I don't just zone out and talk to John during Ms. Walker's class, the proper grammar would've been "Mom + me." But, anyway, I'll continue reading.

"and you will always be respected. You have such a beauti-
ful, caring, gentle spirit, use it for good and God, and no one
will be able to rob you of your dignity. Learn to be comfortable
with who you are, and know that YOU are always LOVED
and always will be... I hope next year I can be there with you.
Remember Olivia, love is all this family will ever be about.
HAPPY BIRTHDAY MY SWEETS! God Bless you Always!
LOVE DAD :)"

But, I don't even care. It's too late. I can move on with my life without him. Of course I miss him, but, he didn't slow my shine up one fucking bit. I had my birthday sex, and I'm going out this weekend for more. Honestly, I just hope he hasn't jumped off the deep end, yaddada? He's come such a long way since the shooting, and I really thought he was done using this time.

On Sunday, I went to church with Elle. Grandma Soul, my grand-Aunts and my Auntie-aunties were there too. But, Lawrence wasn't, and Vivian stopped going after they separated. My Grandma Soul made a big stink of the whole ordeal. She told the Pastor, or some-one close to him, that it was my birthday. So, they called me up in front of everyone and ran through the whole tradition. In our church the tradition is for the birthday person, or persons, to stand on stage with the Pastor, and whatever semblance of a choir that showed up that day. The Pastor and choir would sing, and you, the birthday person, would stand on stage holding a basket. The band would kick up, and usher boys stalked the outside of the aisles also holding satin-lined baskets.

The congregation sang the birthday song. "Happy birthday to you, oh happy birthday to you!" folks sang while throwing their cash into my baskets spread throughout the room. "May you find Jesus near every day of the year! Happy birthday to you, oh happy birthday to you! And the best year you've ever had!"

It was great, but I don't want to talk about it. I'm sick and tired of worrying about him. It's time I worry about myself -- even though there's nothing to really worry about.

I'm actually pretty excited for this weekend. I'm supposed to go to Laurie's house to party with her, Nikky, Charlotte, and the rest of the guys. John has been acting pretty bipolar lately, but maybe it's because he got this really ugly haircut. I think I'm starting to get used to it now though. I also think I've realized that I like John better when he's high, but I don't know. Maybe I just like *myself* better when I'm high? Either way, I can't believe I'm actually sixteen!!

| 40 |

Chapter Forty

May 22nd, 2008

My birthday weekend actually turned out to be pretty funked up. But, I'm still processing everything, so I'm still not 100% sure about what all actually went down. I'll just break it down from the beginning of the weekend, if you don't mind?

The weekend "officially" started on Saturday night. Of course we all partied together on Friday night too, but that's just routine at this point. Everyone except for John was there, because he "had other business to attend to," but it was a blast and a half anyway. Then, on Saturday, Laurie and Nikky woke me up early with a bunch of texts and told me to get ready. They ended up taking me out to a fancy little brunch. It made me feel hella special. Coincidentally, Laurie's parents were out of town, so over brunch she and Nikky filled me in on their plan for the night.

"We're throwing you a super VIP house party!!!" They both celebrated after our servers sang Happy Birthday.

"Oh, word?" I said as if Nikky hadn't already spoiled the surprise on my actual birthday at the beach when we were all drunk.

"Yeah," Laurie exclaimed, "it'll only be us and the guys. So, it's just a small kick back, but we're about to get lit!"

After brunch, we went straight to Laurie's house to start getting ready for the party. I didn't bring any extra clothes to change into because I didn't know if we were actually having a party or not. Laurie offered me "literally anything" of hers that I wanted to wear, but I decided to just show up as myself. I washed my face and applied a new face of makeup, but wore the same jean overalls and white tunic shirt I picked out to wear to brunch. I looked like a Black Jamie Sullivan from *A Walk to Remember*, which probably would've made Lawrence proud.

Any other partygoer could've easily mistaken that Nikky was the birthday girl. She had packed a bag of pretty party-appropriate clothes. When Nikky stepped out of the bathroom she was wearing a crop top and some dark purple sequin high-waisted short shorts. Laurie wore full-length jeans with me, and didn't overdo it with makeup either.

"Great! There's some thick, gooey pomegranate juice all over my panties," Laurie shouted at us from the bathroom, "I can't get laid tonight!"

Nikky and I consoled her heavily before returning to our frufing and selfies. Charlotte was first to come meet us at Laurie's - she brought Steve and Mark along too. Then, Nikky started texting Miles and the guys. By the time the sun went down the whole gang was there.

Once the guys got to Laurie's parents house we all rushed through the living room and headed straight for the kitchen. We blasted "Too Close," by Next, and "Tootsie Roll," by the 69 Boyz, and took a few rounds of group shots. First, in the name of my birthday, then in the name of Laurie's parents being out of town for the weekend, and then in the name of me again. It didn't take too long for John and I to make our way to Laurie's little brother's room.

John and I rolled around in the bed for a while before losing all of our clothes. For a sixteenth birthday gift to myself I went to get tested for STDs, even though I was already 100% confident I was clean. Outside of John I had only ever been with Justin; and, no way John had anything wrong with him. The doctor at Planned Parenthood gave me some free crazy colored condoms during my appointment which ended up coming in handy. John and I laughed at my stash for a while, then he picked the blue glow in the dark one.

Right when we started having sex, maybe two pumps in, John's mom called him. He couldn't not answer her call or else he may have gotten in trouble. John's parents are all touchy and sensitive ever since the expulsion. So he always tries to answer them.

"Hello?" John answered. "Why am I panting?" he repeated back to his mom while smiling at me, "I'm racing my friends down the block."

He lied so quickly I was impressed. Then he hurried her off the phone, and looked back down at me. I was ready to keep going. But, John had lost his... stamina, if you know what I mean. So, we decided to get dressed and go back out to the party.

When we returned everyone was hammered. John and I took a few more shots in the kitchen to catch up. Everybody was in the living room. Charlotte, Peter, and Nikky were dancing together. Steve was laying on the floor underneath the coffee table beating the bottom of it to the beat. Miles was trying to dance with Laurie, but she was out of rhythm, which complicated things. Justin was taking pictures; and, Mark danced circles around John and me trying to encourage us to get up and dance too. I was still pretty horny, so I straddled John on Laurie's dad's favorite brown leather love chair and sucked on his neck.

"Come on, man, at least get up so we can go get some more booze!" Mark complained, "look at Steve's pathetic bitch ass lying on the floor! He needs an injection of alcohol pronto."

"Don't you dare move," John whispered in my ear. He was as hard as a rock. But our friends had other ideas. John is the only one with a fake ID *and* a driver's license. So, he just looked at me and rolled his eyes. He knew he had to go. But, I waited for him to calm down in his pants a little bit before I stood up and joined the girls and Miles on the dance floor.

"Ugh," John yawned while looking over to me on the dance floor. He telepathically told me that he wanted to do bad things to me, and I gave him a smirk while tilting my head to the side in return. John started shaking his head "no" to me, and then he turned to his newest puppy dog, Mark.

"Ok. Let's go! What are you standing around looking at me for? Come on." John clapped his hands at Mark, "let's go."

Peter, Mark and Steve left with John. But, Miles and Justin stayed with us girls. We danced in the living room until Miles yelled out "SHOTS!" Then, we all rushed to the kitchen and had a few more rounds. Before I knew it I found myself dancing on Laurie's kitchen countertops with her, Nikky, Justin, and Charlotte.

I blinked and we were all laying on Laurie's parents bed looking at the ceiling like it was a sky full of stars. The room was dark, but the Bella Luz nightlight from the hallway provided a familiar little glow. I remember Miles and Laurie were spooning, and he was kissing the back of her neck. I laid between Nikky and Justin, and Charlotte was on the edge. All of our legs were intertwined, and Justin was rubbing my earlobes.

"Women have sensory points that arouse them, remember?" he said, "this is one of them right here. Now, I just have to remember how *you* like it."

I was smiling, even though I was confused about how we had all transitioned there. Just as I was about to get up for some water, the rest of the guys came crashing onto the bed. John laid on top of me and kissed me, then rolled over, blocking Justin.

"Was Olivia just about to hook up with Justin again?!" Mark yelled out, only halfway jokingly to the group. Everyone started bursting out laughing. Then, John grabbed my hand and put it on his lap over his crotch.

"Oh yeah? Did you want me to leave you and Justin alone?" he whispered.

I blinked and opened my eyes to an empty room except for John and me. From there, things progressed quickly. I could barely make out his face, but I remember that I saw he was smiling. I remember saying "shut up" and kissing John, and that the door was closed, but then, all of the sudden everything went black.

When I came to, I was in motion. I remember kissing John but feeling like I was going to be sick. I remember the room was spinning and I felt like I wanted the world to just pause for a second like it did in my middle school D.A.R.E. program. I just wanted to catch my breath. I remember John being on top of me and I remember him kissing me. I remember John taking off his shirt and me telling him to "wait," and that I needed a second to close my eyes, think and rest. I remember him stopping and telling me, "OK 30 second break."

Then, I blink, and the world goes black again. The next thing I remember is waking up the next morning naked and sore with John sleeping beside me in his boxers. I think when I went to sleep he must've just finished for himself, right? Like, that's pretty gross of him, but I don't know. It's not like I wouldn't have let him finish if I had been awake, you know? So, I feel like it's not, like, too *too* horrible, you know?

When we got up in the morning we both sorta just went to join the rest of the group. Laurie was in the kitchen cooking crepes for everybody, and she looked like she had been attacked by a vampire overnight. Miles was sitting on one of the barstools lined up at the counter, patiently, smiling. He was next to Mark and Peter, and they all started snickering when John and I walked in holding hands. They patted John on the back and pounded his fist. I squinted at them for their immaturity, and laid down in the second, smaller living room attached to the dining area with Nikky, Charlotte, and Justin. We laid on the floor with our eyes closed, painfully hung over, until Laurie told us it was time to eat.

After breakfast I signaled to my girlfriends that I needed to talk to them privately. I caught eye contact with each one individually and motioned over to the main living room with my eyes. Laurie told the guys to start doing dishes so we could have a second, and we all met in the main living room - hunched around closely in a circle.

Charlotte spoke first, she was too excited to wait, "so, how was last night?!"

I didn't quite give them the story they expected to hear. I told them I didn't fully remember what had happened but that I woke up naked. They laughed awkwardly. Charlotte picked up the talking stick first, "it sounds like you had a pretty good time then!" Laurie didn't say anything, she just looked at me, and reached out her hand and squeezed my knee. Nikky saw this and quickly jumped in saying, "bitch, you better go get back on that god't damn horse! You better give it another go!" We all sorta laughed, and Charlotte cheered me on saying, "*yes*! Yes!"

So, I did.

I went back to the kitchen and gave John a hug. I pressed up against him as closely as I could and whispered, "meet me in the bedroom," like I was an adult. In the bedroom I tried to have sex with John, but to my surprise, and confusion, neither of us were able to perform. He was hard for a while, but I wasn't getting wet for some reason. Obviously, John noticed, and it made him self-conscious or something, so he lost his boner altogether.

We didn't really talk about it. I tried to give him a handjob, but he just shook his head and said, "no, no. This isn't going to work for me," and that was that.

We both got dressed and went back out to the kitchen - where the idiot guys responded the exact same way they had earlier, greeting John with high fives and neanderthal-like displays of toxic masculinity.

It was just another party with more bullshit.

Chapter Forty-One

May 29th, 2008

I'm still mad at Vivian, but now for something new. It turns out my health & wellness teacher, Mr. McMullen, had the actual audacity to email Vivian and tell her I was "misbehaving" in his class.

When Vivian confronted me on Sunday, I acted all bold and tried to act like Mr. McMullen was senile. "I don't even know what you're talking about," I shouted at Vivian, "everybody talks in that class! It's typical teenage behavior!"

I incorrectly felt self-righteous. Vivian had been being hella strict all weekend and I had no idea why. So, by the time she decided to finally confront me on Sunday, I was already at my peak annoyance. Plus, she decided to confront me when I was peeling off my acrylic nails - which already hurts like a bitch and frustrates the hell out of me. So, if you ask me, Vivian really just picked the absolute worst time in the world to confront me, but... hey. I'm not allowed to say anything about that because I'm a kid, right?

"He said you've been smoking weed in his class, not just talking while he's trying to give some lame ass lecture, Olivia. Ms. Walker was the one who complained you were talking too much in class! She emailed me and we already fought about that earlier this year, do you remember? Smoking weed IN CLASS?!" Her eyes were as wide as

Lawrence's, "what the hell is going on with you? This is *not* just 'typical teenage behavior.'" Vivian said, hip popped out to the side and all.

I stood there like a dumbass and sorta just scratched my head while waiting for an excuse to manifest. "Mom, you don't even know what the fuck you're talking about, OK?"

Vivian lifted her chin up towards me signaling her superiority, "oh really?" I could tell she wasn't buying, but I continued.

"Yeah! Really! I'm like the only Black kid in class and Mr. McMullen only focuses on me because I stand out. He's confusing me with some of the other students because he's a racist, Mom!"

"Oh, he's a racist, Olivia?" I could tell Vivian was being sarcastic, but I continued to play like I was clueless.

"Yes, Mom. What? You don't believe me? You really think I'd stare you dead in the face and lie to you like that? Really, Mom?" I was staring her in the face lying, but I still couldn't believe my own Mom would think so lowly of me. I looked at her offended, like she was the crazy one in the scenario.

"I don't even know any more, Olivia. You're going to have to talk to your dad about it. Apparently he's the expert on this type of shit, right? He's been telling me you were up to no good for a while now, and he wants to have a talk with you."

Turns out Vivian wasn't even bluffing. She had talked to Lawrence long before confronting me, *again*, and they already had an elaborate plan in place, *again*. Vivian confronted me on Sunday, and Lawrence called me after school on Monday trying to initiate a lameass heart-to-heart conversation.

"Olivia, you know even though I was MVP at your age, I still only have one or two friends who are from when I was in middle school and high school, right?"

"No, I didn't know," I sarcastically said. It was obvious that Lawrence hung out with an array of sketchy people. I didn't worry myself by caring about the details. It was also clear he was planning to gloss over my award-winning voicemail, and the fact that we hadn't been speaking.

"Well, it's the truth," Lawrence retorted. "These people you kick it with now aren't your real friends, E. They're your followers. You hear me?" I nodded my head "yes," but only to shorten the same repeated lecture I'd been hearing since I was Elle's age.

"You're a leader, Olivia, and people will always follow along with whatever you say and do. That means you have an extra responsibility. Sometimes being a leader means going against the grain, going against what all your little friends think is cool, and that's alright. Being a leader means you're going to be lonely a lot of the time, but that's part of it." I grunted in acknowledgement so he could continue. "So, you have to be strong enough to stick to your convictions, walk with God, and know you're too good to be wasting your time with any sort of drugs or little wanna-be thugs who don't know what they're talking about."

I didn't say anything. Before the silence became deafening, Lawrence demanded confirmation his impact was on point as projected, "right?"

"Right," I responded.

"Your mother's been telling me that you've been messing up at school, talking back to her, and, basically, damn near losing your fuckin' mind like you don't have no sense. She says you've been acting disrespectful and yelling at her? Is that true?!"

I didn't answer.

"You hearin' me, girl?!"

"Yeah, I hear you, Sir."

"Oh, 'yeah?!'" Lawrence sounded bewildered, but I didn't pay it any mind. It's not like his raised voice bothers me any more. Plus, what is he going to do from Washington? I'm in California!

"Yes, sir," I said in a less "smart" tone of voice.

"Yeah, that's what I thought," he started calming down.

We hung up after a few more hours of Lawrence lecturing me. He spoke in his most authoritative tone and repeated key points multiple times. Then, eventually, he naturally shifted from what it means to be a leader to what it means to be Black, per usual. It's like he still doesn't think I know that to be Black means to exist in the world like a deer in headlights. As Lawrence puts it, to be Black "means I can't run around acting a fool like the rest of my little friends."

It's always the same hypocritical lecture. I'm not sure if that was the deep talk Vivian actually had in mind, but it was all Lawrence was capable of, so I took it at face value.

On a separate, but related, note I ended things with John this week. I'm pretty sure he was cheating on me, and I always promised myself I wouldn't turn into my parents, so I had to give him the axe. Last week was the final straw. I caught John driving with his ex, Susie. Of course he made up some lame ass excuse about why they were hanging out, but it is totally obvious that they're fucking, you know?

Here's what happened. I was driving Nikky home when we coincidentally pulled up next to John and Peter at the stoplight. Susie was sitting in the back seat bopping along to whatever lame ass stereo station they were listening to. John and Peter's faces just about fell off, but Susie was still oblivious. She actually started smiling and waving at us.

I was fucking frozen with some phony halfjerked smile slapped across on my face. But, Nikky totally covered for me - she was acting like nothing was wrong even though she knew perfectly well what was going down. We sat there, awkwardly, until the intensity of our tension turned the light green. Then, John sped off like it was a race that he knew he'd win.

Nikky pulled out her cell phone, while I silently processed what had just gone down, and she called Charlotte.

"Bitch, we had an emergency change of plans and we're on our way to your house right *now*. Get ready to meet us downstairs."

Nikky hung up on Charlotte before Charlotte could respond, and then looked at me.

"Are you OK? You're going to be OK. Don't worry. We've got you," Nikky confirmed. Then, she unplugged my iPod that was playing music through the car stereo and replaced it with hers.

Nikky played, no, blasted, "Shake it Off," by Mariah Carey, until we got to Charlotte's house. She switched between singing along to the song and cursing John's entire existence for the rest of the ride. I sang along sorta numbly. We parked outside of Charlotte's house, and harassed her with calls and texts until she came downstairs. Mark tried to come outside and talk shit to us, but Charlotte made him bug off.

"You're not invited! Get out of here, Mark!" Charlotte pulled him off the car by the neckline of his royal blue tall tee, and then hopped into the back seat.

We drove around the block, just to be sure we were completely alone, and then parked on the side of the street. When I parked, Charlotte flipped from cozy to up right and center manspreading the space between the two seats. Nikky turned around and started telling Charlotte what had just gone down with John at the stoplight. Charlotte switched her eye contact back and forth between Nikky and me, even though I wasn't speaking, and said "oh *hell no*," at all the appropriate moments. Then, she finally broke out with a word.

"John doesn't deserve a fucking single second more of your time, Olivia." Charlotte, like Nikky, spoke ferociously out of defensiveness. Men don't realize that when they betray one woman they betray all the other women in her life. My girls take my pain personally. Nikky and I nodded along to Charlotte.

"Say that shit, Charlotte," Nikky said while motioning her hand up in the air to add additional hype. They were both working overtime to gas me up with a full tank.

"No, I'm for real," Charlotte continued, "I know Erik has an axe buried deep inside his closet somewhere." Erik is Charlotte's guardian who takes care of her and Mark. Charlotte pointed backwards with her thumb towards her house.

"We could go get that shit *right* now."

We all started laughing, and I declined the offer.

"It's cool, girl, really. I'm good."

"Hell no. Let's go get that fucking axe, girl," Charlotte said with a straight ass *Set It Off*-ass face.

"We'll chop them the fuck up, and show them who they *don't* want to fuck with," Charlotte continued rallying. Nikky was right behind her, "yes, sis!" Of course, I was the only hesitant one. Laurie would've been the voice of reason we needed, but she's been grounded since my birthday party.

"I feel like there's a *way* better way to handle this situation," I ventured with a smile.

"Really? What is it?" Nikky challenged, as if Charlotte had been seriously suggesting we go take an axe to John and Susie's necks. Nikky was abnormally activated.

"I don't know, I could just end it like a normal person, right? Like, I don't have to go to 100% just because I caught him hanging out with his ex."

Nikky and Charlotte looked at me blankly. Then, they turned to each other and exchanged nonverbal words back and forth. My eyes bounced between the two of them while I tried to decode their convo. But, to be honest, I was in too much of a state of shock to keep up.

"He doesn't deserve to go on fucking with Susie like it doesn't even matter!" Nikky finally shouted up to the ceiling.

"You right," Charlotte added, bowing her head down in an attempt to calm Nikky down.

Nikky was obviously displacing her feelings about her own infamously unfaithful boyfriend onto my situationship. But, somehow I was able to steer them to an alternative resolution. One that didn't involve ruining my entire life in the process, no less. I convinced Nikky and Charlotte to let me end things with John on my own terms, and, by God's grace, they agreed. Nikky even finally agreed to let me craft and send the text message in my own time and in private. Not that it ended up being a big deal or anything.

The next day John didn't say a word about my text but he was acting like a complete jerk when he drove me home from school. I think he was trying to act extra cool because Peter was with us. Peter was sitting in the passenger seat like a real fucking gentleman.

But, little did John know, Peter really *is* a real fucking gentleman. On the way home we stopped to get gas. John stood outside the car, staring at random older women, waiting for the gas to fill with a cocky little look on his face. As soon as he was obviously distracted, Peter turned around to me sitting in the same bitch seat Susie was in the day before, and started confessing.

"So, how are you and John doing?" he asked as if he didn't already know.

"I think we're good," I said, trying to sound neutral.

"Please don't tell him I told you this, but John has been telling all the guys that you were really bad in bed last weekend."

"He *what?*" I was shooketh.

"Yeah, he said you were laid out like a starfish and that you wouldn't move."

Peter turned back to face front as John pulled the tip of the nozzle out. "I'm sorry," Peter said softly.

The rest of the car ride home was normal on the surface. But, inside me a storm was brewing. Everything had changed. I had been in denial about John, but Peter confirmed what I already knew. Now the wait at each stoplight felt like an eternity. My dirty insides felt like they were about to come up all over John's precious back seats. All at once I was realizing the reason your parents always tell you to wait before having sex isn't because they hate you. It's because they already know once you have sex with someone you can't turn back. I know I've said this before, but it's really true.

John walked me to my door, which wasn't the normal flow of things. I think he was trying to get out of the dog house or something? He probably just knew it was time to end it, to be honest. The whole walk to my door all I could think about was Peter. The idea of him sitting in the car, with the radio playing on "scan," felt creepy. Did he really expect me not to say anything? Not to defend myself? Not to acknowledge what my fuck buddy non-boyfriend was saying about me publicly?

Why do "nice guys" sit back, befriend, and normalize all the shitty things boys like John do? Are these really the "nice guys" of our wet dreams? 'Cause I'll be honest, in my opinion, this is how the patriarchy continues. A gang of "nice guys" telling their female friends to stay silent and to not tell anyone just ain't it for me.

Realizing I had become "one of those girls" the guys talk about "in the locker room" gave me strength to dump John like the fucking "Bad Habit" he is. It gave me the strength to give John, and Peter, and the rest of them a real story to talk about.

"I think we should end things," I told John after he hugged me goodbye.

John's face didn't change or react. He just looked through me and said, "yeah, I agree."

And that was that.

12

THUGLIFE

| 42 |

Chapter Forty-Two

June 5th, 2008

Turns out that whole thing I said about ending it with John "like a normal person" was totally overrated. It turns out I'm a person who perfectly expresses her imperfect emotions. It turns out I'm just like every other recovering teenage type-a personality.

I snuck out, and took Vivian's car with me. My first stop was picking up Laurie now that she's finally off punishment, Charlotte and Nikky were next. We had already been texting about it, so they came dressed ready to complete a mission. They were armed with masks and black gloves to conceal their identity. I had the supplies.

Honestly, the masks were way more for fun than they were to actually conceal our identity. I mean, of course it was us. And, we didn't give a fuck if John caught us. I even sort of hoped he did just so he could see the amount of purehearted fun we had at his expense. The masks just added intensity.

We drove around singing along to the music until the night turned back to black. Then we went to John's house to stake out a place where we could wait and watch to see his reaction when he got home.

When John finally pulled up he was with his ex, Susie, and Peter, his sidekick. Me and all my girls jumped out of the car with a roar. Nikky screamed out, "THIS IS FOR SPARTA," and soon we all started yelling, "WAR" and "ATTACK!" We charged John, Susie, and Peter with baseball bats in hand like we were child savages from *Lord of The Flies*. Charlotte was the only one without a bat. Instead, she used her infamous axe - swinging it wildly in the air.

Nikky was first. She wound up her bat and let loose on John, beating him until I got close enough to join in. I kicked John in his nuts until I was sure he'd never breed children, and then Charlotte chopped off his dick to complete the job.

Susie was disgusting. The image of her stupid smiling face in John's back seat was finally gone from my memory. It was replaced with a new image. The image of Susie gushing blood from her nose and her mouth, crying, begging Nikky to not curb stomp her. But Nikky didn't listen. She was too busy shoving all her built up emotions towards her cheating jock boyfriend onto Susie. Nikky went full throttle. She jumped on Susie so hard Susie's four front teeth popped out like Pez candies. Then, Laurie beat on Peter a while longer just for the hell of it.

"I have to make sure he doesn't interfere," Laurie jeered while Peter whimpered to the ether. We must have sounded like a pack of hyenas because a couple of John's neighbors started watching us from their windows. Some of them even stepped outside. They all cheered us on. Even the dogs joined in by barking, and nobody even *thought* about calling the cops. They knew what an asshole John is, so the whole neighborhood encouraged our public service. Folks were happy and celebrating. It was great.

Sike.

Just kidding.

But, seriously, when John, Susie, and Peter pulled up they didn't see us or even notice Vivian's car. We waited a while after they went inside before Nikky called Peter pretending like she wanted to hang out. Really, she was just making sure that we had a good amount of time before anyone would be leaving the house. Once all that was confirmed, we masked up and then dripped out of my car one by one. We stayed low to the ground and snuck over to John's car making as little noise as we could while giggling until we were almost in tears.

Son of a womanizer, he even left his windows down for us a little bit. A gift from God herself.

"I think I can unlock the doors," Nikky fired off.

"Yes, oh my gosh. Do it," Laurie responded.

I was too distracted smashing eggs on the hood of John's car to stop her. Charlotte had the jar of peanut butter open and was smearing handfuls of it around the outside-terior or whatever. I heard Nikky shout, "yes," in a whispered tone, and looked over to see her opening the driver's door, "I'm in!"

"SHH," we collectively snorted at Nikky.

"Sorry," Nikky said normally, "*sorry*," she repeated in a whispered tone. She opened up her personal jar of peanut butter and started mixing it in with the eggs. At this point, Nikky was still just on the sidewalk. Then, to everybody's surprise, she sat down in the driver's seat, pulled down her pants, and started peeing.

"Who else has to go?" she posed to the group, with a shit eating grin on her face.

We acted like we were kids going on a long road trip. One by one, everybody "at least tried," and each of us made a little something-something come out the best we could. Then, we continued to coat John's car in the egg and peanut butter mix Nikky invented. To complete the job, Laurie pulled out the Costco sized plastic wrap and spun it around the car in as many creative directions she could think of. By the end, we were all involved - handing off the plastic wrap like it was a relay talking stick. We were dancing, tugging, and pulling it as tight as we collectively could.

Together, we made an art car out of John's White pussywagon Buick.

It was fucking beautiful.

| 43 |

Chapter Forty-Three

June 12th, 2008

School is officially over and I don't want to kick it with anyone any more. Decorating John's car was definitely a Tyler Durden-esq highlight of my life. But, now that that's all over, I don't want any part of the outside world.

Especially with my relentless ass "friends" who won't take the hint. Nikky, Laurie, and Charlotte keep calling me, wanting me to come hang out. Miles keeps showing up uninvited at random times like he used to, and I have to act like I'm not home. Which, I guess is actually pretty easy because I've been keeping all the blinds closed anyway. Emotionally, everything is red - a dark, dim, angsty red. I don't know what it is exactly. All I know is that I'm not feeling *it* lately, and there seems to be nothing in the universe to pull me out of the funk.

The adults singing erroneously at the barbeque and the kids playing in the pool feel like too much work. I'm just too overwhelmed by their incessant happiness. I've been alone vegging out at home by myself so far this summer, and, to be honest, even that feels like too much work. It's like the band in *Titanic* is following me around all the time.

So, I'm drinking my way through the golden colored tequila hidden above the stove to help out my mood. If Vivian notices the missing alcohol during her night cap, then she doesn't say anything about it. She still puts the liquor in the house in the same two places: under the sink and above the stovetop. I've only been sick from drinking once or twice, and both times were when she was at work, and I made it to the toilet in time. So, she never knew. Usually I just pass out in my bed and sleep it off, hoping that when I wake up I'll feel better.

But, I don't; and, Vivian doesn't notice.

You know who does notice me though? Elle. She'll stand in the doorway while I'm drinking in the kitchen and just look at me, or she'll purposely bounce on the end of my bed when I'm half asleep and still sipping. She goes on and on talking about her day and taunting me to address her as if I'm not busy and unavailable to her. It's annoying, creepy, and strangely comforting. But, I love Elle, she gets me the best. Before I know it, we're tripping down memory lane together.

Then, the more the room starts to spin, the more she dips. She disappears, and she's gone, and I can't find her. Like when I'm out with my friends, I miss Elle. I feel alone without her.

Anyway, next year I'm going to a different school. So, I'll be able to meet new friends who understand me better than the misfit crew I grew up with. I won't have to avoid John any more. I won't *ever* have to talk about what happened at my birthday party again, or answer Nikky's questions about why I'm "being so emo." I won't have to see Justin and Steve in the halls and pretend nothing's changed. I won't have to avoid eye contact with Laurie and Miles, or nearly jump out of my skin when Mark sneaks up on me. Next year I can have a fresh start and refocus back on school and my future. Whatever that holds. Next year will be a new school and better for sure, for sure.

Less nightmarish.

Like last night. I was drunk in my room again, and Elle was there. She kept going on and on telling me yet another fucked up story about Lawrence. Her stories are always about Lawrence. Mine too, huh? At first I was venting about Lawrence, "always remember how fucked up he was to you, Elle, and no matter how jolly he might've seemed, how totally distant he *actually* was," I reminded her.

Elle's been all about Lawrence since I stopped talking to him last summer, and it's so sickening. I've been trying to forget him, and all she does is bring him up all the time. So, last night I had to remind her of the past. "He caused you so much pain and insecurity, Elle! Come on!"

"I know, Ollie," Elle unresolvingly responded, "but nobody can take his place."

"Yeah? Well that sounds absolutely miserable, Ellesha! Think about your first example of how a 'man' is supposed to act. What type of example did he set? Huh?" I paused and waited for Elle to respond, but she wouldn't. She just kept playing with the BB-gun hole in her Mr. Teddy Bear and kicking her feet off the side of my bed. I continued, "I mean, seriously! Did Lawrence teach you what it means to feel safe? Or how to be loved? Or what it feels like to feel protected? Or how to take care of yourself? No! He was the first person to hypersexualize you, Elle. He was the first one to objectify you. He taught you how to hate yourself. Don't pretend you don't remember!"

"We're not in the 90s any more, Olivia," Elle said, almost too mature for her age, "deep down you know he's a good person."

"That's my point! No he's not," I said, not letting her off the hook.

I was just so mad she couldn't see the connection to how he treated her as a young girl, and what had happened at my birthday party. And, I was mad about it. Raging and furious! Like, how could she really *still* be a Daddy's girl after everything? *Everything*! That's not right, right?

Especially now that he's relapsed for the Nth fucking time! If she had learned anything, you would think that she would learn to never love an addict because they can't love you back. Silly girl, tricks are for kids.

"When has he ever had your back? What about all those times he rambled on about how you can't trust anyone? How many girl-friends of his have you met? Do you remember all the names, Ms.

Rememberer? All those disgusting times he made you rehearse giving hugs to random hypothetical men? All those times he spoke disrespectfully about women? All those times he told you you looked like a sex worker in your favorite clothes?"

"He does that 'cause he's sick, like you. He's hurt, like you. But, if there's good in him, then it's in me and you too."

"He's literally been lecturing us since as far back as you can remember! He's criticized your physical appearance, he's yelled at you for not being what he wanted, he slut-shamed you since before you were even out of diapers, Elle. Do you know what 'slut-shaming' is? Of course not! You were a child!!"

At that point, I sat up out of bed and we had a 50-second stare off before I continued - because sometimes enough is just enough, yaddamean?

"I know you remember what I'm talking about, Elle! That wasn't the solid example of a father that you needed!" I'll be honest I was screaming by this point, "It wasn't! And now look what's happened! Look at who you'll turn into! Aren't you upset? How aren't you enraged? Someone has to be at fault. If you're not holding Lawrence accountable for fucking you up like this, if you're not blaming him, then I don't know who else is left!"

Elle stared at me until I met her eyes, then started speaking, "now who's lying about what they remember, 'Ms. Rememberer'? You don't remember what happened to Lawrence to make him act the way he is? " Elle squinted her eyes, "I *know* you remember, Olivia. I still remember what he told us, so how could *you* forget?"

She proceeded to paint the picture he had painted for us years before. She sounded just like him as she continued to defend him.

"He told us the whole story that one time when he woke us up in the middle of the night. It was around the same time that he stole from Vivian's purse, and you remember that don't you? Let's remember together. Come on. I'll help you. He had been gone all day, and he had missed dinner, but everything was calm and cool when Vivian woke us up - you remember don't you? The only lights on in the apartment were the ones from the fish tank and the oven. Vivian made everyone hot chocolates, Jasper chilled out on the linoleum kitchen floor, and Lawrence held us up to the fish tank so you could feed the oversized Jack Dempseys. Remember? Then, we all gathered at the yellow kids table with royal blue legs, and Lawrence told us why he is the way he is.

"Remember? He said, 'your mother and I have been talking about this all week, and your Daddy agrees. I want to talk to you. You ought to know why I'm always so honest with you about the world, E. Your mother says the way I talk to you sounds scary sometimes since you're so little. Even though we have a close relationship, and I've never heard you say to me that I'm scary. So, I guess I'll just have to take her word on that. But, you know your Daddy wouldn't lie to you, right? No lying!'

"You said 'duh' while bouncing on his knees and looking at Vivian, who smiled and rolled her eyes - *remember all that?* And then he said, 'right. So, I need you to listen to me when I'm telling you how to carry yourself because I know what I'm talking about. When your Daddy was a little boy he was hurt by someone very close to him, Ellesha. I was just about your age, and nobody believed me when I tried to tell them because it was someone so close.'

"You asked, 'what happened, Daddy?'

'It was my uncle, Ellesha. He molested me. We were at a family gathering at your Grandmother's house. It was one of those sun shining days after church when everyone heads over to your Grandma Soul's house to kick back, play cards, and eat. Your aunties were cooking in the kitchen like they normally do, and most of the men were watching football in the living room. My uncle was a big, old, loud guy, and he wasn't even my real uncle. He was actually dating your Grandma Soul and we just called him 'Uncle' because we knew he wasn't our real dad. Well, anyway, 'Uncle' called me into your grandma's room, and had me go over to their bed to show me a 'gift' he bought her. But, then he sat me on his lap and started rubbing on me. He told me to touch him and asked me if I wanted a lollipop, but I didn't know what that meant when I was your age, Ellesha. Your Daddy didn't know any better. Then, when I finally got out of their bedroom, I went straight up to your Grandma Soul and the Aunties in the kitchen.'

"You asked for more information, per usual. You said, 'what happened, Daddy? What did they say?'

'I told them exactly what had just happened and what 'Uncle' had said and done. I was so scared! I was sweating and crying. I had wet my pants in the room, but I didn't even notice it. And do you know what your aunts and grandmother said to me at that moment?'

"You shook your head 'no.' And he kept talking, 'they told me to not run wild in the house, and to not talk grown up on grown folk business. They didn't believe me. Your grandmother didn't try to comfort me. She just shooed me out of the kitchen and told me to 'go get cleaned up.' She told me to let her keep cooking, so I did. I told her 'yes, Ma'am' and cried it out by myself in the bathroom upstairs.'

"We all sat at the yellow kids table together and cried. Vivian reached her hands across the table to you and telepathically comforted Lawrence. Jasper rested his head on my lap, and licked Lawrence's damp hands that were wrapped around my knees. You were young but you understood enough to feel betrayed by Grandma Soul. He explained himself to you, 'that's why your Daddy is so harsh on you about how you carry yourself. That's why I taught you how to hug men - so they can't just grab on you. You gotta know that no one can be trusted, because I didn't know that when I was your age, Ellesha. I want you to be prepared and be ready. Question what people say and do if you feel it is wrong. Tell me, talk to me. Remember that I'll always be there for you. I'll always believe you. Even if I have to turn on my own little brother. I don't care. I'll send your Uncle Marlon to jail to protect you, Elle, I don't give a fuck. If anyone ever hurts you, even family, I'll kill them. I'll take care of it. You just tell your Daddy who hurt you, and that'll be that.'

"Mom interrupted, 'Or tell your Mommy,' per usual.

Then Dad continued, 'right, or your Mom. Just tell one of us, or someone who you trust enough to tell one of us, and we'll take it from there. Nobody ever has the right to touch you where you don't want them to, or to make you touch them in ways you don't want to, OK? 'No' should always be enough. And if it's not, you remember that it's never your fault, alright? Trust your gut. Have a plan. And remember to tell someone. I don't want you to hurt like your Daddy is right now, OK? So always tell someone. We'll always believe you.'

"Remember?!" Elle crossed her arms across her chest like she was the boss.

She spoke slowly and with intention. "I know you remember the devastating demons Lawrence was fighting when you were my age, Olivia. So, what's your issue? What are you doing? What darkness are you trying to drink down?"

I laid back on my bed, and tried to forget what Elle was telling me. When I closed my eyes, Elle left, and I haven't seen her ever since.

| 44 |

Chapter Forty-Four

June 19th, 2008

Well. Here's what it is. It's that the types of things you want me to come in here and talk about are the exact types of things I'd never even write down in my own diary. Therapy isn't for everyone; and, I think we can both agree that I've been a particularly difficult patient to work with, right? I told you things never add up in my life.

Especially when I speak about myself in the third person.

Obviously my childhood was a total shitcident that I'd do anything to forget. That's why I'm here. The nights full of arguments, and the times Lawrence had me help him steal money from Vivian to feed his drug habit - sure, I would love to forget those memories. But, when Lawrence relapsed last summer it sort of brought up all this old stuff and I can't shake it. I'd be running the streets with my friends and get hit with a flood of fucked up memories I had been trying to forget. Memories I didn't know how to process without Elle.

Or, I mean, without me.

I think it honestly started when I was five years old. One day out of nowhere, Lawrence came home with a newborn baby in his arms. Even back then I was mature enough to understand that the baby wasn't my mom's. It was the baby of a woman who I barely even knew, if at all. I wasn't sure who the "Mom" was, I just knew Vivian wasn't part of that picture. I wouldn't have been so sad about it all if it meant I was *really* getting a "new baby sister," in the *Family Matters* type of way Lawrence tried to pitch. But, that wasn't what was about to happen, yaddamean?

Having a baby with a different woman meant starting a new branch. More than that, it was going to mean more fights at home, more time apart, more nights of Vivian crying alone, et cetera. Having a baby with a different woman meant hang up calls from private numbers, jealousy, competition, and shady tequila-induced voicemails from both sides of the aisle. At 5 years old I knew all of this without words because I was once the surprise little sister to Lawrence's other family.

"I never even expected him to stick around," is how Vivian justifies it, "I never expected him to love you so much and to want to be better so badly. I didn't know it would turn out like this."

Blah, blah, blah-blah, blah.

So, I'm the one being judged for making up an alternate ending? Who cares?! Everybody stretches reality to make it more manageable.

Vivian and Lawrence knew I always wanted a sibling; and, sure, a 2.0 version of me would be great. But, in reality, what I *really* needed was different. Little me always needed a bigger me; and vice versa. I prayed for an older sister to distract me on the days Lawrence slept until Vivian came home from work. All the times they fought through the night, I imagined a braver, badder, bossier version of myself who could make Lawrence stop. All the times I helplessly found myself feeling the void, feeling helpless and scared and alone, I wished I had a cool sister to dress up and escape into a fantasy worlds with.

I made my dreams my reality. Not in the romantic way like most people brag about. But, in the "you need to go back to therapy," type of way, as Vivian put it. She encouraged my imaginary friend with so much pride and joy when I was five, six, and seven. When she figured it was "just" a coping mechanism for her separation from Lawrence, and the continued ensuing trauma. Ten years later, her reaction is way different.

Now, ten years later, the imaginary friend is just a lie that's about as old as I am. Parenting a child with post-traumatic stress disorder, schizophrenia, and general mental disillusionment takes compassion and attention. It requires time and an understanding job with flexible hours - something Vivian's never had. Trying to do it alone while still recovering from your own life traumas will make any person turn cold.

Vivian has turned to ice. She knew I was drinking. She knew I'd been barely passing my classes since we moved to California. She knew I hung out with a "mature" group of friends, but she's a hippie who tried to focus on the positive. Mark and Steve may slice the nipples off a statue from her great grandmother while she was at work, but she'll pass it off as "developmentally appropriate" behavior. Plus, they made up for it by spelling out "PLEASE FORGIVE US VIVIAN" in rocks outside our front door, so... What can you do? Get back to work. Nikky may act like Regina George, and Charlotte may smoke a lot of weed, and Laurie may be as free as an underwear model, but "that's feminism, baby!" Miles may... well, really, Miles doesn't do anything wrong, which is why he's the only one supposedly allowed over when no one else is home.

Anyway, Vivian watched me dissolve from disappointed to disconnected after we moved to California. After Lawrence relapsed *again* post-shooting, Vivian was desperate for a different life. As soon as we got settled she made me start therapy. Over the past few years she must've made me go see like twenty different "specialists" or something, just so she didn't have to deal.

Talking to a parade of strangers about what was going on felt like swimming in pins and needles. Remembering the past for what *really* happened made my stomach turn. A type of churning that's hard to stop. I wanted nothing to do with that past, because, honestly, what would I do with it? With all the memories and untold stories I'd been storing up silently? Talk about it to you and answer your questions, and then what? Have to look at more sorry faces like the one you had on your face during the session when I told you about riding on the motorcycle with Lawrence?

Blah. Gross. Can you imagine if we had actually acknowledged back then that it was only me and Jasper? Can you imagine that I was actually alone all along? The whole idea gave me heebie jeebies. No thanks.

So I caught the hint and shut the fuck up about "Elle" until Vivian stopped sending me to shrinks. That break from therapy lasted about as long as her rebound relationship after Lawrence: just two years. Then, when Lawrence relapsed last summer, I decided I could too, and here we are today.

Recalling my old friend, Imagination, was a no-brainer. I decided to be my own best friend again. To not just fantasize about an older sibling, but to actually *be* the bigger, better abled body throughout all the childhood memories interrupting my day-to-day. Elle had evolved too -- just like Benjamin Button. She grew from being my imaginary older sibling, to my not-so-imaginary younger self. Exactly what I needed, per usual.

My intention was to recreate the ethical and magical world the Disney Channel taught me to believe exists.

Want to know the real kicker of it all though?

I still wasn't enough.

I still wasn't able to protect myself. You can never ever rewrite history, huh? Not even when simply retelling these phony ass half realities to you. I couldn't rewrite history so much that "Elle" didn't ever get sick on the plastic wrapped couch of some random dope fiend friend of Lawrence. My memory wouldn't allow me to stop recycling it all. I couldn't stop missing my dad, or stop wanting his approval, or stop idolizing everything about him. There was no way to skip over the shootings, his or mine. Ditto with his relapses, and the memory of being homeless. I couldn't retell "Elle's" story without reviewing the times I went to bed wondering and worrying Lawrence wouldn't ever come back home. I tried to remember the good times, but you know how trauma works itself out in the brain. I couldn't rewrite history, I was only able to repeat it.

Isolating, lying, drinking, smoking, sneaking out, dating someone I barely even knew, living in shame -- these are the traits of someone like Lawrence. Not someone like me. But, the more I continued spiraling this past year, the more I also realized Elle's role in it all. I began to really understand that the more I avoid the truths of my father's addiction, the less I heal my childhood, and the more I become an addict like him.

It's crazy how non-universal my little story full of stereotypes is, isn't it? I'd laugh, but then I'd probably start crying; and I've already done enough of that in here. I probably owe you a whole Costco sized order of tissues by now, huh?

They're "tears of triumph," as you call them.

It was something about the generational trauma which cycled through my sixteenth birthday that made me finally want to give up the lie. My predicted trajectory ricocheted back and slapped me across the face without warning. Since my birthday I've been reflecting, and trying to face things on my own more. I don't have to be afraid anymore because the worst has already happened. Now, I just want to get better.

So, I've decided to stop sitting around questioning "why me," and start figuring out what I'm going to do with my own life, you know? To stop trying to rewrite history, and instead focus on what I want *my* story to be. No more pulled shades. No more relying on a made up need to protect "Elle." No more mirroring Lawrence, or using him as the excuse to mess up my own life. His mistakes will not be my mistakes. I am not my father, and I don't have to repeat his past.

There's a better route. There's a way to learn from my ancestors - and that includes Grandma Soul. I want to forgive them all. I want to cherish all the good and grow from all the bad. I want a better story for our family's legacy. A new chapter for us. One free of recycled trauma.

That means I can't ignore my pain anymore. I want to feel it, so I can finally fucking heal it. I want to represent something different to my family and my friends. I want to overcome my darkness, and not get held down by the trauma handed down to me, yaddamean?

That trauma is for generations before me to work out and answer for - not me.

No more party favors.

Let's start the serious work.

| 45 |

Reflection Questions

1. How do you relax? Name 7 techniques.
    -
    -
    -
    -
    -
    -
    -

2. What is your favorite thing to do on a rainy day?

3. Where do you feel the safest in the world? Name 3 special places.

4. In what ways may you be neglecting yourself or your self-care tools?

5. In mental health terms, being "triggered" refers to a broad collection of mental, physical, emotional, and/or behavioral reactions that someone may experience when presented with a reminder of past trauma. In what situations are you likely to be triggered?

What thoughts do you have when "triggered"?	What emotions do you feel when "triggered"?
How do you behave when "triggered"?	How does your body react when "triggered"?

6. Who can you count on to care about you? How do you utilize their support?

7. What gives you the courage to face painful experiences from your past? How does reflecting on past painful experiences shift how you carry the experiences going forward?

8. What are good risks you've taken in your life and how did going outside of your comfort zone pay off?

9. How do you practice authenticity in your social life?

10. What have you learned about yourself by reading this story?

11. What in life last made you laugh?

12. What does your dream life look like? At the end, list 3 things in your current life that you're grateful for.

13. What is the last thing you said "no" to that was difficult? Why was it difficult? How did it make you feel to say "no" anyway?

14. When was the last time you judged yourself (or someone else)? Reflecting upon that moment now, can you acknowledge any grace for yourself (or the other person)?

15. When was your last goal planning and achievement tracking session? Bonus: Open up your calendar; when is your next one?

16. What are your strengths and what makes you unique? At the end, list 5 of your favorite affirmations.

- **Strengths:**
- **Uniqueness:**
  -
  -
  -
  -
  -

Resources

If you, or someone you know, has a drinking problem or is looking for an AA meeting visit: https://www.aa.org/

If you, or someone you know, has a problem with narcotics or is looking for an NA meeting visit: https://na.org/

If you, or someone you know, is worried about a person with a drinking problem visit: https://al-anon.org/

If you, or someone you know, is having suicidal fantasies or is feeling hopeless visit: https://suicidepreventionlifeline.org/

If you, or someone you know, is worried about a person who experienced sexual violence visit: https://www.rainn.org/

For information about pregnancy visit: https://www.plannedparenthood.org/learn/pregnancy/pregnancy-options

For information about sexual health visit: https://www.plannedparenthood.org/learn

For counseling about pregnancy visit: https://www.plannedparenthood.org/get-care

If you, or someone you know, is worried about a person in an abusive relationship visit: https://www.thehotline.org/

If you are questioning if a relationship is abusive or not visit: https://www.thehotline.org/identify-abuse/

If you, or someone you know, is struggling with anger management visit: https://namass.org/

If you, or someone you know, is a male survivor of childhood sexual abuse or incest visit: https://1in6.org/

If you, or someone you know, is destitute or looking for shelter visit: https://endhomelessness.org/

If you, or someone you know, is looking for a destitute person visit: https://www.miraclemessages.org/

For information about food resources visit: https://www.fns.usda.gov/partnerships/national-hunger-clearing-house

For legal assistance or information about your rights visit: https://www.aclu.org/ OR https://www.nlada.org/

References

The entertainment industry has the power to both imitate and dictate reality. Time period storytelling, in my mind, therefore required cultural references that subtly revealed the norms of the world the characters were living in. I hope you enjoyed all the nostalgic references sprinkled throughout this story! Here is a list of songs, albums, movies, and television shows that were integral to creating *They Don't Love You Like I Love You.*

THE MIXTAPE

"Hold Up" by Beyoncé	"Semi-Charmed Life" by Third Eye Blind	"Say You'll Be There" by Spice Girls	"Walk Don't Walk" by Prince & the New Generation	"Hungry like the Wolf" by Duran Duran
"Beautiful Soul" by Jesse McCartney	"Get it Shawty" by Lloyd	"Shortie Like Mine" by Bow Wow feat. Chris Brown and Johntá Austin	"Girlfriend (Remix)" by Avril Lavigne feat. Lil Mama	"Gett Off" by Prince & the New Generation
"Wake Me Up When September Ends" by Green Day	"Smells Like Teen Spirit" by Nirvana	"Don't Cha" by the Pussycat Dolls	"Lose Yourself" by Eminem	"Sex-O-matic Venus Freak" by Macy Gray

"Still" by Macy Gray	"Flow" by Sade	"Your Song" by Elton John	"Thriller," by Michael Jackson	"Back in One Piece" by Aaliyah and DMX
"Clean Up, Clean Up" by Barney	"Good Times" by Subway	"Thizz Dance" by Mac Dre	"Parallel Universe" by Red Hot Chili Peppers	"Float On" by Modest Mouse
"The Ants Go Marching" by Barney	"Blossom" by Carole King	"Build Me Up Buttercup" by the Foundations	"I Think I'm In Love" by Jessica Simpson	"Let Me Love You" by Mario
"Dear Mama" by Tupac	"Boulevard of Broken Dreams" by Green Day	"Rock With You" by Michael Jackson	"All The Things She Said" by t.A.T.u.	"X Gon Give It To Ya" by DMX
"All Night Long" by Mary J. Blige	"Try Again" by Aaliyah	"Complicated" by Avril Lavigne	"Good Day" by Ice Cube	"Happy Birthday" by Stevie Wonder
"How I Wish It Would Rain" by the Temptations	"U Make Me Wanna" by Usher	"Sweet Thing" by Mary J. Blige	"Fat Boy" by Jewel	"Area Codes" by Ludacris feat. Nate Dogg
"Underneath it All" by No Doubt	"Stan" by Eminem	"Thinkin' About You" by Britney Spears	"Life Uncommon" by Jewel	"All I Have" by Jennifer Lopez
"Into You" by Tamia feat. Fabolous	"I'm Like A Bird" by Nelly Furtado	"Bring it All to Me" by Blaque feat. *NSYNC	"I'm Not Missing You" by Stacy Orrico	"Something Real" by Phoebe Snow
"Get Low" by Lil Jon and The East Side Boyz	"Ghost Ride the Whip" by Mistah Fab	"Sgt. Pepper's Lonely Hearts Club Band" the Beatles	"Misty Blue" by Dorothy Moore	"Paradise" by Sade

"Slow Dancing in a Burning Room" by John Mayer	"Reflection" by Christina Aguilera	"Hallie's Song" by Eminem	"Makes Me Wonder" by Maroon 5	"U + Ur Hand" by P!nk
"Sexyback" by Justin Timberlakefeat. Timbaland	"Lovers & Friends" by Lil Jon & The East Side Boyz feat. Usher and Ludacris	"Too Close" by Next	"Party and Bullshit" by The Notorious Biggie Smalls	"Tootsie Roll" by the 69 Boyz
"Always On Time" - Ja Rule Feat Ashanti	"Bad Habit" by Destiny's Child	"I Can See Clearly Now" by Jimmy Cliff	"The Nearness of You" by Norah Jones	"If I Were A Painter" by Norah Jones
"Something in the Way She Moves" by James Taylor	"River Deep Mountain High" Tina Turner	"What's Love Got to do With It?" by Tina Turner	"Call Tyrone" by Eryka Badu	"Switch" by TLC
"Fast Car" by Tracy Chapman	"Maps" by Yeah Yeah Yeahs			

COMPLETE ALBUM EXPERIENCES

FanMail by TLC	*Good Times* by Subway	*My Life* by Mary J. Blige	*Writing's on the Wall* by Destiny's Child	*Stadium Arcadium* by Red Hot Chili Peppers

MOVIE WATCH LIST

Eternal Sunshine of the Spotless Mind	A Walk to Remember	Parent Trap	John Q	Training Day
The Nutty Professor	Legally Blonde	Fight Club	Soul Food	The Lion King
The Butterfly Effect	Bride of Chucky	Jaws	Rat Race	Mary Poppins
Where the Heart Is	Thelma & Lousie	Hulk	Mean Girls	Double Take
How to Lose A Guy in 10 Days	The Jungle Book	Boomerang	Little Women	Romeo + Juliet
The Wizard of Oz	Cheetah Girls	Zoolander	Holes	Set it Off
The Preacher's Wife	Osmosis Jones	Titanic	Norma Rae	Kill Bill
Charlie's Angels	You've Got Mail	Toy Story	Glitter	Fools Rush In

SHOW WATCH LIST

Saturday Night Live	*That's So Raven*	*Ally McBeal*	*Barney*	*Cops*
Sex and the City	*The Simpsons*	*Family Matters*	*Jackass*	*Gilmore Girls*
Courage the Cowardly Dog	*Powerpuff Girls*	*Sister, Sister*	*Dragon Tails*	*The Magic School Bus*

CLOSING WORDS

THANK YOU FOR READING MY BOOK!

Love,
Carlie

www.ingramcontent.com/pod-product-compliance
Lightning Source LLC
Chambersburg PA
CBHW060246100726
47907CB00003B/784